THE
MANSERVANT

THE
MANSERVANT

MICHAEL HARWOOD

KENSINGTON BOOKS
www.kensingtonbooks.com

KENSINGTON BOOKS are published by

Kensington Publishing Corp.
119 West 40th Street, NY 10018

All Kensington titles, imprints, and distributed lines are available at special quantity discounts for bulk purchases for sales promotion, premiums, fund-raising, educational, or institutional use.

Special book excerpts or customized printings can also be created to fit specific needs. For details, write or phone the office of the Kensington Special Sales Manager: Attn. Special Sales Department. Kensington Publishing Corp., 119 West 40th Street, New York, NY 10018. Phone: 1-800-221-2647.

eISBN-13: 978-1-61773-312-3
eISBN-10: 1-61773-312-1
First Kensington Electronic Edition: March 2015

ISBN-13: 978-1-61773-311-6
ISBN-10: 1-61773-311-3
First Kensington Trade Paperback Printing: March 2015

10 9 8 7 6 5 4 3 2 1

Printed in the United States of America

For Alan. The man for whom the phrase
"My other half" was invented.

ACKNOWLEDGMENTS

To my agent, Sharon Bowers, to whom I will be eternally grateful for believing I could write a novel simply because I told her I could.

To my full-time friend and part-time mentor, Clare Cathcart, who has a brain almost as big as her heart.

And finally, a heartfelt thanks to all my past clients. The lords, ladies, dukes, and duchesses, and their esteemed guests for whom I have spent the last twenty years slaving over a hot stove. Now seems like as good a time as any to let them know that it's not just walls that have ears—it's cooks too.

PROLOGUE

—⊶⊶◦⊷⊷—

"An Englishman's home is his castle."

Six words that, when strung together and spoken out loud, are guaranteed to have me jamming my fingers in my ears and humming "God Save The Queen" for all I'm worth. Of course, I know what the phrase means, and it's certainly true that we English are a house-proud bunch, but I know firsthand about what goes on behind the thick, cold stone walls of a real-life castle, and believe me it's not something that any right-minded person should aspire to.

From the very first time I set eyes on Castle Beadale, it occurred to me that if you were to give a pen and paper to a small child with the instructions "Draw me a castle," it's what they would draw. Austerely bleak and imposingly baronial with its four castellated turrets and mullioned windows, it really is your archetypal medieval castle. A little more Bram Stoker than Walt Disney perhaps, but a perfectly formed castle nonetheless. The only thing missing is an actual moat, but in its place there's a wide natural lake fringed with bull rushes snaking around the front of the house, which from a distance gives the impression of Castle Beadale's being situated on its very own island.

The castle is large by anyone's standards, but almost entirely hidden from outside of the estate on which it sits by a combination of nature and clever design. You could know the surrounding area like the back of your hand and never set eyes on the building itself unless you were invited inside its high boundary walls. It occurred to me one day that in a sense Castle Beadale had been hiding from the outside world for almost five hundred years. Perhaps it's this sense of never being observed by outsiders that lies at the heart of its problems. After all, let's not forget it was the aristocracy who first coined the phrase "N.P.L.U."—*"Not people like us."*

The minute I set foot in Castle Beadale I was utterly seduced by life below stairs. It was the familial atmosphere between all the other servants that got me, and I was made to feel right at home from day one. In fact I remember thinking in those early days that it felt a bit like coming home.

Life behind the green baize door was a version of the domestic setting I used to fantasize about as a child: a warm and welcoming kitchen filled with the smell of home-cooked food and a mother hen who took pride in feeding her brood. The reality of my childhood was that every minute my mother spent in the kitchen was a minute lost in the pub, so her idea of a suitable meal for a growing boy was a tin of new potatoes served with salad cream, eaten alone and straight from the tin.

Castle Beadale was not my first taste of domestic life, but in my previous jobs the atmosphere had generally been one of backstabbing and rivalry. But at Beadale it really felt like the family I had never had, and that suited me very well indeed.

Those employed in domestic service with any level of success will always tell you that the secret to being a good servant is knowing exactly where the invisible dividing line between master and servant is. I always prided myself on knowing precisely where that line was and sought never to cross it, but all my problems started when it was my new employer, not I, who chose to overstep that mark.

CHAPTER 1

The moment I found Martyn's bound and gagged body face-down on the bed of the presidential suite, I saw my career prospects spiraling down the drain like dirty bath water.

I'd seen a lot of unpleasant things during my time on the eighth floor: a freshly laid turd on the Egyptian cotton sheets, used sanitary towels floating in the bath, and countless carelessly discarded condoms, but until now never a dead body. Let alone the body of someone I actually knew.

Martyn and I weren't exactly what you would call best friends, but we got on just fine. Along with other guys from the hotel we'd spent more than our fair share of drunken nights in the fleshpots of Soho and Vauxhall, and I had always enjoyed his company. But as I stared at his lifeless body contorted into such a tawdry position, I couldn't help but think that this was going to be a lot harder to sweep under the carpet than the usual detritus that followed a wild night at the Landseer Hotel.

Initially I thought I had the situation contained. Remembering the training I had received for just such a situation, I locked the door to the suite and calmly picked up the phone to call the hotel manager.

As I waited for him to pick up I found myself staring at Martyn's body with a morbid curiosity that shocked me almost as much as the sight itself.

"Malcolm Henderson, how may I be of service today?"

"Mr. Henderson, it's Anthony. We have a code orange on the eighth floor."

The line fell silent for a few seconds before he spoke. "I see. Don't leave the room, and stay calm. I will be up shortly to assess the situation."

As I went to replace the receiver the room was filled with an ear-piercing scream. I swear it was so shrill it must have had half the dogs in Mayfair running for cover. I dropped the phone and spun around just in time to see Consuela, the head housekeeper, fall to her knees, clutching her crucifix and crossing herself with a ferocity seldom seen outside the Vatican.

"*Oh mi dios, los santos nos protejan,*" she screamed, gazing up at the ceiling.

Eventually her words trailed off into an incomprehensible ramble as she rocked back and forth like a mad woman.

I found a sheet and draped it delicately over Martyn's body (as I'd been led to believe was the proper thing to do by Jessica Fletcher) and set about trying to calm Consuela whilst we waited for Mr. Henderson to arrive.

The following morning the *Sun* newspaper carried a full-page photograph of a handwritten note on the distinctive cream vellum headed notepaper reserved for the VIP suites. The note read:

Sorry about the mess.

I had long held a suspicion that much of Consuela's image as a simple Andalucían mountain girl was something of a front, and when I saw the headlines the next day I knew I'd been right all along.

You see, when I entered the suite that note had been carefully placed on the side table. She must have spotted it immediately when she entered the room, pocketing it before screaming the place down. I imagine she flogged it to the press for the price of two EasyJet flights to Alicante before Martyn was even cold.

The papers might well have reported Martyn's death as a suicide, but I knew for a fact that wasn't the case. The words EVERYTHING IS POSSIBLE AT THE LANDSEER were embossed on the hotel stationery, and never more was a company motto interpreted as a statement of fact by its customers. Most of my "pocket money" came from sorting fairly mundane favors for the guests, such as front row seats for that night's performance of *Wicked* or a table for two at The Ivy. But when I had someone on the end of the phone looking to "eat off menu," my inner cash register really started to ring. I had an instinct for what he or she was looking for, and I went to great lengths to facilitate it. Nine times out of ten Martyn would be able to accommodate them, and if he couldn't, I made it my business to find someone who could. If a VIP had a deviant itch that needed scratching, it would never be an assistant putting in the call. Odds were, if the boss could be bothered to pick up the phone and dial my number, he was looking for something he wanted kept quiet. And my secret weapon when it came to indulging the sexual proclivities of some of my more perverted guests was Martyn. Most of the time he was in and out of the suite within the hour, five hundred pounds better off and bragging to me about how little he'd had to do for the money.

"Easier than digging up roads for a living," he used to say.

Martyn's last client had been a Russian playboy with a taste for rough sex and diplomatic immunity, so by the time the body was discovered the gentleman in question was halfway to Moscow in a hastily chartered private jet to be reunited with his doting wife.

Mr. Henderson might have been able to gloss over the fact that Martyn had not been alone when he died, but the gutter press's enthusiasm for a catchy headline and the hint of an untold story made a stay at the Landseer Hotel about as tempting to most of its regular clientele as a swim through nuclear waste. And whilst the manner of Martyn's death might have brought a certain amount of interest in the hotel, it just wasn't the kind one would hope for when trying to sell rooms for three thousand pounds per night.

Up on the VIP floor Martyn had been perfectly placed to hide in plain sight whilst he went about his business. As one of the dedicated butlers, he had always been on hand to meet the needs of our most demanding guests. Young, blond, and with no gag reflex to speak of, he had been by far one of our most popular employees.

And the ladies, to whom he so elegantly served afternoon tea, had had no idea that whilst they pounded the beat at Harrods, Harvey Nichols, and Selfridges, Martyn had been getting a pounding of a different kind from their husbands.

Our agreement had been that he slipped me twenty percent of whatever he made, and we both kept our mouths shut. Looking back it seemed so simple, but if I had thought for just one second that he would wind up dead as a result, I would have put a stop to it months ago. But hindsight is a wonderful thing, isn't it?

I had always been confident that I could keep my half of the bargain, but sometimes Martyn had made me nervous. He had never gone so far as to blab, but more than once, after a few drinks or a sneaky line of coke, I had heard him hinting to some of the other staff about having a "little sideline."

When he died the whole hotel was plunged into a state of shock, myself included, but there were moments when I found myself thinking that at least I no longer had to worry about him dropping me in it. Of course I felt terrible thinking that, but trust has never been one of my strong points.

Nobody would ever be able to prove that I had any involvement in Martyn's sideline, I made quite sure of that. But as the facts of the case emerged through both the press and the inevitable hotel gossip that followed, it became increasingly difficult for the management to believe I knew nothing about the matter. The dramatic fall in bookings was all the ammunition they needed to get rid of me. Exactly one week after Martyn died I was called into Mr. Henderson's office and told I was being made redundant. A month's salary and no notice period. Good-bye, au revoir, see ya later! Just like that, no further explanation required. I can't say I was entirely surprised, but I was acutely aware that without a job to pay my bills I was well and truly fucked.

That week it seemed like my phone never stopped ringing, but in between the "withheld" numbers and ones I didn't recognize, one caller really got my attention.

Normally she's the first on the scene, sniffing for gossip like a pig sniffs out truffles, but despite having waited almost a week she got right to the point.

"Darling," she said in her low, heavily accented voice. "Did you do it?"

"Maria, you are terrible," I said, laughing for the first time in days. "You know me well enough to know that if I'd done it they would have never found the body."

Maria and I had met many years ago when we both worked at the Palace. She had been a housemaid, and I had been one of the Queen's footmen. In those days Maria and I had been an item for a while, but that part of our relationship had ended after she found me on my knees in front of one of the Queen's pages in the silver pantry. Despite the shock of finding her boyfriend with another man's dick in his mouth, she recognized a kindred spirit when she saw one, so we both agreed that we would make much better friends than lovers and have remained inseparable ever since.

Whilst I stayed true to my work experience by taking a job at the Landseer, Maria had no intentions of staying a housemaid for longer than was strictly necessary. It's no exaggeration to say that upon leaving "The Firm," Maria emerged from behind the green baize door a changed woman. She reinvented herself as a high-flying personal assistant, and, after exploiting a few contacts she stole from an ex-boyfriend's laptop, she landed herself a job as PA to one of the world's wealthiest (and best connected) widows. In return for Maria's natural ability to do a hundred things at once, her employer showered her with gifts of Prada handbags, Longines watches, free Botox injections, and envelopes stuffed full of Swiss francs.

Maria took care of every aspect of Madame Szabo's life. From making sure the private jet was sprayed with her bespoke room fragrance before she boarded to liaising with her plastic surgeon in New York, Maria ran Madame's life with military precision and enforced her will with an iron fist (albeit clad in a velvet glove). Many a chauffeur was "let go" because the car was parked facing the wrong way down the street or because he failed to take the hint when Maria said she didn't like his choice of cologne. Maria was not just a PA; she was an SPA: Superhuman Personal Assistant. Her words, not mine, but it was a fairly accurate job title nonetheless.

"We need to go out and get well and truly shit-faced on cocktails, and then you tell me all about it," she said, sucking air through her teeth as she struggled to light a cigarette. "In fact, my darling, let's make it the Connaught, and I may choose to tell you about someone I know who is looking for a butler."

"Maria, I just got fired. You'll be lucky if I can afford to take you to Burger King," I said, feeling a knot form in my stomach at the thought of being skint.

"Darling, what do you take me for?" she asked, deadpan. "It's all taken care of, and I've booked a table at Scott's for dinner later." And with that the line went dead. Two seconds later my iPhone vibrated, signaling a message:

PS, I'm paying 4 dinner.

CHAPTER 2

I arrived early at the Connaught, not really wanting to spend any more time than I had to on my own at home. A tall, Mediterranean-looking waiter appeared at my side the second I entered the bar. He stood close enough that I could smell his cologne. He tried his best to be nonchalant as he surreptitiously looked me up and down.

"May I help you?" He smiled, flashing perfect white teeth that stood out against his dark features.

"I'm joining a friend for drinks," I said, looking around for Maria even though she's never been early for anything in her life.

"Mr. Gowers?" he inquired without consulting a list of any kind, keeping his dark eyes locked onto mine.

"Yes, that's right," I said, trying to sound aloof.

"In that case, Mr. Gowers," he said, with the faintest trace of a smile, "you had better come with me."

I followed and watched as his high, round buttocks strained against the seat of his well-cut black trousers. Moving with an ease that hinted at a dancer's poise, he was, I imagined, waiting tables for tips before his big West End break.

When we arrived at the table, he thrust a drinks menu into my hand and left me to scrutinize it in the designer gloom. The lighting at the Connaught is such that everyone is cast in the most flattering of shadows, and even married couples of some thirty years standing look as if they are conducting a dangerous affair. Reading the menu, however, requires absolute concentration, so I got right down to it and within a few minutes I was sipping a perfectly made dirty martini.

When Maria enters a room, something in the atmosphere changes. It's utterly intangible, but I've seen it happen too many times for there to be any doubt. Wherever she goes men instantly lose their train of thought, and, conversely, their female companions suddenly become very focused. If Maria has any inkling of this phenomenon, she resolutely refuses to acknowledge it. Which, of course, does nothing but add to the effect. And that's how I knew she had arrived without even looking up.

She was, of course, fashionably late, but more than made up for it by looking her usual gorgeous self, all long limbed and tanned from a recent trip to her native Italy; her wild, unruly curls, set free for the evening after a day of being scraped into a severe chignon, fell around her bronzed shoulders. Maria wasn't particularly tall, but the combination of big hair and permanent five-inch Louboutin heels gave her a rather authoritative air. It was an impression that served her well in life, but also made her incredibly sexy. Sometimes I flattered myself by thinking that she made an extra effort with her appearance whenever we met, but in truth she looked this damn good all the time, which made me smile.

The minute Maria's Gucci–clad backside touched the velvet banquette, the bar manager arrived by her side as if from nowhere.

"Compliments of the house, Ms. Rigoni," he said, placing a Negroni in front of her.

"*Molto gentile,*" she said, meeting the bar manager's eye for a split second before turning back to me. "I mean, it's a disaster—who's going to want to spend all that money to stay on the eighth floor after that!"

Maria could drink almost as fast as she could talk, and in a matter of minutes she was banging her empty glass back down on the table.

The bar manager retreated toward the bar, gesturing as he went for another round.

"I know. It's all a bit of a nightmare," I said, thankful of the chance to get a word in edgeways. "What am I going to do, Maria?" I said, resenting the note of self-pity in my voice. "I have nothing. I've got no money in the bank, no job, and a flat that costs me a fortune every month."

It was true; the salary the hotel had paid me was modest, and although there were plenty of people in London who survived on less, they probably didn't live in the heart of Notting Hill or do their weekly food shop at Harrods. My monthly paycheck just about covered the rent, but my champagne dreams and caviar wishes were granted by other, infinitely more scurrilous means. And now that income stream had dried up. By now the alcohol was worming its way through my veins, and I could feel the tension in my shoulders gradually ebb away.

"Anyway, what's all this about someone you know needing a butler?" I said.

"Did you know that Madame Szabo has a daughter?"

"I vaguely knew she had one, but I don't know anything about her, why?"

"Have you heard of Lady Elizabeth Shanderson?"

"Of course. She's all over the press like a rash: *Tatler, Harper's;* in fact wasn't there some feature in *World of Interiors* a few months ago about her new apartment in New York?"

"Well, they are one and the same person!" Maria said with a

flourish, as if she had revealed the murderer in an Agatha Christie novel. "One minute she's plain old Erzsebet Szabo, and the next thing you know she gets hitched to the lord of the manor and is Lady Elizabeth Shanderson." Maria sniffed.

"Her mother tells everyone her daughter had an arranged marriage. The only difference is that Elizabeth arranged it herself!" Maria threw her head back and laughed loudly at her own joke.

"So she's reinvented herself as the lady of the manor, so what?" I asked.

"Darling, you wouldn't believe it. The voice is the best bit. When she speaks, she makes Camilla sound positively common!"

"I see, and I take it Lady Elizabeth is looking for a butler?"

"As ever, *mia caro*, you are only half right," Maria said smugly.

As we talked, Maria shifted slightly in her chair, and her glossy painted lips pursed ever so slightly as I felt her foot brush mine. A few moments later our second round of drinks arrived, but, as the hot Mediterranean waiter bent down to carefully place them on the table, I felt the pointed toe of her shoe jab me sharply in the shin. I stifled a laugh for fear the waiter would think he was the source of my amusement, but was distracted when Maria leaned forward so that her mouth was near his ear.

"My friend wants your number," she said without bothering to whisper.

"Maria!" I hissed. "I never said that." I looked up at him, hoping to see a shrug of the shoulders or a conspiratorial roll of the eyes, but he was staring straight at Maria.

"In that case you had better tell him to look under his drink." And with that he turned and made his way back through the crowded bar. Maria and I both suddenly looked down at the martini glass placed in front of me, and there, clearly visible through the base, was a name and number scribbled onto the napkin upon which the glass sat.

"Ha!" Maria exclaimed before snatching the napkin for closer inspection. "I knew he liked you. And who could blame him?"

I groaned, knowing exactly what was coming next.

"You are so handsome, Anthony," she said, pinching my cheek like an Italian *nonna*.

"Oh, Christ! Maria, please, not this again," I wailed.

"Darling, I mean it; just look at you! With your movie star looks. Dark hair . . . blue eyes . . . and that body! You could be a model—have you thought about that?"

"Seriously, you need to shut up now," I said, reaching over and grabbing the napkin from her hand.

"His name is Marcello, which makes him Italian, so be careful, *mia caro*," she said, changing the subject.

"Why's that then?" I asked.

"Because Italian men are all beasts!" she exclaimed. "And I should know."

"Beasts?" I said, raising an eyebrow. "I certainly hope so, Maria. I certainly hope so."

With my late evening entertainment all taken care of, I turned my mind back to Maria's cryptic little guessing game.

"So, if it isn't Lady Elizabeth looking for a butler, who is it?" I asked.

"Her husband, Lord Shanderson," Maria said.

I thought about it for a second and realized that, in all the photographs I had seen of Lady Elizabeth Shanderson, I had never seen one of her with her husband. Plenty of her draped around Elton and David and quite a few of her sandwiched between Anna Wintour and Suzy Menkes in the front row at Chanel, but to the untrained eye she appeared to be a single woman.

"I have to confess, Maria, that I didn't even know there was a Lord Shanderson."

"Madame Szabo tells me he is something of a country bumpkin; never leaves the countryside without a packed lunch and his passport!" Maria laughed.

The picture Maria was painting was not a rosy one. I had visions of bowing and scraping to some tweed-clad old fart and spending my days chipping horseshit off riding boots. I could practically smell wet dogs just thinking about it. The thought of being miles from London and all its earthly pleasures was bringing me out in hives. I mean, not only would I have to wave good-bye to all my friends, where was I going to find a gym in the middle of the countryside? I had been working on my body four times a week for years, and I wasn't prepared for my hard-earned six-pack to turn into a keg for the sake of a job. I could wave good-bye to finding a boyfriend too. The very idea made me feel quite ill.

"Hardly ever leaves the estate," continued Maria, oblivious to the dark cloud crossing my face. "Apparently it's magnificent, like a fairy-tale castle in leafy East Sussex."

"Oh, I don't know," I said. "It sounds like it's in the middle of nowhere, and I'm not sure I'm ready to retire from public life completely just yet. . . . And anyway, I don't believe in fairy tales."

She gave me a look I had seen a thousand times. It was a look that said she realized she was going to have to work that little bit harder to get what she wanted. Pinching the bridge of her nose and inhaling deeply, she pressed on.

"Anthony, listen to me. You are thirty-two years old with no job, an overpriced apartment, and no means of paying for it. Unless, that is, your landlord suddenly decides to accept cashmere sweaters and Prada shoes as payment."

She was right—for years I had spent everything I earned on designer clothes and other luxuries I couldn't really afford. As my mother was fond of reminding me, I had a rich man's taste with a poor man's pocket.

"What happened last week was far too close for comfort if

you ask me. Are you absolutely sure that Martyn didn't tell anyone else what you and he were up to?"

"Maria! I wasn't up to anything," I said rather indignantly.

"Bullshit, Anthony—you were in it up to your neck and you know it. You may not have been the one doing all the work, as it were, but you were the Heidi Fleiss of the whole operation, and look what happened to her! And, darling, let's face it; you are never going to earn enough money to live in the style to which you have become accustomed just by working in hotels." Maria sat back in her chair, looking rather pleased with herself.

I had to admit she had a point. If anyone else knew about the level of my involvement in Martyn's business, I would be royally fucked. And not in a good way.

"And the Shandersons pay way better than anyone else," Maria continued without pausing for breath. "In fact, with your CV you could just about name your price." She knew damn well that would get my attention; money always does.

I grew up with a mother so fiscally irresponsible that for most of my childhood we were on the run from one angry landlord or another. My mother let money either fall through her fingers or straight into the till of the nearest pub. Come to think of it, she was no better these days; it's just that I didn't have to live with her anymore, thank God. That kind of upbringing scars you; it really does. Having no money means losing control, and I don't like losing control. I had to get a job and fast.

"And, if it's lack of men that's putting you off leaving London, then don't let that worry you," she said, reading my mind.

"Maria!" I protested, hand clutching an imaginary string of pearls in mock horror. "I don't know what you mean."

"Brighton is only thirty minutes away from the estate, and there are more available men in that town than even you could handle—you could fuck to your heart's content on your day off." This she delivered as her coup de grace, knowing that I would not be able to resist the heady cocktail of money and the promise of regular sex.

"Okay, now you've got my attention," I said, softening to her powers of persuasion. "Not that it's any of my business, but it seems like an unlikely coupling between Lord and Lady Shanderson. It doesn't look like they have all that much in common."

Maria rolled her eyes as if speaking to a slightly dim-witted child. "Darling, they have more in common than you could ever know." She leaned toward me in the way she did when her story was about to get interesting.

"As you know the Szabos are one of the wealthiest families on the planet," she whispered.

"Yes, of course."

"Believe it or not they started off as simple Jewish Hungarian peasants, but when old man Szabo fled the homeland before the war he stuck a pin in a map and guess where it landed?" she asked.

"New York?" I guessed.

"Wrong! That came later. His pin landed smack bang in the oil fields of 1930s Texas. Within two years he'd struck black gold, and within ten he was one of the richest men in America." She thumped her well-manicured fist down on the table like a full stop.

"That's all fascinating, but what's that got to do with why Elizabeth or Erzsebet or whatever her name is wound up married to Lord Shanderson?"

"Because, my sweet, the Szabos can buy and sell most small countries ten times over, but the one thing they have always failed to achieve is respectability. They have a reputation for being rather gauche Hungarian peasants, so Elizabeth made it her mission to snare an English gent and silence the critics by becoming a fully paid-up member of the British aristocracy. All she had to do was find someone with the right pedigree who needed her money as much as she needed a title, and it was guaranteed to be a marriage made in heaven. It's a tried and tested formula that's been working for centuries."

"It can't just be about the money; surely he has plenty of that of his own," I said.

"Well, like so many of your aristocracy, he was as poor as a church mouse before old money bags came along. The family fortune was all but swallowed up in death duties after World War II. That house was practically derelict before she financed the renovations, and according to Madame Szabo he loves that house more than anything else in the world. Been in the Shanderson family for centuries, and through lack of funds he was forced to watch as it crumbled before his very eyes. It took millions upon millions of Szabo money to get that house back on its feet—way more than he could ever stump up." Maria paused for dramatic effect before adding, "Now do you think they've got nothing in common?"

"Okay, I get it, but I have a question. What happened to his last butler?"

"Madame Szabo didn't say—probably just moved on; you know how it is," Maria said dismissively.

"I'm still not sure," I said. "I hear Lady Shanderson is terribly difficult to work for. There are always stories appearing in the press about how demanding she is. It seems like not a week goes by that some disgruntled employee isn't suing for wrongful dismissal. Just the other day I read that one of her chefs was taking her to court after getting the boot. Her grounds for sacking him were that she didn't like the way he cut her strawberries at breakfast—and that doesn't sound like the behavior of a sane woman."

"I keep telling you, it's as a personal butler to Lord Shanderson, not Lady, and anyway, I don't think she is as bad as the press makes out. You know what the papers are like; they love a pantomime villain. And anyway, she has her own butler, so you probably would hardly see her. Madame Szabo tells me her son-in-law is a sweetheart, a real English gentleman."

I didn't say as much, but I knew exactly why Maria was giving me the hard sell on this job. If she managed to find a suitable candidate, Madame Szabo would be so grateful she was sure to demonstrate her gratitude with a Chanel handbag or maybe even a little blue box from Tiffany. It was well known that Madame Szabo would stop at nothing to give her little princess what she wanted, and in this case Maria had clearly been given the task of making it happen.

"I promise I'll give it some thought, but for now let's drink up and go have some supper."

"Good, I'm starving, but give me a minute. I need to pop to the ladies."

As soon as Maria left the table I took my iPhone and the napkin out of my jacket pocket and keyed in Marcello's number. I texted him:

What time do you finish tonight? —Anthony x

I watched from across the room as he felt his phone vibrate and discreetly read the text under the bar. In two seconds flat I received a reply:

Very late but can take a break in 5 meet me at the goods entrance if you fancy it. —Marcello

Maria arrived back, but didn't bother to sit. "*Avanti!* Come on; I'm starving," she said impatiently.

"Babe, meet me at the restaurant and order me another cocktail. I'll be there in ten minutes; there's something I need to do first." Maria just shrugged her shoulders in that way Italians do, before adding, "Ten minutes, no more."

I quickly walked her to the door, but, when she turned right to walk to Scott's of Mayfair, I turned left toward Grosvenor Square. Just a few yards past the main entrance to the hotel was an alley that I guessed would lead me to the goods entrance. I walked down a short way past industrial bins and piles of empty crates, and sure enough there was Marcello. He was huddled in a fire escape doorway, hugging himself to ward off the cold night air. It was dark, but his exquisite features were highlighted by the yellow glow of a streetlamp. As soon as he saw me, his face broke into a grin.

"*Buonasera,*" he whispered in a low, sexy voice.

"I'm not here for pleasantries," I replied, pushing him back into the darkness of the fire escape. He gasped as he fell against the door, but before he had a chance to speak I clamped my mouth onto his. His breath tasted of cigarettes and hastily swallowed mints. As my tongue feverishly searched the inside of his mouth, I pushed one hand deep into his thick curly hair and grabbed a handful; my other hand pushed hard on his chest so that he couldn't move. Through the flimsy fabric of his work shirt I felt nipples as hard as football studs. I pulled at the buttons until a couple gave way, allowing me to slip a hand inside. As I explored the contours of his gym-hard pecs, I began to detect a trace of stubble and instantly felt my attraction to him falter. Call me fickle, but if there's one thing guaranteed to turn me off a guy, it's excessive grooming. It might be a cliché, but I like men to feel and smell like real men. I quickly slid my hand out of his shirt and moved it south to his crotch, where sure enough something hard strained against the front of his pants.

"Wow! You are so handsome," he said, stroking my face. But the tenderness of his touch was so unexpected that I recoiled from him before I could stop myself, instantly feeling a stab of regret. In fact the whole thing was starting to feel like a dreadful mistake. What on earth was I doing here fumbling in the darkness with a total stranger? It was as if someone had turned on all the lights, and what had started in my head as an erotic tryst was exposed for what it really was: a seedy grope in a stinking goods entrance with a total stranger who cared no more for me than I for him.

"Sorry, mate," I said, suddenly pushing him away from me. "Not tonight."

"I don't understand," he said, looking genuinely shocked. "Why did you bring me out here if this is not what you want?" His voice now had an edge to it, and he wasn't bothering to whisper anymore.

I just shook my head, unable to explain myself.

"Oh! I get it. You have a boyfriend. Is no problem—me too. Don't worry; nobody has to know," he said, moving toward me again.

"No, seriously, I have to go." I felt terrible. I was embarrassed, and I could tell he was too, as neither of us could bear to look at one another. As he set about tidying himself up, I turned my collar up against the chill winter air and began to walk back up the alley.

"If you change your mind call me, *sì?*" he shouted after me.

"Yes, of course," I replied. "I'm sorry, Marcello."

As soon as I was in the glare of the streetlamps on Mount Street I stopped and reached into the pocket of my jacket. Scrolling through the numbers in my phone I arrived at Marcello's and pressed Delete. I walked briskly toward the restaurant, propelled by a sudden and ravenous hunger.

When I arrived at Scott's I half expected Maria to be sitting at one of the outdoor tables. Even though it was bitterly cold, huge gas-fired heaters blasted hot air into the canopy, making it possible for diners to sit in shirtsleeves whilst they chain-smoked between courses. But as she was nowhere to be seen I headed inside. I was greeted by a maître d' sent straight from central casting.

"Table in the name of Rigoni," I said as he wordlessly ran a finger down the page of an enormous leather-bound ledger.

He grunted when he located the booking and gestured for me to follow him into the bowels of the discreetly lit restaurant to a table where Maria was chatting on her phone, oblivious to the disapproving looks of her fellow diners.

The atmosphere in Scott's of Mayfair is thick with money and tradition. Much like many of its clientele, Scott's has had its fair share of facelifts over the years, but the things that matter most to the very rich remain the same: The table linen is so heavily starched you could hurt yourself on it, there is a crystal glass set out for every eventuality, and the black-and-white-clad waiters maintain a haughty disdain at all times. It's the kind of restaurant that makes you automatically sit up straight in your plushly upholstered seat.

"*Sì, sì, grazie. Ciao!*" Maria said into her phone, ending her call abruptly as the waiter pulled out a chair for me and laid a white napkin across my lap.

"What's all this then?" I said looking down at a bowl of caviar surrounded by blinis.

"Caviar," she said matter-of-factly. "The fact that you are jobless and penniless is no reason for lowering one's standards. Sit, eat."

"Osetra?" I asked.

"Don't be ridiculous!" she said, heaping a mound of the stuff onto one of the tiny pancakes with a mother of pearl spoon. "Beluga—infinitely better."

"And twice the price," I added, laughing.

"Madame Szabo is paying, so eat up like a good boy."

"I've had a chance to think about it," I said, changing the subject.

"Am I going to like what I hear?" Maria asked through a mouthful.

"I'll update my CV and e-mail it to you in the morning. I'd be happy for you to forward it to Lord Shanderson for his consideration." I felt a huge sense of relief as I said the words.

"Darling," Maria said, leaning over the table and taking my hand, "don't bother with a CV—you've already got the job. You start on Friday."

CHAPTER 3

The following morning I was woken up by the sound of an e-mail arriving on my iPhone. As soon as I began to fumble down the side of the bed for it, I realized just how hungover I was. With every tiny movement my brain slammed into the side of my skull, and my tongue was so dry you could have struck a match on it.

When I finally managed to focus on the tiny screen, I saw the e-mail was from Maria, sent at the unlikely hour of 7 a.m.

Maria Rigoni, you sly bitch! I thought as I began to read.

It had obviously been composed before she had turned up at the Connaught, and she had simply pressed Send this morning before turning over and topping up her beauty sleep. I began to laugh, but it hurt so much I quickly stopped.

The e-mail contained a map of how to find Castle Beadale, and details of my accommodation, what my salary was (she was right; it was very generous), and what uniform I was being supplied with. Castle Beadale was obviously an old-school kind of place, as I would be expected to wear the full monkey suit: traditional tailcoat, striped trousers, gray waistcoat, matching silk tie, and, best of all, white gloves.

How very *Remains of the Day*. Things started to look up when I got to the part about my accommodation—the charmingly named Rose View Cottage. Judging by the name I imagined a chocolate-box cottage with roses around the door and a tiny two ring Aga in the beamed kitchen, but then I suddenly had the horrible thought that Rose View might just be 1950s prefab next to the cowsheds. I hoped to God it was the former and not the latter, because if Maria ever came to visit she'd be calling for a cab back to London at the first whiff of cow shit.

The e-mail ended by saying that I needed to be at Castle Beadale by Friday lunchtime at the latest. It was now Wednesday, so it didn't leave me with much time to get myself organized.

I dragged myself out of bed and padded barefoot through to the kitchen of my tiny flat. I had moved here when I started at the Landseer, and although it's only rented I'm very attached to it. It's at the top of what once would have been a very grand house in Stanley Gardens, just a stone's throw from Portobello Road, and would have formed the servant's quarters when the house was built at the turn of the nineteenth century. Being in the attic the ceilings slope dramatically on either side of each room, causing most people to smack their heads at least once on their first visit.

One whole wall in the living room was dedicated to my vast collection of framed Polaroid photographs. Most had been taken the summer I arrived in London after I bought a vintage Polaroid in Portobello Road market and became obsessed with documenting every aspect of my burgeoning social life.

Many pictured me with people I no longer recognized, and some were of people I'd rather forget, but my absolute favorite was of Maria and me, impossibly young, tanned, and semi-naked on a Greek beach. We had gone there the year we first met and had lived off cheap beer and Greek salad for a whole week. She and I often remembered that holiday as being the best on record and vowed to try to relive it in style one day.

I stood, as I often did, transfixed by the wall of Polaroids, as each tiny photograph brought vivid memories flooding back. Some were happy, some not so much, but those memories were the glue that bonded me to my life in London and to this little rented flat.

As I waited for my precious Gaggenau espresso machine to warm up, I gazed out of the small kitchen window at the private gardens below. I had watched the seasons change the face of the garden for five years and felt a knot in my stomach at the thought of leaving it behind.

As a kid I had lived in so many different places that the idea of suddenly packing up all my things and moving house made me feel uncomfortable, but I knew deep down that I didn't really have a choice in the matter.

Even so, there was always a chance that my new job wouldn't work out and then what? If I gave the flat up completely I'd have nowhere to come back to. And what would I do with all my stuff? I could hardly turn up on Friday with a removal van. I would have to find someone to look after the place and pay the rent for at least six months until I knew whether or not I could hack it in deepest, darkest Sussex. And I knew just the person to call.

I dialed Chris's number and waited for the ring tone to tell me whether or not he was in the UK. The familiar sound told me that he was on home turf, but after a few rings the call went to voice mail.

"Chris, it's your very favorite person here—at least I will be when you hear what I've got for you. Call me, and I will reveal all. Bye!" I hung up knowing he wouldn't be able to resist a message like that.

Chris and I had become friends many years ago when he

worked as an under butler for the late Queen Mother. Under normal circumstances the Buckingham Palace staff and the Clarence House staff would avoid each other like a dose of the clap, but for one long, torturous month every summer they were forced to work cheek by jowl when the Queen and the Queen Mother traveled to Balmoral for their annual summer holiday. The rivalry between the households was long held and deep-seated, but soon after meeting it became obvious that neither Chris nor I wanted to play any part in the bullying and backstabbing that went on below stairs. He had a quick mouth and a sharp brain, so any bitchy comments aimed in his direction were deflected effortlessly and with aplomb. Thankfully, he looked out for me too. In those days I was considered fresh young meat, so I had bigger things to worry about than snide comments. During my first trip to Balmoral I was practically stalked by one of the Queen Mother's old footmen, Mr. Mills. Chris warned me about him, but I took little notice until one day when he followed me into the silver pantry, locking the door behind him.

"I like to play a little game with all the new boys," I remember him saying. "It's a bit like hide-and-seek."

The dirty old bastard then put the key down the front of his uniform breeches and told me if I wanted to get out I had to retrieve it myself. Even back then, I was nobody's fool, so when he stood back and thrust his hips at me I shoved my hand down the front of his trousers and rummaged around for a few seconds before taking his scrawny old balls in my hand.

"Now there's a good boy," he moaned, just seconds before I squeezed as hard as I could.

When he doubled over, screaming in agony, the key shot out of the leg of his trousers, and I calmly unlocked the door to find Chris standing there. Mr. Mills pushed past us both and scuttled off into the dark recesses of the castle like a cockroach, leaving Chris and me howling with laughter.

"I think you and I are going to get on just fine," he said when he finally composed himself enough to speak.

Chris continued to look out for me that summer, and I suppose in a way he's never really stopped.

When the Queen Mother died in 2002, all sixty-five members of the Clarence House staff were turfed out on their ears. Some of them had been there since their teens, but when it came right down to it that counted for nothing. If there had ever been any doubt as to how ruthless the British monarchy is, it was promptly removed when "Backstairs Billy," the Queen Mother's favorite footman, was evicted from his grace and favor cottage just days after her death. Less than a week later his home for over forty years was turned into a ticket office and gift shop, in preparation for the opening of Clarence House to the public. He died just five years later, but not before describing his fall from royal favor as like being "stabbed in the back with a diamond encrusted dagger."

But rather than join in with the chorus of complaining, Chris pulled his finger out and fulfilled a lifelong ambition by applying to be a purser for British Airways. Unsurprisingly, given his pedigree, he'd been in the job for less than six months before they put him in charge of the first-class cabin, and he couldn't have been happier. The first-class passengers loved his witty but respectful banter, and he adored flitting back and forth between LA, New York, and London. The one thing he was unhappy with, however, was his living situation. He had recently split with his boyfriend, Barry, but the two of them were stuck with a mortgage neither could really afford. Chris earns good money, but it's nowhere near enough to cover both his share of the mortgage and the rent for a flat. Barry had made it perfectly clear that he had no intention of budging his fat arse out of the flat and has always behaved appallingly whenever they are together. I'd always suspected that he'd knocked Chris about during various stages of their relationship. I'd asked Chris about it, and whilst he's never actually confirmed my suspicions, he sure as hell hasn't denied them either.

So my plan to invite him to stay at my place would provide a safety net of sorts and hopefully make the future look an awful lot less scary for the pair of us.

My phone vibrated, and just as I suspected it was Chris.

"What's up, girlfriend?" His American accent was the worst I'd ever heard, but it was guaranteed to make me laugh.

"How's wedded bliss?" I asked sarcastically.

"Don't ask. You should have seen the state of this place when I got back from New York yesterday. Barry's refusing to do any housework whatsoever. It's a fucking pigsty." All traces of humor had gone from his voice now. "Anyone would think he was trying to drive me out. Anyway, forget him. What is it you have to tell me?"

"Well, first of all I should tell you that I've been fired from the Landseer," I said.

"What?" Chris screeched, his voice shooting up an octave. "I thought you'd never leave that place. What on earth are you going to do?" he demanded.

"I have a new job. I'm going back to butlering," I said, pausing for dramatic effect.

"You. Are. Going. Back. To. Butlering," he said in staccato, as if exploring the exact meaning of each word. "I don't believe you."

I laughed out loud at his certainty. That's Chris all over: If he doesn't believe something, it must simply be untrue.

"I've been offered a job in the country," I said, bracing myself for his reaction.

"Oh! My God, it's worse than I thought."

"Yes, but that's where you come into it," I said, trying to calm him down. "I wondered if you would like to move into my flat for the next few months or just until I know whether or not I can hack it in the country."

The line went so quiet that at first I thought I'd been disconnected.

"Really?" he asked eventually in a small voice. "Move into your flat in Notting Hill? The one right next to Portobello Road, the one overlooking the beautiful private garden? Hang on a minute, let me think." He paused. "Hell yes! When can I move my stuff in?"

"I have to be out of here by the end of the week, so you can move in at the weekend if you like."

"Anthony Gowers, I don't know what I've done to deserve you. Thank you, thank you."

I felt a sudden surge of happiness. Happy to be helping Chris get away from that pig of a boyfriend and happy that my flat would be cared for whilst I eased myself into rural life. If it didn't work out for me, then the worst that could happen was that Chris and I would have to share the flat until he sorted something else out.

"What are you doing tonight?" I asked.

"Well, I was going to indulge in a spot of anal bleaching, but if you come up with anything more interesting, I'd be all ears," he replied.

"Good. Come over here—I have a bottle of Laurent-Perrier Rose with our names on it. Be here around 8 p.m.," I said, before hanging up.

With a couple of hours to kill before Chris was due to arrive, I pottered around the flat trying to get my head around what needed to come with me to my new job and what should stay. In the true spirit of procrastination I first rearranged all the bottles of cologne on the bathroom shelf. When I was happy with the results I got to work folding my ridiculously thick towels so that the embroidered Landseer crest was clearly visible on each—I doubt there was a single employee of the Landseer who hadn't stolen at least a couple of these towels over the years. When I got to the bedroom I flung open the large double wardrobe and tried to take in all of its meticulously organized contents. On the top rail were suits and jackets organized in order of color from left to right, starting with my favorite Helmut Lang suit (very fitted jacket and ridiculously narrow trousers that did wonders for my rear view) through to a slightly frivolous white linen jacket picked up in the Harvey Nichols sale one year but which I had never worn. On the day I bought it Maria took one look and declared it "far too vulgar unless worn on a yacht." Being nothing if not an optimist I decided to hang on to it just in case.

In the other half of the wardrobe was my vast collection of cashmere sweaters. Every shade and hue was there, and each one lovingly folded and interleaved with tissue paper. In times of great stress nothing brought me more pleasure than an hour or two folding sweaters until the inside of my wardrobe looked like a branch of the Edinburgh Woollen Mill. Suddenly a lump formed in my throat when I realized that Martyn had actually helped to pay for most of the designer gear in front of me, but I was also struck by how terribly urban my clothes were. There would be little opportunity to wear my handmade Church's brogues or my silver nylon Prada raincoat in rural West Sussex. I knew that if I were to make a decent attempt at country life I would need to invest in some appropriate attire; a Barbour jacket and some wellies would do the trick. For once in my life I would attempt to blend in.

I finished straightening a row of shoes until they were mathematically perfect and then went into the kitchen in search of champagne flutes. As I was blindly feeling around in the back of the cupboard, the phone rang. I let the answer machine pick up as my need to find decent glassware was greater than my need for double glazing or whatever else I was about to be sold over the phone.

Nobody of interest ever calls me on the landline; I don't know why I pay for it, I thought as I eventually found what I was looking for and gingerly removed them from the cupboard.

I walked into the living room just as the tiny plastic box squawked to life, and the second I heard the caller's voice I felt the flutes slip from my fingers and smash into a thousand jagged pieces on the wooden floor.

"Hi, Tony—It's your mother. . . ."

CHAPTER 4

I stood rooted to the spot, horrified, as my mother's voice filled the room. With every word she uttered I felt my blood pressure rise. Even the tiny speaker failed to mask the booze-soaked tone of her voice.

"Long time no see, son," she slurred. "I saw the papers the other day, and I thought I'd call to make sure you're okay. Anyway, you're not in so I guess I'll see you soon. Bye, Tony."

"Don't call me Tony!" I screamed at the box before landing a kick on it that wrenched it from the wall. "And not if I see you first, you drunken old cow!"

Once I'd calmed down a bit I began to think about what she had said: *I saw the papers the other day.* At first it didn't make sense, but then I remembered that one of the tabloids had managed to snap me coming out of the goods entrance of the hotel the day after Martyn died. I had thought nothing of it at the time, but the following day I was wrongly named as Anthony Gowers, "Hotel Manager." Mr. Henderson had been furious at first, but when he realized it meant his name was going to be kept out of the scandal, he said no more about it. I couldn't have cared less, as by then I knew my days were numbered at the Landseer, but my mother obviously thought I'd been promoted.

Typical, I thought. *Never one to miss an opportunity to squeeze a few quid out of her only son.*

An hour later, the broken flutes replaced and the shards of glass cleared away, I showered and changed in time for Chris's arrival. I needed to see a friendly face more than ever after my mother's impromptu call.

He arrived dead on eight o'clock, but given the events of the evening so far I double-checked it was him before buzzing him up.

"Sweet Mary and Joseph!" he said when I opened the door. "You look like you've been crying."

"Only tears of frustration," I replied, ushering him into the flat.

Chris wasted no time popping open the champagne and pouring us both a glass.

"I think you had better tell your Aunty Christine what's been going on," he said, draping himself over the sofa like a forties film star. He listened patiently as I told him about my mother's call, and when I finished he sat bolt upright and raised his glass.

"I propose a toast," he said. "I propose a toast to pastures new and letting go of the past."

"That's two toasts," I said, chinking my glass against his.

"So it is," replied Chris, topping both our glasses up and chinking once again.

The champagne didn't last long, so we moved on to Grey Goose served over chunks of ice chipped from the freezer compartment with a bread knife. Both of us were now sprawled languidly on the floor with the bottle between us.

"So you had better tell me about this new job you have signed up for," Chris said, almost missing his mouth with his glass.

"By the end of the week," I said, straightening up, "I will be Lord Shanderson, Third Earl of Beadale's personal butler."

"Shanderson?" Chris asked, suddenly sitting up poker straight. "Not Lady Elizabeth's husband?" he asked.

"The very same. Why, do you know of him?"

"Not exactly." He smirked. "But Lady Shanderson is one of my regular first-class passengers. She's quite a handful."

"If you believe everything you read in the papers," I said.

"Oh! Sweetie, I could tell you stories about Elizabeth Shanderson that you will NEVER read in the papers." Indicating that he had no intention of doing anything of the kind (just yet, anyway), he drew a thumb and forefinger across his mouth as if closing an imaginary zip. "But you know me, Anthony, I'd rather die than spill."

I looked at the clock and was cheered to see that it wasn't even ten thirty. I was now having fun with my old friend, and my woes seemed to be disappearing just as fast as the vodka. The bottle, which had been a third full when we started, was now completely empty, but I wanted more. I'm not a big drinker, but every now and again I get the bit between my teeth and don't want to stop until I am properly drunk. And this was one of those nights. I was also starting to feel very, very horny.

"Let's go out!" I said suddenly, jumping up. Chris held out a hand, which I used to hoist him to his feet with a jolt.

"Maybe just one quick one for the road," he said with a mischievous grin.

By the time we'd excitedly galloped down five flights of stairs and run into the rain-sodden street, neither of us could be bothered to turn back and grab umbrellas. So whilst Chris huddled in the shelter of my front door I stood in the road wildly waving my arms. As anyone who has ever tried to hail a cab in London in the rain will know, it often feels like the drivers are vetting you before deciding whether or not to stop. A few passing cabs had their yellow lights on, but either I looked more drunk than I actually was or I had become temporarily invisible.

"Fucker!" shouted Chris at every passing cab as he blew cigarette smoke into the cold night air. "Show a bit of leg, babe."

"You are not helping!" I said. "Really not helping."

I was about to give up before getting even more soaked when a taxi came around the corner and drew up slowly in front of us. We jumped in without observing the usual protocol of stating our destination through the driver's window.

"Evening, gents," said the driver in a thick cockney accent.

"The Coach and Horses on Ledbury Road, please," I said. The driver clocked me in the mirror and then turned in his seat to speak face-to-face.

"I know it well," he said with a slight grin.

He was strangely sexy when he smiled. Not my type at all but sort of rugged and handsome, mid forties maybe. He was balding, but what hair he had was gray and closely cropped. His short beard was also liberally speckled with gray, but his craggy features were tanned. It was the eyes that did it though. They were bright and mischievous and the color of Wedgwood china.

"Err, great," I said, stumbling over my words. "Let's get going then."

I smiled weakly at him, but caught myself biting my bottom lip. He winked suggestively before turning his attention back to the road.

The drive to Ledbury Road was a short one, and, although Chris chatted nonstop all the way, I kept one eye on the driver's mirror and watched as his eyes flitted between the road and me. When we drew up outside the bar Chris did his usual trick of being the first out of the cab so that I was stuck with paying for it.

"I'll get us a drink in," Chris said, before squeezing past me and running for the door.

"How much?" I asked the driver though the glass partition.

"Just give us a fiver," he replied, shooting me that sexy grin again.

"The meter says seven pounds," I said, handing him a ten-pound note.

"Yeah, well, sometimes it's good to break a few rules, innit?" he said, handing me back a fiver.

"Cheers then," I said, pulling my coat around me to disguise the growing bulge in the front of my jeans. I headed toward the bar, but as I squeezed past the two burly bouncers I turned to see the taxi still by the curb with the engine running. The driver smiled before pulling away and disappearing toward the Bayswater Road.

The bar was throbbing as usual and filled with the kind of random mixture of guys that made it my favorite haunt. I hate the kind of places that attract just one kind of guy; bars for bears or bars for gym bunnies, that kind of thing. It just strikes me as terribly restrictive. I mean, how are you supposed to know what kind of mood you are in? I like to think of my taste as very democratic. I surveyed the room for familiar and unfamiliar faces alike before spotting Chris weaving through the crowd, carrying a couple of drinks and bouncing in time to the music.

"Cin, cin!" he said, handing me a large vodka. We chinked glasses before falling into the companionable silence that makes it possible for two friends to cruise a room without looking single or desperate. After ten minutes of being lost in the music and the scent of a hundred horny men, I turned to Chris to ask him if he wanted another drink. But I was too late; he was already locked deep in conversation with a tall black guy who had his enormous hand clamped to Chris's backside as they chatted.

I watched Chris's new friend knead his arse like a master baker at work until I felt a firm tap on the shoulder. Assuming it was someone I knew, I turned around smiling broadly, but

was greeted instead by the taxi driver holding two pints of
lager. He obviously registered my shock at seeing him in this
place, so he spoke first.

"I see your mate got lucky."

"What are you doing here?" I said, accepting the drink he
was holding out to me.

"Well, like I said, sometimes it's good to break a few rules."

"Lager isn't usually my drink," I said, taking big steadying
gulps of the cold beer. "But seeing as you offered . . ."

"That's not all I'm offering," he said, almost causing me to
choke at the forthrightness of his statement.

He was smiling, but the look in his eyes told me he was
deadly serious. I stood back to get a better look at him. He was
solid like a rugby player with broad shoulders and a surprisingly narrow waist. He was taller than I expected too. In the
cab, where I could only see his body from the shoulders up, I'd
imagined him to be a little soft around the middle, maybe even
with a beer belly. But looking at him now, up close, it was clear
he spent his fair share of time in the gym.

"I'm Frank," he said, holding out a hand the size of a shovel.

"You certainly are," I said, shaking it firmly. "I'm Anthony."

He squeezed my hand tightly and used it to pull me close
enough to him that our chests were touching and his mouth
was close to my ear.

"You look like you need a real man, Anthony," he growled
into my ear. "You know, someone to, err, take control of the
situation. If you know what I mean."

Suddenly the loud dance music pumping from the speakers
dwindled to a barely audible hum, and the only sound was that
of my own rapid breathing. All witty remarks and smart-arse
responses evaded me. I took a deep breath before answering.

"As a matter of fact, Frank, I'm usually in the driving seat if
you know what *I* mean," I said, trying to sound cool. "And I
find there aren't that many real men around these days."

"Well, maybe all that is about to change," he replied, keeping his eyes firmly locked onto mine.

He released my hand, and we hastily downed the remains of our drinks. I halfheartedly signaled to Chris to not only tell him I had gotten lucky but also to see the look on his face when he saw with whom. I needn't have bothered though as he was busy eating the face off the black guy in a darkened corner, oblivious to everything and everyone in the room. I'd have to share the intimate details of my conquest over a coffee some other time.

I followed Frank down the street until we came to his cab. He unlocked it and climbed in the driver's seat.

"Get in," he said urgently, and I obeyed, climbing into the back. He drove, only just this side of the law, directly to where he'd picked us up earlier. His voice came through the taxi's intercom.

"Where to exactly?" he asked.

"Park anywhere near here," I said. "We are right outside my place."

He pulled into a space just yards from my front door and was out of his seat and holding the passenger door open before the engine had died.

As I fumbled with my keys Frank ground himself into me, forcing me against the door. Once inside the communal hallway I quickly led the way, sprinting up the stairs, two at a time, him hot on my heels.

In the flat I reached for the lights, but before I had a chance to hit the switch he was on me. The dark of the flat was punctuated only by a faint yellow glow rising up from the street-lamps below the living room window, and in the half-light we pulled at each other's clothes until in a matter of seconds he had kicked off his shoes and was naked from the waist up whilst I, somehow, was wearing only my white Calvin Klein Y-fronts. I felt strangely vulnerable, not a sensation I was used to, but it felt deeply arousing. I stood before him instinctively awaiting instructions.

"Get over here," he said, lowering himself into the over-stuffed armchair in the corner of the room.

I moved toward him. With one of his big hands he took me by the arm and bent me over his knee where the rock-hard bulge in his jeans dug into my solar plexus.

"I bet you are a bit of a naughty boy, aren't you?" he said as his hand circled my cheeks through the thin white fabric.

I squirmed and tried to get myself upright again but then, very suddenly his hand came crashing down on my backside, forcing my whole body into a jolt. I should have seen it coming, but I was wound up into a state where all common sense was gone. Another slap came seconds after the first, and I felt him twitch beneath me.

"You like that, don't you?" he said.

The truth was I didn't know what I felt. Part of me wanted to jump up and tell him this wasn't my kind of thing, but a greater, much more powerful voice in my head was telling me that he was right. I liked it, and I liked it a lot. I had only known the guy for a couple of hours, but there was something about him that had me completely hypnotized. My chest was pressed firmly into his thick muscular thighs, and I could feel my heart pounding, and I'm pretty sure he could too.

"Let's go to bed," I said.

"I like a man who knows what he wants," he said, easing me off his lap and onto the floor.

Standing slowly he flexed his biceps and puffed out his chest, which was covered in a thick layer of dark hair. His hands moved slowly, undoing his belt followed by the buttons of his jeans. I stared, transfixed by this slow motion striptease. The only sound in the room now was my heavy breathing.

Eventually he eased his jeans down and stepped out of them, revealing a pair of tight black designer briefs.

"Nice pants," I said, reaching up and hooking my thumbs into the waistband and slipping them down in one fluid movement.

"I can tell you've done that a few times before," he said, sending them sailing across the room with one flick of his foot. He was now standing over me completely naked, and I quickly realized he possessed that rare thing that's utterly impossible to fake—confidence. I stood and pushed him in the direction of the bedroom, and once through the door he allowed himself to fall back onto the bed and I immediately fell on top of him. Between a volley of frantic kisses Frank reached over and located the switch for the bedside lamp. When he flicked it on, the bedroom was flooded with a warm glowing light.

"Let's leave it on," he said as he began to kiss my neck. "You are way too good-looking for me not to be able to see you."

I'm not sure what I expected to happen once we were in bed together (particularly since I could still feel a faint stinging sensation on my arse cheeks), but I wasn't expecting him to be so incredibly tender. My usual habit of automatically taking charge sexually flew right out of the window along with what few other inhibitions I possess the very minute he laid his huge hands on me. I'd never before been with anyone who made me feel so inclined to surrender to him, and I realized I liked it. A lot.

I have to be honest; I thought he would bolt as soon as he got what he came for. That's usually the way it works, but he didn't. All that sex and alcohol must have made me suddenly very tired, and I assumed that as soon as he saw me yawning and my eyes drooping he would head for the door, but he didn't. Instead he put his arms around me and engulfed my body with his. We must both have drifted off immediately, because the next thing I remember is being woken by the sound of the alarm on my phone. It was 8 a.m.

CHAPTER 5

"Frank, wake up," I said gently, shaking him by the shoulder. He stirred and moaned, but showed no signs of actually waking. I looked admiringly at his naked body. Last night had been dark and carnal, but there against the whiteness of the sheets I saw him, quite literally, in a new light. I studied him carefully as he slept, and my eyes were immediately drawn to the large, new-looking tribal tattoo that wrapped around the top of his arm and snaked over his shoulder. I'd never really wanted to have one myself, but on a body like Frank's I found it a real turn-on. He stirred suddenly and rolled onto his other side, revealing another tattoo on his left shoulder that I hadn't noticed the night before. It was an old-fashioned swallow trailing a banner, and on it were the words:

MANDY & FRANK FOREVER

I was stroking it absentmindedly when Frank opened his eyes and smiled up at me.

"Morning, mate," he said sleepily.

"Hi, you okay? I mean, do you need to be anywhere? We have slept right through."

"If you want rid of me, you just have to say," he said, laughing.

"No, no, not at all," I said. "It's just that I thought you might have to get back to somebody or something. I don't want you to have to answer any awkward questions."

He laughed lightly and shook his head.

"No worries on that score, mate; young, free, and single as they say."

"And Mandy won't be wondering where you are?" I asked.

He looked at me for a second and then let out a booming laugh.

"Ah!" he said, patting the tattoo on his shoulder. "That. Let's just say that in mine and Mandy's case, forever meant two miserable years and a very expensive divorce a long, long time ago."

"Coffee?" I asked breezily, desperate to change the subject.

"Nah, mate—can't stand the stuff. Bit more of a tea drinker really," he replied.

I padded into the kitchen and began frantically searching the cupboards for tea. I never drank it, but usually kept some for guests.

"Earl Grey aright for you?" I shouted through to the bedroom.

"Er, PG Tips?" he replied. Eventually I found some Fortnum and Mason's English breakfast tea that I figured was the nearest he was going to get. I fired up the Gaggenau for my coffee and boiled the kettle for tea.

"Nice and milky with four sugars," he said from the doorway, making me jump.

"Four sugars?" I asked, slightly appalled. "You'll rot your teeth."

He had a towel around his waist, but it fell to the floor as soon as he moved across the kitchen. He slipped a broad arm around my waist and pulled me to him, clamping his mouth onto mine. His breath was sweet with the taste of mouthwash, reminding me that I hadn't yet brushed my own teeth.

"My breath must stink," I said, placing a hand over my mouth and pushing him away, suddenly embarrassed.

"Nah! You taste just fine to me," he said, pulling me back.

We stayed locked together kissing passionately until the kettle came to a boil, letting out an ear-piercing scream.

The noise of the kettle, or maybe just the promise of a cup of tea, forced us apart, but not before I had taken in the sight of Frank standing stark naked in my kitchen. For a second I couldn't take my eyes off him as he leaned casually against the kitchen counter. He made no attempt to cover up, and his sheer lack of self-consciousness sent a torrent of blood rushing to my groin.

"So what's with all the boxes?" he asked, breaking my filthy train of thought.

"I'm moving," I replied. In truth I didn't know what else to say, as I was only just getting my head around what I was about to do.

"Not too far I hope," he said, finally retrieving the towel and casually knotting it around his waist.

"Funny you should say that. I'm leaving London for a while. It's a work thing."

"What do you do for a living then?" he asked. For some reason the question completely wrong-footed me. Exactly what was it I was going to be doing? It was easy when I was at the Landseer; I would just answer, "I work in a hotel." Nobody ever asked any more questions beyond "Which one?" But now I wasn't sure I could be bothered explaining that I was about to become a manservant.

"I'm a sort of personal assistant," I said. "But my boss needs me to be at his house in Sussex," I added for good measure.

"Sussex ain't far," he replied, taking a deep gulp of tea.

And then, whilst those three words hung in the air, I sud-

44

denly launched myself at him, sending the contents of his mug flying across the marble worktop. I flung my arms around his broad, muscular neck and planted a big, passionate kiss on his lips. We stayed like that for a couple of minutes before he pulled away, smiling broadly.

"Something I said?" He grinned.

"As a matter of fact it was."

And it was then I realized for the first time since my evening with Maria that what Frank said was absolutely true. West Sussex is not the dark side of the moon; it's only a couple of hours away from London. A couple of hours away from home. I now felt ready to leave for Castle Beadale.

We showered together, but my tiny bathroom was so small it prevented us from getting too carried away. It did, however, allow us to explore each other's bodies under the guise of simply getting clean. As fast as his strong hands lathered up every inch of my body, the hot water rained down and rinsed it clean. When it was my turn he held his arms above his head and turned his face into the stream of water. I massaged his broad chest and ran my fingers through the thick hair, slowly working down his torso. My hands moved around his waist and dwelled for a time on his high, round buttocks. His cheeks tensed when my soapy hands began to explore them, but he relaxed when I moved farther down his legs, paying particular attention to his thick, bulging thighs. I couldn't help thinking that if we had found ourselves like this in one of the huge showers at the Landseer, we would have been fucking like teenagers by now, but the restricted space of my shower cubicle meant that this was as far as it was possible to go. Not to mention the fact that I had expected to be packed and ready to leave by now.

"So what you doing for the rest of the day?" Frank asked as we toweled ourselves off in the bedroom.

"I have to finish packing. I'm supposed to be leaving tomorrow."

"So soon?" he said, pulling on his jeans. "I might have to come and see you in Sussex."

I could feel myself smiling at the thought of Frank's nipping down to Sussex to relieve the tedium of country life, but pulled myself together when I glanced at the clock. I knew I had to get rid of him if I was going to get anything done, but the truth was I was enjoying his company too much to ask him to leave.

"Don't take this the wrong way," I said eventually, "but I really need to get on, and having you here is acting as something of a distraction—a very nice distraction, but a distraction nonetheless."

"How you getting to Sussex?" he asked.

"Erm, train, I guess. I hadn't really given it much thought."

"Don't bother; I'll drive you. I can take the morning off and be back in London by mid afternoon."

I stared at him over a pile of clothes. He smiled and took my chin in his hand.

"I'll pick you up here at 9 a.m.—that work for you?" he said, before bending down to kiss me lightly on the lips.

"Oh! That's really nice of you, but I can get the train, it's no problem. . . . I wouldn't like to impose. . . ." I babbled ever so slightly, stunned at his offer.

"It's an offer of a lift, Anthony, not a marriage proposal; don't worry," he said matter-of-factly before pulling on his leather jacket and heading toward the door.

I searched his face for any sign that I'd offended him, but saw nothing. He didn't even appear to mind that I was kicking him out. He just smirked when he registered my look of concern.

"If you really don't want me to drive you tomorrow, just text me and let me know; otherwise be ready at 9 a.m." I watched him descend the stairs two at a time before he stopped on the half landing and turned back. "Don't be late—the meter will be running." He winked, and moments later I heard the front door of the building slam shut with a bang.

It wasn't until he was gone that I realized we hadn't exchanged phone numbers, so I couldn't cry off even if I wanted to. I felt a slight sense of irritation that I wouldn't be able to make my excuses. He was totally sexy, and the night before had been great, but I had to face the fact that I was never going to see him again after he drove me to Castle Beadale. I mean, I couldn't really imagine going out with a taxi driver. What on earth would we talk about?

Slumping back onto the sofa I surveyed the piles of clothes, books, and assorted junk littering the living room floor and realized the sight was no longer causing a knot in the pit of my stomach. A day earlier I had sat in exactly the same spot dreading all the upheaval of moving to a strange place and leaving everything and everybody I loved behind. But for reasons as yet unclear I was feeling infinitely more positive about the whole thing. Indeed, as I packed the last few things with renewed vigor, I could have sworn I felt the stirrings of excitement in the place where dread had been just twenty-four hours earlier.

By late afternoon everything I wanted to take with me was packed into two large holdalls. The rest of my stuff was boxed up to make room for Chris to move in. I'd already e-mailed him with detailed instructions on how the dodgy central heating worked and contact numbers for the landlord in case of emergency. All that was left to do was to hide the spare front door key under the mat, and the place was as good as his. But until then I was alone in the flat for the last time.

I padded through to the kitchen in search of a glass of wine, but just as I was about to open the fridge I saw, amongst all the postcards and utility bills stuck to the door, a small yellow Post-it note with Frank's name and number on it. He must have stuck it there before he left. I punched the number into my phone and made a mental note to text him later to politely tell him I'd be taking the train. I also nervously recalled his last words before he left: "The meter will be running." *Yes, much better idea to go by train,* I thought, pouring myself a very large glass of Sauvignon Blanc. *With the state of my finances I can't risk a taxi fare all the way from London to Sussex.*

It didn't take long for the wine to magically evaporate from my glass, but as soon as it did I was gripped by a raging hunger. I hadn't eaten anything all day, but I really couldn't be bothered to leave the flat, so I searched the cupboards for something vaguely edible. I love to eat, but I'm not much of a cook. While I'd been working at the hotel I had either eaten at work or headed straight out to a restaurant every night of the week, so I had very low expectations when it came to foraging for food in my own cupboards.

To my amazement, hidden behind various half-empty bottles of spirits and unopened containers of protein powder left over from a short-lived health kick, I found a packet of instant noodles. I studied the cooking instructions on the packet whilst waiting for the kettle to boil (I told you I wasn't much of a cook) and in less than five minutes I had sufficiently quelled my hunger to concentrate on sending a few e-mails, updating my Facebook status, and checking out who'd looked at my Gaydar profile in the past twenty-four hours.

By seven p.m. I was exhausted and surrendered to the voices in my head telling me to turn in for the night. I laid out some clothes for the morning—a smart casual look consisting of chinos, Ralph Lauren shirt, and brown Prada lace-ups—and climbed into the still unmade bed. I pressed my face into the pillow on the side where Frank had slept and breathed in the faint trace of his smell. In seconds I was sound asleep.

The next day I woke early, realizing immediately that I hadn't contacted Frank to tell him I'd decided to take the train. I showered briskly, and by eight thirty I was fully dressed and impatiently tapping my fingers on the kitchen counter as I waited for the Gaggenau to warm up. The idea of heading out of the door without at least one double espresso inside me was utterly unthinkable, but even so I didn't want to be late. Once poured, the thick, treacly brew barely touched the sides before it was finished, the cup washed, dried, and wrapped carefully in tissue paper before being stashed in my suitcase. My caffeine habit is a habit in every sense of the word and extends as far as the vessel from which I consume it. My cup of choice is a prized possession and goes everywhere with me. Stolen from Bar Italia one drunken night in Soho many, many years ago, it serves as a constant reminder of those heady days when youth and time are taken for granted. These days it's chipped, and the logo has been rendered barely visible by hundreds of harsh dishwasher cycles, but it still has the power to make even second-rate coffee taste half decent.

I decided to wait for Frank downstairs and began the task of dragging my two bags noisily down the stairs one at a time. Leaving them in the hallway, I bounded back up the stairs to lock up the flat. I did so at high speed for fear I would change my mind and thrust the keys through the letterbox with a flourish. As they landed with a rattle on the other side of the door, I shivered with excitement. About what exactly, I still wasn't sure.

Out on Stanley Gardens I scanned left and right for Frank's taxi and felt a slight sense of irritation at the fact that, despite his having been quite insistent I be on time, he himself was nowhere to be seen. As I contemplated calling him, a car horn sounded loudly on the other side of the street. I scanned the line of vehicles and to my utter astonishment saw Frank behind the wheel of not a black London taxi but a bright yellow sports car. I stood rooted to the spot, surrounded by bags I knew instantly had no chance of fitting into this tiny and vaguely ridiculous car. Frank beamed wildly as the roof automatically retreated into the boot.

"So whaddaya think?" he shouted.

"I think that's not a taxi; that's what I think," I replied, omitting to add that it was the most hideous car I had ever seen. "I'm not sure I'm going to get my bags in the back of there."

"Come on!" he shouted cheerfully. "It'll be a laugh!"

But I wasn't laughing; in fact this was starting to feel like a really bad idea. I had thought I was going to be turning up at my new place of work in a relatively respectable London taxi. Instead, I would be arriving at Castle Beadale in what looked like a car stolen from a hairdresser.

"Frank, listen. I don't think this is going to work for me; maybe I should get the train after all. Why don't you just give me a lift to Victoria Station?"

He leapt out of the driver's seat and crossed the road to where I was standing, motionless and open-mouthed.

"Come on, Anthony," he said breezily. "You were much more fun the other night."

He tugged at the handle of one of the bags, but I wasn't ready to let go just yet.

"Is this your car?" I asked.

"Not exactly," he replied, managing to wrestle both bags from my vise-like grip and marching over to the car. I followed him and watched as he slung them effortlessly into the back of the car. "I borrowed it from a friend."

Rather irritatingly the bags did fit, albeit snugly, into the tiny recess behind the two seats. But I still wasn't entirely happy, as I had visions of them flying open in transit and disgorging their contents all over the hard shoulder of the A23.

I looked over at Frank, ready to continue my protests, but when I saw the look of sheer enthusiasm on his face I just couldn't bring myself to do it. This total stranger had taken the day off work, borrowed this ridiculous car, and offered to drive me two hours out of London—for what? Well, apparently just because he was a nice guy. "Okay, you win," I said, climbing into the passenger seat.

"I usually do," he said, starting the engine.

The drive out of London, as usual, seemed to take forever. We headed south to Victoria and sailed past the station where I could have caught the train. Brixton and Streatham were a noisy blur, but by the time we had left the motorway just south of Croydon the urban sprawl of London was replaced by the gently sloping hills of the South Downs.

With the directions on my phone, I was acting as navigator by shouting instructions over the deafening noise of the wind. We had attempted to play the radio, but it was pointless with the roof down, so I made do with the scenery and the occasional bit of lipreading between Frank and me. I started out worrying about what the drive would do to my hair, but after about half an hour I honestly couldn't have cared less. At times I raised myself up in the seat so that the wind whipped my face, and Frank pushed me back down by placing a hand on the top of my thigh and squeezing tightly.

About ninety minutes out of London Frank turned off the main road and pulled into a petrol station located on the outskirts of a small village. The kiosk attached to the petrol station looked as if it served as the main village shop and had a steady stream of people coming and going with newspapers, groceries, and the like.

"Do you want anything?" he asked, rummaging in his bag for his wallet.

"I'm fine, thanks," I replied, checking my windswept reflection in the rearview mirror.

Frank walked across the forecourt and joined the queue inside the small shop. I watched the scene through the large picture window as if it were a TV screen with the sound turned off. The young girl behind the counter appeared to get more and more irritated with an old man she was serving, and even from where I was sitting I could see her rolling her eyes as he painstakingly counted out the price of his newspaper in small change. When I glanced over at Frank he was looking at the girl with a face like thunder. He stepped forward and placed a gentle hand on the old man's shoulder before speaking to him. Whatever it was he said caused the old man to smile and nod vigorously before stepping back to allow Frank to count out the money on his behalf. In a matter of minutes the old guy was heading off up the road with his newspaper tucked under his arm.

Well, Frank, aren't you the man of the hour? I thought.

As exhilarating as open-topped cars are, even a short drive is guaranteed to leave the passengers looking like shit. One look in the mirror proved I was no exception. My eyes were watering so badly I looked like I'd been crying. I checked all the pockets in my jacket, but found nothing to wipe them. I thought there might be a pack of tissues in the glove box, so I popped it open and had a rummage around. I felt something like a handkerchief wedged in behind a pile of old parking tickets. When I pulled it out the tickets came with it, spilling onto my feet. But when I began to scoop them up, not all of the papers turned out to be tickets. Tucked in between them was a small handwritten note on lurid pink notepaper. I looked up and saw that Frank was still waiting to pay for his petrol, so I quickly unfolded the note and began to read:

> *Babe, don't wreck my car or I swear I will have*
> *to kill you. Have fun and behave yourself!!!*
> *Love you, xxxxx.*

I held it in my hand for a few seconds, but then I saw Frank bounding toward the car with an arm full of snacks and drinks, so I stuffed it hastily into my pocket.

"Bloody hell, mate—you all right?" Frank laughed as he

climbed into the driver's seat. "You look like you've been bawling!"

"Crying?" I said, my hand brushing the pocket containing the note. "No chance; I'm not really the crying type."

As Frank pulled out of the station forecourt he stroked my thigh affectionately.

Borrowed the car from a mate? I thought, smiling at him. *Sure you did!*

According to my directions Castle Beadale was only another thirty-minute drive, which I was glad about as I was starting to see Frank in a slightly different light. I felt a bit let down at the thought of his lying to me, but then again he had only been my "good-bye-London fuck," so why should I care one way or the other?

He had said he was divorced and that he was single, but why should I believe him? He wouldn't have been the first guy I ever slept with who was living a double life. But then again he seemed to know an awful lot about how to please a man in bed, too much to be simply dabbling behind his girlfriend's back. I felt a faint stirring in my lap at the thought of exactly how good he was in the sack.

I put it to the back of my mind, figuring I had more important things to focus on for now.

To his credit, Frank kept on trying to rekindle the conversation as best he could even though it was obvious my mood had changed.

"You excited about your new job?" he asked, squeezing my shoulder.

"Yeah, I really am," I replied.

"You seem a little tense, but I suppose that's normal on your first day."

"Listen, Frank, I really like you, and the other night was great. I mean, really great, but how's about we just stay mates from now on?"

"Bloody hell!" he said, taking his eyes off the road for a second to look at me. "Where did that just come from?"

"Oh, just ignore me," I said, smiling at him. "I'm just being stupid. Probably something to do with all the upheaval of moving."

He shook his head and laughed as if I had just spoken to him in Cantonese or something.

"According to my instructions," I said, changing the subject and checking my phone, "we have to drive round to the back of the castle and park in the old stable yard. All visitors must enter through the servants' entrance."

"Fuck! How big is this house?" he asked.

"If you look over there you can see for yourself," I said, pointing to a gap in the high boundary wall.

Frank slowed the car and pulled it up onto the grass verge, where we both climbed out and just stared in silence for a few minutes. It looked like part of the gray stone wall had been taken down for repair, and through it I could see the solid outline of the castle perfectly picked out against a clear blue sky. I have no idea why, but I was rather taken aback by how much like an actual castle it was. I'd been expecting a grand English country house like Castle Howard or Blenheim Palace, but Castle Beadale was nothing of the sort. "You told me it was a house," Frank said, breaking the silence. "That, my friend, is a fucking castle!"

"Yup, I'm about to be the butler in a real-life castle."

"I thought you said you were a personal assistant," Frank said, raising an eyebrow.

"Yes, well, it looks like neither of us are beyond telling a few little white lies, doesn't it?" I said, climbing back into the car and waiting for him to do the same.

"So"—Frank grinned with a glint in his eye—"what you really are is a manservant. I like the sound of that—a lot!" His hand slowly wandered over to my thigh and began to massage it.

"How we doing for time?" he said, leaning in to kiss me.

"Frank, I'm not sure if this is a good idea. I mean somebody could drive past and see us." The words were tumbling out of my mouth and my brain was telling me that this was a really bad idea, but even so I found myself wrapping my arms tightly around his neck and succumbing to his volley of kisses.

"Frank, I must get on," I said, eventually pulling away from him.

"Sure, I understand," he replied, starting the engine.

The road clung to the perimeter of the estate, and when it narrowed to a single track I felt sure we had somehow missed the entrance, but as we drove slowly under a dense canopy of trees it opened up again, and the green was replaced by the gray of the stone wall. Two minutes later we arrived at the gates of Castle Beadale.

In contrast to the traditional wrought iron work of the gates, I noticed a very modern CCTV camera, beneath which was a high-tech intercom system with two buttons: one marked VISITORS and one CASTLE. When the gates silently swung open I took a deep breath, readying myself for my final farewell with Frank and the beginning of my new life at Castle Beadale.

"Looks like they're expecting you," he said, rolling the car slowly forward over a cattle grid and onto the estate.

"What happened to dropping me at the gates?" I asked.

Frank said nothing, just pointed at the vast gap between us and the tiny outline of the house in the far distance.

"Still wanna walk?" He laughed as he slowly drove toward the castle.

The grounds stretched out in every direction, so much so that it was impossible to see where the estate ended and the real world began.

The unsealed road meandered through the center of the estate, which was wild and unkempt. I'd been expecting formal gardens by Capability Brown with straight lines and frivolous topiary, but instead it felt like we were driving through remote Scottish Highlands. And it felt like we were being watched.

Out of the corner of my eye I saw something move behind the cover of a densely wooded copse, but tried to ignore it. The car juddered as we rolled noisily over another cattle grid, and seconds later a dozen or so huge stags bolted from the cover of the trees, scattering in every direction. I slammed my foot on an imaginary set of brakes at the same time as Frank applied more gentle pressure on the real ones.

"Wow! I've only ever seen one of those on the label of a bottle of Scotch," he said with a faint trace of wonder in his voice.

"Just make sure you don't kill one of them—it wouldn't be the best way to start my new job."

As the castle drew nearer the road forked, and a hand-painted sign marked TRADESMEN directed us off to the left, through an ivy-covered arch leading to a large cobbled stable yard. Frank brought the car to a complete halt and turned off the engine.

"So, this is good-bye, is it?" he asked.

"Looks like it," I said, reaching for the door handle. He leaned over and took hold of my wrist.

"What's up?" he asked.

"Honestly, it's nothing. I just really need to go."

I looked across the yard and noticed a farmhand leaning on his shovel outside one of the stables, eyeing Frank and me suspiciously. The old guy was making no attempt at concealing his curiosity, and I was tempted to ask him what he was staring at, but then, looking back at Frank behind the wheel of his ridiculous yellow sports car, I realized it was pretty obvious.

"But you got all weird with me after we stopped for petrol. Is it something I said?"

At that moment all I wanted to do was get out of the car and start my new job. I didn't want a scene, especially with Farmer Giles watching my every move. But there was something about Frank that made me act irrationally, and the next thing I knew I was frantically rummaging around in my pocket.

"There!" I said, tossing the note at him. "I don't know whose car this is, but tell your 'mate' thanks for the loan." Frank stared down at the tiny piece of paper like I had just tossed a live grenade into his lap.

"Where did you find that?" he asked, beginning to laugh.

"This is not funny, Frank!" I barked at him. "You are a great guy. I like you, I really do, but it could never work between us. So this is good-bye. You've made a mug out of your girlfriend . . . or boyfriend. It doesn't matter to me which, but I'd rather you didn't try to do the same to me."

He stopped laughing and was beginning to look a bit sheepish, so I took the opportunity to get out of the car in as dignified a fashion as I could manage. I hoisted my two bags out of the back and allowed them to land with a thud on the cobbles.

I tentatively glanced over at the guy by the stables, but thankfully he now appeared to be more interested in shoveling huge piles of horseshit than in me.

"So, thanks for the lift, Frank. Seriously, I appreciate it," I said, extending my hand into the car for a gentlemanly handshake. He responded by doing the same, but when he took my hand he yanked me firmly toward him, sending me completely off balance and headfirst into the car. He said nothing, but planted a huge, passionate kiss on my lips that, given my rather awkward position, I was unable to resist. When he moved his head away from mine, he spoke.

"I can explain if you'll let me. I do not have a girlfriend *or* a boyfriend, I swear. But there is a vacancy going for the latter. If you want to apply, I could fast-track your application." He winked.

I could feel my face flush with a mixture of embarrassment

and lust as I struggled clumsily to plant my feet back on the cobbles. Eventually, after some undignified flailing around, I was out of the car and upright again.

"Well, that was embarrassing," I said, smoothing down my ruffled hair. "The last thing I want is the entire estate to know I'm gay. This is not London you know! For all I know they still put gay people in the village stocks and pelt them with rotten fruit around here."

As I strode away from the car my cheeks felt hot, and my heart was pounding wildly inside my chest.

"Call me when you have had a chance to settle in, and maybe you'll let me explain," Frank shouted, but I didn't bother to turn around. I heard the car move slowly out of the yard, and after he was gone I stood in front of the door marked DELIVER-IES. I took a breath before ringing the bell, but was stopped in my tracks by an unfamiliar voice.

"Bell doesn't work," the old farmer shouted, pointing his shovel in the direction of the door. I cursed Frank under my breath for putting on such an embarrassing show in front of one of the locals. The one thing I could ill afford to happen was for this little display to get back to Lord Shanderson. I'd be on the next train back to London before I'd even had a chance to unpack.

"Cheers," I said, forcing a smile. "I'll bear that in mind."

I knocked hard on the door, willing someone to open it quickly as I could feel the farmer's eyes burrowing into me from across the yard. My knock was immediately rewarded by the sound of barking dogs. The canine chorus persisted for a few minutes until I heard footsteps from the other side and a voice that silenced the cacophony almost at once.

"Shut up, you stupid animals. Otherwise you'll all be going down, and it won't be in bloody history!"

The door opened to reveal a tall, willowy woman dressed rather austerely all in black.

"Hello, I'm ..."

"His Lordship's new butler, yes, I know. We've been expecting you."

She ignored my outstretched hand as well as my two cumbersome bags and simply headed down the dimly lit corridor, leaving me on the doorstep. I lugged the bags over the brass threshold and began wheeling them behind me, trying to keep up.

"Be careful of the tiles," she barked over her shoulder. "This floor has just been buffed; I don't want it covered in scratches, thank you."

Jesus! This woman was quite the welcoming party, I thought as I struggled to carry the bags without their coming into contact with her precious floor.

She stopped abruptly at one of the doors off the corridor and opened it, signaling for me to enter. It led into a huge, brightly lit kitchen filled with the unmistakable smell of baking bread coming from an ancient range neatly tucked into a cavernous fireplace. In the center of the room was an imposing pine table surrounded by old chapel chairs. Its surface looked freshly scrubbed, and in the center was a battered enameled jug filled with wildflowers. This was the kind of country-house kitchen interiors magazines constantly tried (and failed) to replicate, but it was obvious from the ancient copper pans, the pitted flagstone floor, and the rickety old dresser filled with mismatching jars of preserves that this was the real deal.

"Vera will be here shortly to show you your accommodations, but in the meantime I suppose you should take a seat," she said, waving a bony finger in the general direction of a chair. She left the room without another word, letting the door slam behind her.

On the far side of the room above a row of ceramic Belfast sinks were large picture windows looking out over farmland at the rear of the estate. I was just admiring the view when a voice from behind made me jump.

"Have none of those buggers offered you a cuppa?"

I turned to see a short, squat woman I guessed to be in her sixties, wearing a dirty old Barbour jacket and a knitted bobble hat. Her cheeks were flushed, and she was holding a wooded trug filled with vegetables still covered in wet mud. When she banged it down I couldn't help thinking that whoever had scrubbed that table wouldn't thank this woman for covering it in soil.

"I'm Vera," she said, pulling off a gardening glove and shaking me by the hand with firmness that took me by surprise.

"Nice to meet you, Vera, I'm—"

"Anthony, yes, I know. We've been expecting you."

She shook off her coat and slung it on the back of a chair en route to the range.

"Right, let's have that cuppa," she said, sliding the kettle onto the hot plate of the Aga. Something told me now was not the time to ask if she had any Guatemalan espresso.

"That would be lovely, Vera. I'm parched."

I watched her glide around the kitchen fetching clean cups, taking a sugar bowl out of the cupboard, and filling a small jug with milk with a practiced ease that suggested this was entirely her domain. On the other side of the kitchen a face appeared around the top of a split door leading out to the garden.

"Vera, His Lordship asked me to let you know that he won't be back for tea. He's just gone off to the saddlery in Westcourt Village," he said in a West Country accent.

I literally gulped when I saw whom the voice belonged to. He was about six feet tall with tousled sandy hair and a light covering of stubble along his strong jawline. I could only see him from the waist up, but he looked like he was wearing riding gear.

"Come in, George; don't just stand there," Vera said.

He reached in, unbolted the door, and strode purposefully into the kitchen.

"BOOTS!" Vera yelled at him.

As he bent down to pull off his muddy boots, the fabric of his jodhpurs stretched across his thighs, almost causing me to spill my tea. Now I could see the whole picture, he instantly reminded me of the brooding love interest in a Jilly Cooper miniseries I saw on TV as a horny teenager. Ever since then equestrian wear has held a certain erotic fascination for me that I've never really been able to shake.

"Time for a cuppa, George?"

" 'Fraid not. His Lordship wants me to ride out one of his horses before he gets back," he said, smiling warmly at Vera whilst managing to blank me out completely.

"Wouldn't mind a bit of cake to take with me though." He eyed a plate of Victoria sponge on the table between us.

"Hi, I'm . . ." I said, standing up to greet him.

"Yeh, I know who you are," he replied, ignoring my outstretched hand. I felt my cheeks flush as my hand just hovered there, waiting to be shaken.

Arsehole! I thought, pretending to look at my watch and sitting back down.

Vera was too busy wrapping a huge slice of cake in waxed paper to notice George's bad manners, but I was fuming.

"There you go, George, now bugger off!" Vera said, beaming with what looked like genuine affection.

George pecked her on the cheek and headed back out the door without even looking at me, let alone saying good-bye.

"Such a lovely boy," Vera said when he was gone.

"Really?" I said. "I thought he was a bit rude if I'm being honest."

"Oh, don't pay any attention to George; he's just a bit shy, that's all. He's not long out of the army, so we are still trying to housebreak him." She laughed.

Moments later the door half opened again, and George's face peered round it. He was smiling this time.

"Sorry, totally forgot me manners—welcome to Castle Beadale, Anthony," he said with a wink before heading out the door.

"Top up?" Vera asked with the teapot already hovering over my cup.

I smiled and nodded, so Vera poured the tea and placed the pot between us on the table.

"So, Vera, what do you do here?" I asked.

"What don't I do here?" she said, letting out a booming laugh. "I'm chief cook and bottle washer. Been here forty years next June."

"You must have been not much more than a child when you started," I said, trying to work out the maths.

"Not quite, but not far off either. I keep telling His Lordship I'm still waiting to find out if I've got the bloody job! I started as a kitchen maid straight out of school. Back in the sixties we were one of the only houses in Sussex to still have a full complement of staff. When I joined there were footmen, under butlers, parlor maids, ladies' maids, cook, scullery maid, Mr. Johnson the butler, and Mrs. Heathcoat the head housekeeper. I remember there being two sittings for staff meals, there were so many of us. Oh! Those were the days," she said wistfully. "We try our best now, but it's not easy running a house this size with only a handful of us. That's why we are all so glad to see you, dear. Why don't we drink up and I'll show you to your accommodations."

"How far is my cottage from the main house?" I asked her.

"Cottage?" she replied with a look of surprise.

"Yes, I was told that the job came with a cottage. Rose View, in fact."

"Ah! Yes, about that. Rose View is being, erm, renovated at the moment, so we'll have to put you up in the house for now."

I was a little stunned at the prospect of not getting the chocolate-box cottage I had been promised, but tried not to let my disappointment show. Right now I just wanted to shower, change into my uniform, and get to work. It wasn't the time to start haggling about the details, but I'd take up the matter with His Lordship just as soon as I got the chance.

I quickly finished my tea and with luggage in tow I followed Vera out of the kitchen and down the windowless corridor into the depths of the castle. She stopped at the foot of a flight of narrow stone stairs, waiting for me to catch up.

The corridor walls were lined with dozens of framed portraits, and Vera smiled as she waited patiently for me to take them all in. The pictures appeared to start at the farthest end of the corridor, nearest the back door, as naïve oil paintings stretching back to what I guessed, judging by the clothes the subjects were wearing, was the eighteenth century. As we moved farther along the pictures moved forward in time from early photographs at the turn of the twentieth century and then, at the far end where Vera was standing, into color photographs taken in the 1970s.

"Play your cards right," Vera said, "and you could find yourself up there one day."

"What do you mean?" I asked. "Who are they all?"

"Those, my boy, are all the servants who have worked at Castle Beadale over the years. It's something of a tradition here. Every master of the house has a portrait done of his servants on the tenth anniversary of their coming here."

"Where are you then?" I asked, scanning the photographs for one that might just look like a youthful Vera.

"I'll let you figure that one out in your own good time," she said over her shoulder as she began to stride up the stairs.

I dutifully followed, and after what seemed like endless flights we reached the top of the house. I was puffing and puffing whilst Vera, clearly conditioned by years of climbing these very stairs, hadn't so much as broken a sweat. She shouldered a swing door that opened into a long, narrow passage lit by skylights in the sloping roof. On each side, a dozen or so doors were each painted with a number in faded gold paint. This floor of the castle had obviously been designed to house the servants and, for the time being at least, it was about to do so again. With its scuffed paintwork, yellowed with age, my first impression was that this floor had not been used for many a long year.

"The good news is that you have the whole floor to yourself," Vera said cheerfully as she stopped at a door at the very end of the corridor. A small brass plate on the door read:

Mr. Johnson

"After you," she said, gesturing to me to enter.

Despite the faint whiff of mothballs, the room I found myself in wasn't at all what I had expected. The utilitarian feel of the hallway was a world away from the luxury of Mr. Johnson's, now my, room. Curiously, it appeared to be circular in shape and had a tented ceiling held in place by a heavy brass chandelier.

The bed, which dominated the room, was an ancient four-poster hung with drapes perfectly matching the ceiling as well as the curtains framing a row of Gothic arched windows. The bed had been turned back, hotel style, to reveal a large embroidered letter *B* in the center of the top sheet.

"Wow!" I said. "Not what I had expected from the servant's quarters."

"This used to be Mr. Johnson's room. He was a man of great taste and a very loyal servant."

I strolled over to the windows to admire the view of the lake, and only then, as I studied the gently curving walls, did I realize where exactly the room was positioned within the castle. I was in one of the turrets I had seen from the road.

"I believe Gloria hung your uniform in the wardrobe," Vera said, breaking my train of thought. "So I should leave you to get settled in." She headed for the door, but as she passed she stopped and gently patted my cheek.

"We are all terribly glad to have you here, Anthony." And with that she left the room, closing the door behind her. I flopped down onto the bed and stared at the ornately draped ceiling.

I needed to get ready for work, so I headed for the bathroom, looking forward to an invigorating shower. I opened the only other door in the room to be confronted by my butler's uniform alone in a shallow wardrobe set into the wall. I scanned the room and realized with a slight sense of dread that there was no en-suite. With a heavy heart I padded out of the turret in search of a bathroom. Somewhat optimistically I tried the first door I came to, but when I turned on the light it turned out to be nothing more than a dusty storeroom full of old trunks and tea chests. Thankfully, the next one was the bathroom. However, in place of the hotel-style wet room I had been hoping for, I was greeted with something that seemed like it had been preserved in aspic sometime back in the 1930s. It was meticulously clean, and the chrome fittings on the roll top bath in the center of the room positively gleamed, but it was obvious that this room, as well as the others on this floor, had escaped the Szabo millions lavished on the rest of the castle.

I ran a bath and splashed in a liberal dose of Jo Malone's Wild Fig and Cassis Bath Oil stolen from the hotel. I might have pulled the short straw on accommodations, but I could see no reason not to indulge in a little bit of luxury.

I undressed in the bedroom and padded naked down the corridor back to the bathroom to discover it was thick with sweetly scented steam. Slipping into the hot water I found the bath was much bigger than most modern versions, and I could easily stretch out, allowing my head to slip under the water without my toes touching the opposite end. The scent from the bath oil was heady and rich, and in just a few minutes I was in a deep state of relaxation.

I began to run through the events of the week, and instantly my mind settled on the night I spent with Frank. With eyes tightly closed I dunked my head under the water, but when I surfaced I was snapped out of my dream by the sound of creaking floorboards. Wiping the thick foam from my eyes and ears I swung round to see where the noise was coming from. There was nobody there, and sinking back into the water I reminded myself that old houses often create quite a racket without any help from humans. Plus, Vera had assured me that I would have the whole of the top floor to myself. Then I heard a very human cough.

Heart pounding, I spun round, sending a tidal wave of scented water over the rim of the bath. There, standing in the doorway, was George.

"What the . . ." I said, not sure whether or not to stand up or sink back down below the water out of sight.

"Sorry to startle you," he said, not bothering to look away. "Vera asked me to pop up and let you know that His Lordship will be back within the hour."

Even though I had been shocked to see him, I was delighted to see George was still wearing his riding jodhpurs, but now his flannel shirt was untucked, and as he spoke he stroked his midriff absentmindedly, revealing a glimpse of a washboard stomach with a light covering of dark blond hair.

"Very kind of you, George, but you could have called me or something." I fumbled down the side of the bath for a towel only to realize that it was still hanging on a stand on the other side of the room. George followed my gaze and strode over to where the towel was and grabbed it. When he finally held it out to me, he did so just out of my reach. I stood up and I took it, trying to conceal myself as best I could, but the towel was half the size of the ones I had been used to at the hotel, so it wasn't easy.

Rather than knot it around my waist I chose to use the towel to dry my hair. I couldn't see his face as I rubbed my hair vigorously, but hoped he was feeling a little more embarrassed by now and that he would pick up on the fact that, if he chose to creep up on someone in the bath, he might get more than he bargained for.

"So George, how long have you worked at Castle Beadale?" I asked from behind the towel, but I got no reply. When I peered out from behind it he was gone. Smiling, I headed back to the bedroom to change into my uniform.

CHAPTER 6

It was years since I'd worn such formal dress, but it felt reassuringly familiar. Despite the fact that I had forwarded only my waist, inside leg, and chest size to an e-mail address given to me by Maria, the uniform fitted so well it could have been tailored for me on Savile Row. The gray pinstripe trousers broke at just the right point on my patent Oxford shoes, and the black worsted tailcoat nipped in flatteringly at the waist, revealing just the right amount of gray silk waistcoat. I admired my reflection in the full-length mirror as I tied the gray silk tie into a half Windsor knot. Brushing away an imaginary speck of lint, I puffed out my chest and marveled at the effect good tailoring has on one's posture. The results were nothing short of miraculous, and, feeling an inch taller than before, I was forced to admit that I looked bloody good in a morning suit. Finally, picking up the white cotton gloves, I headed for the servant's stairs, bounding down them two at a time until I was once again on the ground floor of the castle.

Approaching the kitchen I could hear voices, so I knocked before entering.

"Ah! Here he is." Vera beamed as I entered the room.

Gone now were her dirty gardening clothes, and instead she was wearing an old-fashioned floral apron over a crisp white blouse. Her hair was pulled into a neat chignon, and she was wearing a generous coat of lipstick. Had she not spoken first, I would have barely recognized her.

"Hello, everyone," I said to the various people who turned in unison to face me, "I'm . . ."

"We all know who you are," said the woman who had opened the door when I first arrived at the castle. She was smiling this time, but it looked like it took a bit of an effort. "I'm Gloria, the head housekeeper," she said, extending a thin, veiny hand.

Compared to how frosty she had been just a couple of hours earlier, it seemed like Gloria was, for some reason, putting on a show of friendliness in front of the others. When I shook her cold and clammy hand I was filled with a sudden sense of dread, and I prayed my face wouldn't betray what I was thinking. Her handshake was weak and limp, but I did my best not to recoil. Weak handshakes give me the creeps, and Gloria's more than most.

"Anthony, this is Wendy," Vera said, waving over at a dowdy-looking woman peeling potatoes into the sink. "She comes to help me with the cooking here."

"Hello," Wendy said, looking up from her potatoes with a thin smile.

"And this is my son, Tom," Vera said, resting a hand on the shoulder of a young man who sat at the table nursing a mug of tea. "He is Lord Shanderson's driver."

The young man smiled, but said nothing.

"Speak up!" Vera barked. And then, so quickly he didn't see it coming, she swiped him around the side of the head with the back of her hand. I gasped, but realized no one else had so much as batted an eyelid.

"Sorry, mum," Tom said. "Nice to meet you, Anthony." This time he stood up and shook my hand firmly, looking me straight in the eye.

"That's better," Vera said, softening her tone considerably.

"And last but not least, this is Kylie. She comes in to help Gloria around the house turning down beds and lighting fires. Don't you, dear?" Vera smiled at the young girl, dressed rather awkwardly all in black apart from a crisp white apron and sitting opposite Tom at the kitchen table. From what I could see Kylie was much more interested in Tom than in Vera's introductions; she only just managed to tear her gaze away from him long enough to say hello. For a few tense seconds I wondered if she too might feel the back of Vera's hand, but was relieved to find that was reserved for Vera's own flesh and blood.

Introductions over, Vera doled out various tasks to each person before steering me toward the door.

"Gloria, will you show Anthony around the castle or shall I?" Vera asked.

"You'll have to do it; I'm far too busy!" Gloria replied, not bothering to look up from her newspaper.

Vera just smiled and led the way out of the kitchen and into the depths of the castle.

"We'll start at the bottom and work our way up I think, don't you?"

Beyond the servants' staircase was a heavy green baize door studded with brass tacks that opened out onto a huge marble entrance hall.

Going from the relative gloom behind the scenes into this light and airy cavern of a room made me squint.

"I wasn't expecting that," I said.

"Yes, well, this house is full of surprises."

Briskly marching ahead, Vera progressed through all the ground-floor rooms at a cracking pace. Each room opened onto the next, starting with the breakfast room, then the Long Library, the

Yellow Drawing Room, the billiards room, and finally the dining room.

"And this room," Vera said with a sweeping arm gesture,
"speaks for itself."

After a succession of grand rooms Vera had saved the best
for last. The dining table, which was one of the largest I had
ever seen, was groaning under the weight of huge gold center-
pieces and multi-branched candelabras. The walls, rather than
being painted or papered, were upholstered with glossy red
silk, but only minute areas were visible amidst the sea of gilt-
framed portraits sandwiched between the dado and the picture
rail. Those pictures were no doubt all of ancestors of Lord
Shanderson.

As my eyes struggled to take it all in, Vera picked her moment perfectly to flick a switch by the door that sent refracted
light from the crystal chandelier bouncing wildly from every
surface. The effect was incredible.

"Are we expecting company?" I asked.

"No, His Lordship will dine alone this evening."

"Alone? Amongst all this?" I asked, looking around at a
room set out more for a state banquet than dinner for one.

"Yes, all alone—he loves this room, and he's perfectly happy
to enjoy it in his own company." She smiled as she looked
around with what could only be described as absolute pride.

"Better show you upstairs before His Lordship gets back.
There'll only be enough time to show you the master suite, and
then you should lay the table so you've got enough time to help
him dress. Follow me."

Vera led the way out of the dining room through a concealed
door on the far side that led into a small butler's pantry. Tradi-
tionally this is where the plates were cleared to, washed, and
then put away. The fine china would never be allowed to find
its way into the kitchen, where it would surely perish at the
hands of some clumsy kitchen maid. The pantry even had one

of the original wooden sinks designed to protect the fine bone china from chips and scratches. Glass-fronted cupboards housed vast quantities of plates and glassware. The plates were in all shapes and sizes, but each was decorated with a heavy banding of gold leaf and what I took to be the Shanderson crest in the center. The crest was comprised of a baronial shield flanked by two intricately detailed golden griffins, and I recognized it instantly as being the same as the one positioned high above the main gates of the estate.

Vera didn't linger long in the pantry, marching me through into yet another corridor. By now I had totally lost my bearings.

"And that brings us back to where we started," she proclaimed.

"Does it?" I asked, genuinely confused.

"It certainly does, and through there is the kitchen." She pointed to a door opposite the pantry. "The castle is basically built in the round. If you carry on going in one direction long enough you'll always arrive back where you started." She laughed, leaning against a panel in the wall that swung open to reveal a narrow staircase.

"Another surprise?" I asked, following Vera as she bounded up the uncarpeted stairs with a speed befitting someone half her age.

"Years ago, when I started here as a girl, Mr. Johnson used to say 'Vera, if you find yourself stood on carpet, you are in the wrong place!'" She laughed.

On a landing another green baize door brought us out into a richly decorated hallway, at the end of which was a set of heavy mahogany doors.

"His Lordship's room," Vera said, leading the way.

Lord Shanderson's bedroom was very much in keeping with the rest of the house and was liberally stuffed with antiques and works of art. Looking around the room my eyes were immediately drawn to a large Baroque portrait of a lady hanging in pride of place above the fireplace. Its ornate gilt frame and the way it was positioned in the room suggested that it was perhaps a jewel in His Lordship's collection. Once I moved closer I could just make out the words on the tiny brass plaque on the bottom of the frame:

LADY ALICE SHANDERSON BY JOHANN ZOFFANY 1733–1810

I let out a whistle of admiration that Vera was polite enough to ignore.

"Do you know anything about art?" she asked.

"I'm not sure how much I actually know," I said, not wanting to brag. "But it's been something of an obsession of mine all my life."

"Then I can see you and Lord Shanderson getting on like a house on fire."

Tearing myself away from Lady Alice, I followed Vera around the room as she pointed out various things, such as which drawer of the tallboy his collar studs and cufflinks were kept in and where to position his slippers during turndown.

"When we have guests Gloria and Kylie do all the turndowns apart from His Lordship's, and of course when Lady Shanderson is in residence her butler will take care of her room."

"Isn't this Lady Shanderson's room too?" I asked.

"Hers is on the other side of the house," Vera said, before turning her attention to the extravagantly upholstered four-poster bed.

"His Lordship is very particular about his bed," she said, getting down on all fours and retrieving an electric iron from beneath it.

"He likes to have the sheets ironed on the bed. It gives a better finish." She plugged in the iron behind the nightstand and started furiously smoothing out creases from the linen sheets. I just stood and watched as she worked at lightning speed.

"It looks like a bit of a faff, but once you get the hang of it, it shouldn't take you more than a few minutes." She stood back to admire her work, and sure enough it was perfect. "Not bad for a cook, eh?" She laughed. "And then turn the right hand side down to an angle of forty-five degrees, turn the lights down to thirty percent, and whatever you do make sure the blinds are fully lowered."

She moved to the window to demonstrate her point, but before she did I caught a glimpse of the view that Lord Shanderson woke up to every morning. Although it was now dark, the strategically placed outdoor lighting and a bright winter moon meant that I could see the edge of the lake beyond the gravel turning circle at the front of the castle. The water shimmered, and the outline of the naked trees at the lake's edge gave it an eerie look that was somewhere between beautiful and sinister. Before Vera snapped shut the blinds it also occurred to me that the room had exactly the same view as my own; my accommodation was positioned directly above His Lordship's.

"Right then, young man, it's 6:30 p.m., and His Lordship always eats at 8 p.m. if he's alone, so you need to set the table and then wait in the kitchen. He'll ring down for you if he needs a hand dressing—he usually doesn't, but he probably will want to get the measure of you."

I followed Vera out, trying desperately to remember the way back to the dining room.

"Oh! I almost forgot—you'll be needing this," she said, retrieving a small cordless telephone from the pocket of her apron. "I'm extension 218; call me if you need anything." And with that she disappeared down the hallway, humming quietly to herself.

After a couple of attempts I found the hidden panel that concealed the servant's stairs, and in no time at all I was in the dining room.

I then realized that in the rush to take everything in I hadn't bothered to ask Vera what she was cooking for His Lordship's dinner; without this information I couldn't correctly lay the table. But just as I was about to head off to the kitchen I spotted a small printed menu card bearing Castle Beadale's crest, placed at the head of the table:

MENU

CONSOMMÉ

ROAST GROUSE, GAME CHIPS, FRIED CRUMBS, AND BREAD SAUCE

VEGETABLES FROM THE GARDEN

TREACLE TART AND CUSTARD

Although this seemed a surprisingly formal setup for someone dining alone, it happily provided me with all the information I needed to work my magic. Years ago at the Palace I had been known for my speed and accuracy when it came to laying the table, and I still had the wood and brass folding ruler I was taught to use there. It was a well-known fact that the Queen could spot an unevenly laid table at twenty paces, so to avoid this we used the standard issue ruler to measure the spaces between the settings. Conveniently, at Castle Beadale all the silverware was kept in the drawer of an imposing mahogany sideboard, as was the dinner service and linen, so in ten minutes flat I had laid the table with mathematical precision and stood back to admire my work. Having decided that restraint was probably not the order of the day at Castle Beadale, I went for a "Prince of Wales's Feathers" napkin fold that I hadn't done for years. I was delighted that I could still remember how to do it.

Feeling really rather pleased with myself I left the dining room and made my way down to the kitchen, hoping there was enough time for a bit of a sit down and something to eat before being summoned by His Lordship.

Vera must have read my mind because when I walked in the kitchen she was just finishing off making a huge plate of sandwiches.

"There we are, love," she said, handing me the plate. "You must be starving. If I had to guess I'd say that's the first thing you've had all day."

I nodded my agreement and began to devour them. And then, just minutes later as I swallowed the last mouthful, the servants' bell marked LONG LIBRARY rang on the old wooden panel on the wall.

"Right, young man. Quick sticks—time to meet your new boss," Vera said, grabbing the mug out of my hand and all but hoisting me to my feet.

"Wish me luck!" I said as I hurried out of the kitchen and down the hall to the door I hoped would lead me back into the Marble Hall.

My sense of direction was, for once, spot on, and, finding myself outside the door of the Long Library, I took a deep breath before knocking and entering.

The lights had been dimmed, but I could see Lord Shanderson reading a broadsheet newspaper by the light of a desk lamp at the far end of the room. I approached the desk and stopped a few feet in front of it, waiting for him to speak. He stayed silent for a while as I watched a cloud of sweet cigar smoke waft above the rim of the newspaper.

"Welcome to Castle Beadale, Anthony," he finally said before slowly lowering the paper. As he did so I felt the whole room slide out of focus, except for Lord Shanderson's face. And then the terrible realization dawned on me that the old guy in the stable yard, the one who had witnessed Frank's and my messy good-bye, was in fact Lord Shanderson. I suddenly felt sick. Very sick indeed.

"How have you settled in?" he asked.

My mouth was so dry I was afraid no words would form, so

I summoned every available drop of saliva before I opened it to speak.

"Very well, sir, thank you."

"I will need you to drive me after dinner; I have some business to attend to in Brighton, and it's my chauffeur's night off. It shouldn't take more than an hour or so."

As he spoke I studied his face. He no longer bore any resemblance to the old man in the stable yard, though it was clear they were one and the same person. His hair was gray but sharply parted and greased into place. Expensive tweeds had replaced his shabby work clothes. An expensive cologne mingled with the cigar smoke in the air between us, but what surprised me most of all was how handsome he was.

"... don't you think?" he said, snapping me out of my daydream.

"Indeed, sir," I said, despite having missed the question.

"Good; in that case once I have had my after-dinner brandy I'd like you to bring the Land Rover round to the front of the house and wait for me there."

"Not the Bentley, sir?" I asked. I'd seen a sleek black Bentley parked in one of the old stables with the number plate "DS 1." I wondered why on earth he would want to be driven in a Land Rover when such a beautiful car was there for the driving.

"No, the Landy will do just fine. Sometimes I find the Bentley a little, I don't know ... conspicuous?" he said, before turning his attention back to the *Financial Times*. "That will be all, Gowers."

Back in the kitchen I found Vera and Wendy laying the table for the staff evening meal. The most delicious smell was wafting from something tented with foil that sat on the warming plate of the Aga. I couldn't resist having a sneaky peek.

"Oooh! Cottage pie, my favorite," I said, licking my lips.

"Show me a man who doesn't like cottage pie, and I'll show

you a man who doesn't like to eat," Vera said as she fussed over the table. Having thought I was going to be staying in my own cottage, I hadn't really given much thought to what the eating arrangements for the staff would be, but I was impressed at how civilized this was all looking. I watched Vera carefully as she placed a linen napkin and a wine glass at each setting, adjusting a wayward knife or a skewed fork with utter concentration.

"Would you like a small glass of wine with your dinner, Anthony?" Wendy asked, holding out a bottle of half decent-looking red.

"Better not, thanks; His Lordship has asked me to drive him to Brighton after dinner."

"Has he now?" said Gloria from somewhere behind me. "And why would he go and do that?"

"I don't see why that would be any of your business, Gloria," Vera replied, banging the cottage pie down in the center of the table with a thud.

"He said it was Tom's night off," I volunteered.

"Do you know anything about this?" Gloria asked a sheepish Tom, who looked as if he wanted the ground to open up and swallow him.

"I'm going with Kylie to the pictures in Horsham—His Lordship said he didn't need me tonight," Tom said, keeping his eyes fixed on his dinner.

"And now poor Anthony has to stay up till God knows what time waiting for His Lordship to finish doing God knows what in Brighton." She spat out "Brighton" like it was a dirty word.

"I honestly don't mind, Gloria. It's not a problem."

"Not for you maybe," she said as she spooned peas and carrots rather exuberantly onto each person's plate.

The pudding was apple crumble and custard, and before I knew it I'd scoffed down not one but two helpings. I made a promise to myself to go for a long run in the morning before breakfast to make sure all these country-sized portions didn't instantly glue themselves to my arse.

I glanced up at the old clock above the Aga, and seeing that it was just before eight, I brushed myself down and headed to the dining room to light the candles and wait for His Lordship to come in for dinner. But to my horror he was already sitting at the table talking on the phone. I hovered uncomfortably in the doorway for a few seconds, unsure whether or not to enter as the conversation sounded like one I probably shouldn't be party to. He hadn't yet spotted me, so I retreated back into the hallway and began to watch and listen through the crack in the door.

"Elizabeth, we've been here before—are you absolutely sure this time?"

I assumed the Elizabeth on the other end of the phone was Lady Shanderson, so I began to eavesdrop in earnest.

"Good, good. And are you certain you have taken every precaution to cover your tracks? We can't afford for there to be any skeletons rattling around. And there definitely can't be anyone else in the frame."

Whatever his wife's response was to the last question, it certainly made him jump, and even from behind the dining room door I could hear her tiny voice squawking from the receiver he was holding at arm's length. And she didn't sound happy.

"For Christ's sake, Elizabeth, calm down. Given your track record, you can't blame me for asking! And yes, my own affairs are very much in order, thank you for asking. Anyway, I shouldn't have to remind you exactly what's at stake for both of us now. Still, it looks like this little bird is finally coming home to roost." His tone was firm, but his voice was low. "And speaking of coming home it's time for you to do the same. I realize that Beadale isn't exactly The Plaza, but a deal is a deal. I want you to get on the next plane to England. But please,

please, do *not* go and hide at your mother's the minute you arrive; we have a lot to discuss—come straight to the castle."

From my vantage point I had a clear view of his face, and I stifled a laugh when he rolled his eyes dramatically.

"Elizabeth, please don't be so melodramatic. I'd hardly describe Beadale as a prison. This is by far the safest place for you to be over the next few months. You haven't got time to waste, and we both know it's for the best. . . . Hello? Hello?" He looked at the receiver in disbelief before slamming it down on the cradle. "Bloody woman will be the death of me," he muttered just seconds before noticing me standing in the doorway.

"Apologies, sir. I was told 8 p.m. for dinner," I said, quickly lighting the candles and pouring him a glass of claret.

"Take this phone away, and if anyone calls I'm not here."

I took the phone from the table and placed it on the sideboard.

"I'm keen to eat and get going, so please tell Vera I don't require a first course or dessert—I'll just have the grouse."

I couldn't get Lord and Lady Shanderson's phone call out of my head, so I stopped en route to the kitchen to try to make sense of it. Why did she need to be kept safe? And what kind of deal was he referring to? None of it added up, and I found myself wishing more than anything that I could have heard her side of the conversation too. Maybe that would have shed some light on whatever it was they were up to, but as it stood, it sounded like she was about to frame someone for something to settle a debt with her own husband. I started to wonder what the hell I'd let myself in for.

I passed Lord Shanderson's message to Vera, but she didn't look too impressed that two-thirds of her menu was being overlooked when she handed me a heavy silver salver bearing a single bird garnished with all the trimmings. I placed a large domed cloche over it and hurried back into the dining room to serve. I held the heavy platter out at arm's length so that His

Lordship could help himself in the traditional way. As he did so I comforted myself with the thought that after a few months of serving his dinner in this way I would have great triceps.

I topped up his wine and watched with interest as he tore into the tiny bird with relish. It was bloody and rare, and I could smell its gamey aroma from the other side of the table. I've never really seen the appeal of game birds; it all looks like too much effort for not a lot of returns, but by the way Lord Shanderson was stripping every last bit of flesh from the bones I could tell that he disagreed. When he had almost cleared his plate I fetched the platter from the sideboard and offered him seconds of all the trimmings.

"No, thank you, Gowers. Wouldn't want to get fat now, would I?" he said, patting his stomach.

In the flickering candlelight I saw a faint smile cross his face. As I leaned in to pour some wine into his glass, I said, returning the smile, "I don't think there is much danger of that, sir."

With dinner cleared I brought him a large glass of Courvoisier that he barely touched before rising from the table.

"Right, meet me out front in ten minutes," he said, throwing his napkin onto the table and marching out of the room. I quickly cleared away the last few things and blew out the candle.

CHAPTER 7

When Lord Shanderson came out of the castle I was waiting for him with the engine running and the heater blowing warm air into the drafty interior of the Land Rover. As he climbed into the passenger seat I noticed he had changed his clothes and was now wearing jeans and a Barbour jacket. It was strange seeing him in "civilian" clothes; he could have got away with looking like any other average Joe were it not for the very obviously expensive handmade brogues he was wearing.

"Do you know the way to Brighton?" he asked as we bumped our way through the estate, the total darkness pierced only by the beam of the headlights.

"I have a fairly good idea, sir," I replied.

Sure enough, half an hour later, with the dark, winding country roads behind us, we turned onto the floodlit dual carriageway. Nearing the city, the rolling hills of the South Downs morphed into the gray blur of suburbia, and I realized exactly how close Brighton was to Castle Beadale. I'd always loved Brighton and had enjoyed many a dirty weekend there. In fact, when we passed a sign on the very edge of the city that read

WELCOME TO THE CITY OF BRIGHTON AND HOVE, I felt a little flutter of excitement at what possibilities lay ahead so close to my new home.

"Would you like me to drop you anywhere in particular, sir?" I asked.

"Just head for the seafront," Lord Shanderson replied. "You can find a parking space and wait in the car. I shouldn't think I'll be more than an hour."

As instructed, I drove toward the bustling seafront, and in the distance I could see the gaudy lights of the pier picked out against an inky black sea. The traffic was heavy, so at one point we slowed to no more than a crawl until we stopped completely right opposite the Royal Pavilion, probably one of the most staggeringly beautiful but frankly bizarre buildings in Europe. With its extravagant onion domes, exotic towers, and faux Indian façade, it dominates the city center like the architectural love child of Gandhi and Liberace.

"Marvelous, isn't it?" Lord Shanderson said when he noticed me staring at it.

"It really is quite remarkable, sir, yes."

"It was built as a temple to excess, you know. No better than a great big whorehouse in its day." He laughed. "Queen Victoria couldn't bear it, you know. In the end she was so offended by the stories of what her uncle had got up to there, she sold it to the council for peanuts."

"What a terrible party pooper she was," I said, instantly thinking I might have overstepped the mark.

"And nobody likes one of those, now do they?" he replied with a deep and throaty laugh.

Eventually I found a parking space, but before I even had a chance to apply the hand brake His Lordship was out of his seat and halfway up the road. I watched as he disappeared down a side street and eventually out of view altogether.

As soon as he was out of sight I began fiddling with the

radio, hoping to find some decent music to help pass the time. However, the crappy old thing was picking up more static than music, so after a few minutes I abandoned my efforts and took out my iPhone to call Chris. I knew he'd be dying to know how my first day on the job was, and who was I to deny him?

I dialed his number and drummed my fingers on the dashboard as I waited for him to pick up. Just as Chris's voice mail kicked in, the headlights from a passing car filled the interior with light, and I noticed a small black leather wallet on the seat. I hung up without leaving a message. When I picked up the wallet a shiny black plastic card fell out of it. At first I assumed it was one of the "no credit limit" black American Express cards I had seen flashed around so many times at the Landseer, but on closer inspection it was nothing of the sort. It looked like some kind of membership card, and it bore only the words BLACK ORCHID CLUB in gold along with a ten-digit number beneath. I put the card back in the wallet and placed it on the passenger seat, figuring Lord Shanderson would come back for it as soon as he realized he'd left it behind.

The air in the car was so stale and warm that I began to fall asleep. The next thing I knew, a gust of cold wind woke me up when Lord Shanderson opened the passenger-side door and began wordlessly searching for something in the darkness.

"Ah, hello, sir, are you looking for this?" I asked, passing him the wallet and trying my upmost to hide the fact that I had just woken up.

"Oh! Thank goodness," he said, instantly removing the black card and shoving it into his pocket. "Sorry about that, for a moment I thought I'd lost something quite important," he said, smiling at me. The relief on his face could not have been more obvious.

"Not a problem, sir."

"Thank you, Anthony, I won't keep you long," he said, before slamming the door shut and marching back into the darkness of a side street.

The Black Orchid? I thought. *Doesn't sound like your run of the mill gentleman's club to me.*

True to his word His Lordship was back in the car in less than an hour. This time I was wide-awake, and as soon as he fastened his seatbelt I had the engine fired up and was turning the car around to head back out of town. With a slight sense of sadness I watched the bright lights of Brighton Pier and the bizarre silhouette of the Royal Pavilion each disappear behind us as I headed north in silence. When Lord Shanderson eventually spoke, he sounded noticeably more relaxed than before.

"I do hope this hasn't been too long a day for you, Anthony. I don't usually have to engage the services of my butler for driving duties. This was something of a last-minute thing."

"It's a pleasure, sir."

"A pleasure? Excellent. I'm all for a bit of pleasure." He laughed, looking out of the window and shifting a little in his seat.

Few words were exchanged between us for the remainder of the journey, and by the time we arrived back at the castle it was in total darkness except for the lamp in the portico over the front door. I brought the car to a halt, and in the gloom of the interior I could feel Lord Shanderson's eyes on me.

"Good night, Anthony, and thank you."

I waited for him to disappear behind the heavy studded oak door before I turned around to park in the stable yard. I let myself into the house through the back door that to my relief was unlocked. The servants' corridor was also in complete darkness, but I could just about pick out my way by a faint light coming from the kitchen. I pushed open the door expecting to find Vera, but the room was as empty and silent as the rest of the castle. Before I turned off the lights and braced myself for the long climb up to the top floor, I spotted a note in the middle of the table with a glass of something on top of it. The note read:

> Dear Anthony,
> I thought you might need a wee dram to fortify
> you ahead of all those stairs!
> Breakfast at 7:30 a.m. for His Lordship. —Vera x

I sniffed the contents of the glass, and my nose was instantly flooded with the peaty aroma of a fine single malt whisky. I flopped into a chair and swirled the amber liquid around the glass. I sipped it at first, but as the heady liquor wormed its way into my system I started to feel utterly exhausted. I thought it best to skull what remained for fear I would never make it up the stairs if I waited any longer. By the time I got to my room I could barely summon the energy to hang my uniform on the back of the door before flopping down onto the bed.

Old houses never fail to deliver on their reputation of being cold and drafty. Castle Beadale proved to be no exception when the alarm woke me at 6 a.m. the following morning. I writhed and stretched under the thick mound of blankets for at least twenty minutes, attempting to delay the moment when I would have to face the freezing walk to the bathroom. When I sighed at the thought of it, an icy cloud of my own breath hung in the air above my head as if to prove the point. Counting to three I jumped out of bed and slipped quickly into a thick toweling robe stolen from the hotel. Dancing from foot to foot I pulled on a pair of gym shoes and made a mad dash down the hall. I filled the tub, and it wasn't long before huge clouds of steam had taken the chill off the room. Not having a shower was going to take some getting used to, but in the mean time I was rather enjoying the old-fashioned luxury of a pre-breakfast soak.

By the time I had bathed, shaved, and dressed I'd either warmed up or simply become accustomed to the cold. I wasn't sure which, but either way, feeling wide-awake, I bounded down the back stairs two at a time toward the kitchen. I could smell the aroma of cooking bacon all the way from the first floor landing, and my mouth was watering uncontrollably by the time I pushed open the kitchen door.

Inside, the room was buzzing with activity. Wendy was at the Aga frying bacon as fast as Vera could pile it into a waiting silver dish. Alongside the bacon on the warming plate were dishes of deviled kidneys, mushrooms, scrambled eggs, fried bread, and grilled tomatoes. There looked to be enough food for at least a dozen people.

"Do we have guests?" I asked.

"Not as far as I know," replied Vera, placing the lid on a silver chafing dish and passing it to me. "Gloria, is that toast ready?" she barked. "And whatever you do, don't burn that black pudding. Kylie, be a love and give the porridge a good stir, would you?"

"This can't all be for His Lordship," I said, looking at the vast array of dishes spread out in front of me.

"Oh, can't it now?" Vera laughed. "Trust me, my boy, this is normal. But don't worry; you'll get used to Lord Shanderson's excesses soon enough."

Vera picked up two of the dishes and motioned for me to follow her through to the dining room. She placed the dishes in perfect alignment on an electric hot plate on the sideboard, and when I put a dish down she rolled her eyes before making a minor adjustment to its position.

"Right, be a love and run an iron over this before you go and wake him up, would you?" She handed me a copy of the *Telegraph* from under her arm. "There's an iron in the butler's pantry just for the job."

I hadn't heard of anyone's ironing the newspaper for years. One of the old boys at the Palace had told me they used to do it to set the ink so that the royals didn't end up with dirty fingers. Even though I was pretty sure things had moved on in the world of printing since then, it seemed old habits die hard at Castle Beadale.

After a quick once-over with a hot iron I returned the newspaper to the dining room, where I placed it neatly alongside the single table setting before sprinting up the back stairs to wake Lord Shanderson.

I paused outside his room when it occurred that nobody had briefed me on the correct protocol for waking His Lordship. Should I just knock on the door and wait for a response, or should I knock and enter? I mulled it over for a few seconds before rapping sharply and entering as authoritatively as I could.

The room was pitch-black; I fumbled around the furniture toward the heavily draped windows and pulled back the curtains. The bright morning light flooded the room, revealing a sleeping Lord Shanderson only partially covered by a swathe of white linen sheets.

He stirred, but remained sound asleep whilst I took the opportunity to have a sneaky look at His Lordship. It appeared that, beneath the formality of his Harris Tweeds, Lord Shanderson had been concealing a surprisingly fit and toned body. His chest was broad with a light covering of hair that tapered down to a narrow treasure trail before disappearing beneath the sheet. His arms too were broad and generously muscled but not, I guessed, from endless workouts in the gym, but rather from a life lived in the country where looking after his horses was his daily exercise. After all, had I not seen him energetically mucking out the stables himself the day I arrived? Whatever it was that kept him looking so buff for a man of his age, it was working. As he slept I studied his face carefully and began to wonder exactly how old he was. His skin was smooth with only a few wrinkles around the eyes, and his hair was thick and wavy with only a smattering of gray at the temples. His beard, on the other hand, whilst carefully trimmed, was heavily flecked with gray, and it was probably this alone that had made me mistake him for someone older. If I had to hazard a guess, I would put Lord Shanderson at no older than mid fifties, but however old he was, one thing I knew for sure was that he was a damn sight sexier right now than when I had first seen him in the stable yard.

I gasped nervously when he rolled over, fearing he might open his eyes at any moment only to catch me staring, but to my relief his eyes remained tightly closed. I forced out a cough, feeling sure it would wake him, but instead he simply shifted his position. I returned to the window and began to wrestle with the enormous swathes of fabric that made up the elaborate curtains. Eventually I managed to secure them in place by using the heavy, gold-tasseled tiebacks. After I fully raised the blinds, even more light flooded into the room.

"Good morning, Gowers," said a voice from behind me. I breathed deeply and pinched the bridge of my nose, trying to erase all the mental pictures of my near-naked boss before turning to greet him.

"Good morning, Your Lordship," I said with a smile. He was now sitting up in bed and had pulled the sheets back over himself. "Breakfast is ready when you are, sir," I said, trying my best to keep eye contact.

"Jolly good, Gowers. I'm starving," he replied, before throwing off the sheet and springing out of bed. I tried to keep my cool as he stood completely naked in front of me. He remained motionless for what seemed like an age before speaking.

"Would you have me eat my breakfast in the nude, Gowers?" he asked.

"Sir?"

"It wouldn't be a problem for me, but I'm not sure if Vera's nerves could take it, so perhaps you would be so kind as to pass me the dressing gown hanging on the door right behind you."

I turned and hastily grabbed the silk robe from its hanger, holding it out at arm's length for him to slip into. But as he turned his back to me my eyes couldn't help but wander from the nape of his neck down the length of his spine to his backside. The fact that he had an extremely pleasing arse was not what caught my attention though. What did take me by surprise was that on one cheek there was a tattoo. I saw it only for a fleeting moment before it disappeared beneath the folds of his silk dressing gown, but it looked like some kind of Latin inscription.

"*Honi soit qui mal y pense,*" he said, turning to face me.

"Excuse me, sir?"

"*Honi soit qui mal y pense*—evil be to him who evil thinks. It's the motto of the Household Cavalry."

"I'm sorry, sir; I'm not sure I know what you mean."

"My tattoo, I know you just saw it. All the chaps in my regiment had them done."

"Oh! I see, sir. I'm afraid my Latin is rather rusty," I said, stumped for anything else to say on the matter.

"It's French," he replied, smiling and looking rather pleased with himself. He breezed past me and bounded down the main staircase toward the dining room, leaving me just a little bit stunned.

Despite the huge spread laid out for breakfast, His Lordship ate only a couple of slices of toast before disappearing back upstairs to dress. As soon as he was out of the dining room Vera appeared to help me clear away the dishes.

"Such a shame all this food is going to go to waste," I said.

"Don't you worry about that, my dear; nothing edible goes to waste in this house. If the staff don't demolish it, the dogs will."

I followed Vera back to the kitchen where quite a crowd had gathered. I scanned the room and saw Tom, Kylie, Gloria, and

Wendy, and on the far side of the room by the back door, struggling to remove his riding boots, was George.

"Right, you lot—help yourselves, but be quick. I want to get these things washed and put away," Vera said, placing all of the silver dishes in the middle of the kitchen table.

Tom was the first to spring into action, but as he lunged at a dish of deviled kidneys his mother rapped the back of his hand with the wooden spoon she was holding.

"F.H.B!" she barked at him. "What does that stand for, Tom?"

"Family hold back," he said sheepishly before moving aside.

I stifled a laugh and glanced over at George, who was now hovering over a plate of sausages. We exchanged glances before he spoke.

"Morning, Anthony," he said coolly.

"Hi, George, lovely day," I said, but it looked like he was done talking as he just tucked into his breakfast without another word.

I hastily assembled a bacon sandwich for myself and stood leaning on the workbench whilst I devoured it. George began chatting to Kylie and Tom about something work-related that I couldn't quite hear, but every few seconds he glanced over in my direction before quickly looking away again. I found his behavior most confusing. One minute it felt like he was flirting with me, and the next it felt like he couldn't stand the sight of me. This guy seemed not to know what he wanted.

Maybe, I thought to myself, *I could help him find out.*

All of a sudden, the chatter in the room was replaced by the scraping of chair legs on flagstones as everyone seated stood up. I turned to see Lord Shanderson standing in the doorway.

"Please, don't get up, I just came to say that I will be out most of the day. I'm shooting over at Glebe Farm. I'm going to have lunch there. I'll be back for tea."

"Very good, Your Lordship," said Vera.

"And Tom, I'm going to drive myself," he added, before doffing his tweed cap to the room.

As His Lordship closed the kitchen door behind him, a very faint waft of his cologne floated past my nose. A bracing mix of citrus and spice, it wasn't a scent I had ever smelt before, so I made a note to check his bathroom to see what it was.

"Right, you lot, let's not waste the day now His Lordship is out of the house. There's plenty for everyone to do." Vera clapped her hands, which seemed to be universally understood to mean that breakfast was over. If Tom harbored any doubt of her precise meaning, she promptly removed it by taking away his half-eaten breakfast and scraping it into the bin.

"Got any plans for the day?" I asked George as he wrestled with his boots by the back door. He looked up, but yet again he chose to ignore me, leaving without another word.

I knew that my first job of the day was to make His Lordship's bed and tidy his bathroom, so I got right to it, hoping that if I got a move on I might get a few hours to myself before teatime. I planned to take a walk through the estate and get a feel for the place. I thought I might even go for a run if I could summon the energy.

The bed was as he had left it, with the linen sheets practically tied up in knots. I grasped a handful of the top sheet, meaning to simply smooth it into place, but before I knew it I had my entire face buried within its folds, breathing deeply. Pure linen is permanently cool to the touch, so any secret hopes I might have harbored about the sheets still being warm left me disappointed. However, there was a lingering human scent, which instantly sent a jolt of electricity to my groin.

For God's sake, Anthony, pull yourself together, I thought as I began to work on making the bed in earnest. Once I had placed the top cover on and plumped up the pillows, I quickly ran an iron over it the way Vera had shown me and got down on my hands and knees, checking that everything was just so. Eventually, when satisfying perfection had been achieved, I began to move around the room picking up various items of discarded clothing. I picked up a pair of crisp white cotton boxer shorts and noticed that they were handmade and had the initials *DS* embroidered in red silk on the inside of the waistband. It's hard to imagine anyone having bespoke underwear these days, but I guess Drummond Shanderson isn't just anyone. Finally I placed his dressing gown back on its hanger and started on the bathroom.

There were towels strewn everywhere, and he hadn't even bothered to let the water out of the bath.

Jesus! I thought. *This guy doesn't do anything for himself—and I thought he was supposed to be low maintenance.*

As I began to tidy all his toiletries on the washstand, I came across a small glass bottle. It was in the shape of an old-fashioned apothecary bottle with a gray ribbon tied around the neck and a tiny crystal stopper. The label on it read:

BLENHEIM BOUQUET

One sniff of the bottle told me it was the cologne I had smelled earlier. I stood for a moment with my eyes closed, thinking about Lord Shanderson, but quickly pulled myself together and put the bottle back on the shelf where I had found it.

With Lord Shanderson out of the picture for most of the day, I opted for a run to try to shift the bacon sandwich that I could feel weighing down on my conscience as well as my stomach.

The weather outside was damp and cold, but all I had with me was the gym kit I was used to wearing in the comfort of the hotel health club. The skimpy nylon shorts and flimsy tracksuit top weren't really suitable for cross-country running, but would just have to do, and I figured that if I ran fast enough I could generate my own heat. I wasn't looking forward to it, but

I was determined not to let my change in career lead to a change in my waist size.

I managed to avoid bumping into anyone on my way out of the castle, and in a matter of minutes I was beating a path across the fields and building up quite a head of steam. It was ages since I'd been for a proper run, and at first I felt ungainly and a bit out of kilter. I stumbled and tripped a couple of times, reminding me how very different an activity running on a treadmill is, not to mention how much easier it is. I was used to running for forty-five minutes or more, but today I'd been at it for a third of that time, and I was really feeling the strain. Even though the muscles in my calves and thighs were screaming for mercy as I splashed through muddy puddles and vaulted over rickety wooded stiles, I had to admit I was really rather enjoying myself. After stopping for a moment to catch my breath, I laughed out loud when I saw the state I was in. Splattered from head to toe in mud and with shorts that were wet and clinging obscenely to the contours of my thighs, I hoped to God that I wouldn't bump into anyone whilst I looked such a mess.

I decided to run to the farthest edge of the estate, which looked to be about half a mile away and was marked by the high stone wall. After that I would head back to the castle for a good long soak in a hot bath, and be ready to start work again by the time Lord Shanderson returned.

After reaching the wall I leaned on an old tree stump, stretched out my calves, and tried to figure out which would be the best path to take back to the castle. The direct route I had just come on was one option, but I didn't think my legs would cope with the return journey over the rough, uneven ground. But there was also a narrow track running off to the left that disappeared into the woods. I knew that on the far side of the woods was the lake, so by my rough calculation the path could only lead back to the castle. Apart from anything else, even if it were a slightly longer route, it looked as if it would be a bit more forgiving, so I set off with renewed vigor.

Sure enough after ten minutes of running through the woods I arrived at the lake. The path had dwindled to not much more than an animal track, but I followed it along the water's edge until it trailed off altogether, leaving me no choice but to head back the way I had just come. But before I turned around I noticed, through a line of dense trees, the back of an old stone cottage set on slightly higher ground. I scrambled up the steep, muddy bank, which sloped down from an overgrown and neglected rear garden. There was a light on inside the cottage and sweet-smelling wood smoke pouring from the chimney, but when I peered through the window there was no sign of life. I fought my way through a thick tangle of brambles to get to the front of the cottage, and there, coming toward me with arms full of logs, was George.

"Where did you just pop up from?" he asked, looking genuinely surprised to see me.

"I went for a run, and I was trying to get back to the castle when the path I was on just sort of ran out," I said, shrugging my shoulders.

"You look like you've been for a swim not a run," he said, looking down at my soaked kit. "You must be frozen."

"Not quite, but I suppose I'm not really dressed for this weather." I laughed through chattering teeth.

"Why don't you come and dry off," he said, pushing past me and holding open the front door. "It's lovely and warm inside."

By now I was shivering uncontrollably, so the warmth that emanated from the cottage's interior drew me in like a moth to a flame. As I passed inside I noticed a small wooden plaque attached to the front door. Although it was faded and some of the painted letters had peeled away, there was no mistaking what it said:

ROSE VIEW COTTAGE

So, I thought as I entered the darkness of the cottage's interior, *George is living in "my" cottage, is he?*

George kicked off his riding boots and threw a couple of logs into the wood burner before tossing the rest into a waiting basket. He then sank back onto an old battered Chesterfield before speaking. "Sorry about the mess," he said, bending down to pick up an empty beer can. "I wasn't expecting guests."

"That's quite all right," I replied. "I wasn't planning a visit."

The room smelled strongly of leather and saddle soap; bits of broken saddles, riding crops, and other horsey paraphernalia covered every surface, and magazines and books littered the floor. The room had the vague air of student digs, but I felt a twinge of jealousy when I realized it had the one thing I would never have over at the castle: privacy.

I thought it best not to mention to George that he was living in the cottage I had been promised. In fact this was the cottage that Maria had dangled like a carrot back in London when she was giving me the hard sell. I guessed that George had no idea that he was squatting in my dream home, so I decided to keep quiet. For now.

"If you want to dry off, there are towels in the bathroom," George said. "It's up the stairs on the left. The room on the right is my bedroom." He let this last piece of information hang in the air between us for a second before adding, "Feel free to borrow a dry shirt and some track pants from the wardrobe."

The bathroom was tiny, with just a shower cubicle sandwiched between a hand basin and a loo, so I barely had room to move. I did my best to towel myself down, but I was fighting a losing battle with the lack of space. So, deciding it was the best option, I just stripped off my shorts and top and wrapped the towel tightly around my waist and headed for George's bedroom for some dry clothes.

When I entered the room I was stopped in my tracks by the sight of George lying on the bed. He had stripped off down to his boxer shorts and simply raised an eyebrow as he stroked the empty space next to him on the rumpled sheets.

"I feel like we kind of got off on the wrong foot—how's about letting me make it up to you?"

"George," I said, "that's not why I'm here, and you know it."

"Yeh, and I wasn't planning this either, but after watching you in the bath yesterday, I sort of couldn't help myself. And anyway, now you're here you might as well get comfortable." He reached up and gently pulled the corner of the towel, guiding me nearer to him before giving it one final tug and removing it altogether.

"If you're sure you know what you are getting yourself into," I said by way of fair warning.

"I know exactly what I'm doing," he replied.

I doubt that very much! I thought as I fell naked onto the bed, where he wrapped his arms tightly around my neck and began to kiss me with a passion that suggested he'd been starved of male company for a while. I leaned back to get a good look at his body for the first time. There wasn't an ounce of fat on him, and as he moved and writhed the muscles in his shoulders and arms rippled and tensed. He was absolutely beautiful and held himself in a way that reminded me of myself at his age—brimming with the sort of nonchalant confidence only the young can afford. He had no apparent inhibitions, but neither did he seem to realize what a fine specimen of a man he was. Part of me wanted to tell him how hard he was going to have to work to have a body that looked half as good at thirty never mind forty, but why bother? Guys of his age never look that far into the future.

He began to nibble and suck at my nipples whilst his hand worked its way slowly and firmly down the flat of my stomach. He then put his whole body weight on top of me, and I realized it was time to let him know who was really in control of this situation.

George might have been a mass of youthful sinew and muscle, but I was the larger of the two of us, and I used this advantage to take him by surprise, suddenly flipping him off me and onto his back. Whilst he adjusted to the position, I roughly took hold of each of his wrists and held them tightly above his head.

"You were in the army weren't you, George?"

"Yeah, used to be," he said, looking confused.

"Then you should know a thing or two about discipline," I said with my mouth close to his ear.

"Is that right?" he said, suddenly not so cocky.

When I released him he rubbed his wrists before moving his hands tenderly to my waist. But I wasn't looking for tenderness so I pushed them away before rolling him over onto his front.

"Stay where you are for a minute, and close your eyes," I said as I got up from the bed. I quickly bounded down the stairs and grabbed something I had spotted earlier on the table in the living room.

George had done as I asked and was still in exactly the same position when I returned, so he didn't see me place the riding crop silently beside him. I gripped the waistband of his boxers and slipped them gently down over his hips and helped him out of them before tossing them over my shoulder. I took the crop and ran the leather tab at the end of it gently all over his body.

"What's that?" he asked nervously, attempting to look up.

"No peeking now," I said.

I continued to tease him with the tip of the crop for a couple of minutes more, whilst the only sound in the room was his rapid breathing. And then, when I thought he was expecting it the least, I flicked one cheek and then the other in quick succession, once, twice, three times on each buttock. George raised his hips farther and gripped the edge of the bed. He stayed silent with the exception of a sharp intake of breath and a low groan, but not once did he tell me to stop. After a few minutes I stood back to admire my work.

"So, how does that feel, George?" I asked.

He hesitated before answering.

"I'm not really sure," he said eventually.

I placed the crop down on the floor and began to kiss the back of his neck.

But then, just as I began to let my hands wander down his tightly muscled torso, he started to struggle beneath me like a bucking bronco. Eventually his efforts sent me off balance, and he jumped to his feet.

"Are you okay with this?" I asked, even though it was clear he was anything but.

"Yeh, fine, I just got stuff to do, that's all," he replied with his back to me, frantically searching the floor for his clothes. All flirtatiousness was now gone from his voice, and I immediately began to regret having given in to his advances. The last thing I wanted on my hands was George's being overcome by shame every time I walked in the room. I could have kicked myself—why hadn't I just waited until I got the chance to go to Brighton where nobody knew me and I would never have to see the same person twice? I waited a few minutes before speaking again as he studiously avoided eye contact.

"George, if you are worried I'm going to tell anyone about this, you needn't be," I said, grabbing his arm and forcing him to look at me. "I'm as keen to keep this quiet as you are."

"Okay, sorry," he said, and quickly began pulling on his T-shirt and jeans. "But don't go thinking this kinda stuff is gonna happen again, 'cause it ain't."

Before I had the chance to offer him any reassurances, I heard a door slam somewhere below us. George obviously heard it too as he froze to the spot, jeans half on and half off.

"What the fuck was that?" he said, looking utterly horrified.

"Calm down; it's probably just the wind. It's pretty blustery out there."

He finished dressing so quickly it was as though his life depended on it, but when he stood in front of me fully clothed I realized I had nothing dry to change into.

"Hurry up!" he said, staring incredulously as I remained completely naked on the bed.

"I'd love to, George, but the whole fucking point of my being up here was to borrow something to wear—not for a roll in the hay with you. So why don't you do something useful and pass me those track pants and a T-shirt."

He threw the clothes at me and shifted nervously from foot to foot as I hurriedly pulled them on. He seemed reluctant to be the first to head downstairs and waited for me to finish dressing before practically pushing me through the bedroom door.

"Hello?" I shouted down the stairs, as much to placate George than anything else. "See, there's no one there; it was just the wind."

He seemed to relax a bit as we descended the stairs, but when we reached the ground floor a sweet and fragrant scent wafted past my nose. George seemed oblivious to it, but to me it was unmistakable. It was the smell of Blenheim Bouquet. Now it was my turn to be in a hurry.

"I need to get my wet stuff from the bathroom. Don't suppose you've got a plastic bag or something I can put it in, have you?" I said, heading for the stairs.

"No, you stay here," he said, practically barring the way with his body. "I'll get it."

"Fine, whatever," I said, pulling on my sodden running shoes.

Whilst I waited for him to return I couldn't help but notice a bulging brown manila envelope on the mantelpiece with George's name handwritten on it. I could have sworn it hadn't been there when I arrived, but when George returned he just thrust a carrier bag at me and said nothing. It was obvious he wanted to get rid of me, so I decided not to point out the envelope and just get the hell out of there.

I shouted my good-byes from the door, but didn't wait for a reply. I was in no mood to be George's psychologist, but I was more than a bit concerned as to why I had just smelt Lord Shanderson's cologne in the cottage where I was fooling around with his groom. Of course, I could have imagined it; I mean, there was no reason at all why Lord Shanderson would be in Rose View Cottage, and I was pretty sure he wasn't the only person who wore that cologne, but I still didn't like it one bit. My head began to throb as I explored every possible explanation. Unfortunately all the scenarios I ran through ended with exactly the same outcome: my getting fired for gross misconduct.

Exhausted and frozen half to death I arrived at the castle desperate to get to my room without running into anyone, but as I entered the stable yard my heart sank. His Lordship's car was parked in its usual spot.

"Bollocks," I muttered as I headed for the back door.

"Anthony." A voice as loud and clear as a bell came from behind me. I fixed a smile onto my face before turning to greet Gloria.

"His Lordship is back, and he's been asking for you," she said in her emotionless drawl. Jesus, I was starting to dislike this woman.

"Right you are, Gloria. I'll just change and go and see him," I said cheerfully as I hurried into the castle.

"Shit, shit, shit!" I muttered as I bounded up the servants' stairs two at a time.

I changed into my uniform, and as I checked my reflection in the mirror I realized that it could quite possibly be the last time

I'd be wearing it if Lord Shanderson really had seen what was going on with George earlier. I took a deep breath and headed off to face the music.

I bumped into Vera in the passageway as she was arranging a huge vase of flowers.

"Hello, dear," she beamed. "His Lordship's been asking for you."

"So I understand."

"He's in the Long Library," she said, dead-heading a rose with a sharp click of her secateurs. In my confused state even a bit of flower arranging seemed like a metaphor for my undoing.

When I entered the Long Library, His Lordship was in his usual spot at the far end, partially obscured by his broadsheet newspaper. The walk from the door to the desk felt like it was more than a mile, and he made it worse by not speaking or lowering the paper until I stood right in front of him.

"You wanted to see me, sir?" I said with a dry mouth.

"Ahh! Anthony," he said, folding the paper and placing it carefully on the desk. He was beaming from ear to ear, which, considering he was about to fire me, seemed rather cruel.

"I just wanted to tell you what a marvelous job you are doing."

"You did?" I said, my jaw threatening to drop at any moment.

"Indeed, indeed. I have heard great things about you. I hear you are getting on very well with all the other staff, which is so important in a little community such as ours. Very important indeed."

I ran his words though my head to check for hidden meanings, but none were apparent. He seemed genuinely pleased with me.

"Thank you, sir. I am very much enjoying being here at Beadale."

"Bravo! Anthony, I think if you carry on the way you are going you will have a good future here. That will be all." He raised the newspaper to signal that our chat was concluded, so I turned and headed for the door. But before I left the room he spoke once more.

"About Rose View Cottage." My heart began to pound in my chest, and I swallowed hard before turning back to face him.

"What about it, sir?"

"I understand it was promised to you as part of your contract, is that correct?"

"It was, sir, but it's not a problem. I am quite comfortable in the room I'm in." That wasn't strictly true. I wasn't particularly happy being stuck on the top floor with no en suite, but under the circumstances I felt it unwise to push my luck.

"I will arrange for Rose View to be cleaned and prepared for you to move in. I understand it requires a little maintenance, but I shouldn't think it will take more than a couple of days."

"That's very kind of you, m'lord," I said, stunned at what he was saying.

"Well, a deal is a deal, don't you think? And a young man like you would no doubt enjoy a modicum of privacy," he said, turning his attention back to the paper.

I closed the library door behind me and stood in the hallway, taking a moment to let what His Lordship had just said sink in. I wasn't sure what to make of it.

Had he really been at the cottage or had that just been a figment of my imagination? And why was he suddenly prepared to give me Rose View? Not to mention, where would that leave George? Jesus! I hope he didn't expect George and me to share. That's the last thing either of us would want. I had so many questions swimming around in my head that I didn't see Vera approaching.

"Penny for them!" she said. "You look like you've the weight of the world on your shoulders."

"Me? Oh, I'm fine. Absolutely tip-top in fact. So what's for staff dinner?" I asked, keen to change the subject. "I'm starving."

Later that evening the kitchen was buzzing with gossip and the usual work-related chitchat.

Maybe it was just my paranoia, but when nobody mentioned having seen me running in the woods or my detour via Rose View, I felt a huge surge of relief.

"Are you waiting for someone?" Gloria asked out of the blue.

"No, why?"

"Because you haven't taken your eyes off the door since you sat down to eat." She sniffed, shoveling a second helping of Wendy's chicken stew onto her plate.

Annoyingly, she was right. I hadn't been aware I was being so obvious, but I was desperate for George to show up so that I could take him to one side and grill him about this business with the cottage.

And whilst I might have underestimated Gloria's powers of observation, I'd be damned if I was going to let her get one over on me.

"Yes, as a matter of fact I am," I said, all eyes in the room suddenly on me. "I've organized for Brad Pitt to come and take Vera out on the town."

The whole table burst into laughter, all that is except Gloria, who scowled furiously at me.

"I'd better put some lippy on then, hadn't I?" Vera said, before throwing her head back and roaring with laughter.

"No George tonight?" I said to Tom as we cleared away the dinner plates.

"Don't look like it," he said matter-of-factly. "Maybe he's gone down the pub or something; he's a law unto himself, that one."

Tom's attention turned to Wendy, who was attempting to

turn out a huge steamed treacle sponge pudding onto a serving platter.

"You're spoiling us tonight," he said, gazing at the pudding.

I'm not usually a dessert man, but even I had to admit it looked magnificent in a Dickensian kind of way. But my body hadn't seen this many carbs for years, so I decided to politely pass when it was offered to me. But before I had a chance, Vera dolloped a huge portion of it onto a plate, followed by an obscene amount of custard, and placed it in front of me without another word. After just one mouthful I knew that I'd be unable to leave a scrap of it. It was as light as air and sweet, but not sickly so; before I knew it the whole lot was gone.

"I like a man who enjoys a good pudding," Vera said, looking like she was about to give me seconds. "I don't know where you put it, mind; I've seen more fat on a chair leg."

"I'll have to run it off tomorrow, that's for sure," I said, holding my hand over the empty plate to ward off any unsolicited second helpings.

"Yes, I've heard you like to go running in the woods," Gloria chipped in.

I might have known she'd be the first to monitor my movements. I was going to have to keep my wits about me around Gloria.

"You don't get a body like mine by sitting around all day," I said, winking at her.

Much to my delight, Gloria seemed utterly appalled by my response and left the table without another word.

I served His Lordship's dinner at the usual time, and few words were exchanged between us. He had his Cognac and wished me good night, which is the universal master-servant code for "I no longer require your services; go to bed."

Most of the time I sleep like a baby, but that night my mind refused to stop running over what had happened between George and me, and His Lordship's offer of the cottage. Eventually when sleep did come I dreamt about Frank.

In the dream Frank was leaning in the doorway of Rose View looking so very at home he clearly lived there. He was smiling and mouthing words at me that I couldn't decipher. He was trying with increasing frustration to tell me something, but it was as if I were completely deaf. As I struggled to comprehend, the smile fell from his lips and he became agitated. Disappearing into the darkness of the cottage he emerged with a piece of paper on which he furiously scribbled a note. He held it up for me to see, and in large, bold letters it said **CALL ME**.

The following morning after breakfast I took a walk around the lake to get some fresh air. I couldn't summon the energy for a run, and my muscles hadn't quite forgiven me for the last one. But a brisk walk wrapped up against the bitterly cold air was just what I needed to clear my head. Once away from the castle I felt my phone vibrate in my pocket. The mobile reception inside the castle was almost nonexistent, and I had barely spoken to anyone from the outside world since I had arrived, so I retrieved the phone from my pocket with a slight air of desperation.

I quickly connected to the voice mail, eager to hear a friendly voice.

"Hello, Mr. Gowers. It's Bill from Notting Hill Residential Lettings. We've had a report of a disturbance coming from your flat, and I wonder if you could give me a call to reassure us that everything is okay. And by that I mean sooner rather than later if you don't mind. You have my number. Many thanks."

I played the message over again, and as I listened to it a second time my mind began to race. A disturbance? What kind of disturbance?

My heart was in my mouth as I ran through every possibility. Had I been robbed? Or had there been a fire? Maybe Chris had had a party that got out of hand.

I went to dial Chris's number and remembered there was another voice mail waiting for me. It was from Chris.

"Hi, Anthony, it's only me." His voice was small and lacking his usual jokey tone. "Erm, can you give me a call? I've got a slight problem. Nothing to worry about, but I think I need your help. So if you could call me back, I'd really appreciate it. Like, as soon as poss. Bye."

I punched his number in from memory, and after just a couple of rings he picked up.

"Oh! Anthony, thank fuck. I thought I was going to have to send out a search and rescue party to get hold of you." There was a distinct tone of nervousness in his voice.

"What's going on? I just had a phone call from my landlord saying there was a disturbance?"

"Yes, well, I suppose that's one name for Barry," Chris said, spitting his ex's name out like poison.

"Oh! Christ, don't tell me he turned up at the flat! Did he hurt you?"

Chris stayed silent for a few seconds before he answered. I was used to him choosing his words carefully when it came to discussing the train wreck of his personal life.

"He turned up drunk, shouting the odds about how I owe him money and shit like that. I didn't want to let him in, but someone from one of the other flats buzzed him into the building, and I didn't want him airing our dirty laundry in the hallway so I opened the door."

"And then what?" I asked.

"And then he changed his mind about the money and started ranting and raving about you. Saying that you and I were having an affair and always had been, and that all this was part of some master plan of yours to get me to yourself."

I was listening to Chris's outpouring in complete disbelief, pinching the bridge of my nose and screwing my eyes shut to stem the torrent of abuse that threatened to erupt out of me at any second. I felt the cold in my fingers and toes slowly disappear as a surge of anger built up inside me.

"He did WHAT?" I screamed into the phone. "That fucking meathead will regret ever having brought trouble to my door. Tell me, Chris, and I swear to God you had better tell me the truth—did he hit you?" I breathed deeply as I waited for a reply, filling my lungs with painfully icy-cold air.

"Yes."

"Right, I see." I was furious that Barry had hurt my friend and furious that he had infected my home with his poisonous presence. "I will sort it."

"I'm fine, Anthony, honestly. He's gone now, and I doubt he'll be back." Chris's voice had taken on a sort of meek pleading tone that didn't suit him and only made me angrier. It was probably the same cowed tone he had used to get Barry out of the flat.

"You are not fine. It is not fine. Nothing about this fucking situation is fine," I said, blood rushing to my cheeks. "I will make sure that idiot never comes anywhere near you ever again and mark my words—if he does he will regret it."

"What are you going to do about it, all the way down there in deepest, darkest Sussex?" Chris said.

"Trust me on this one, Chris. I know just the person to call."

I had calmed down a bit by the time I ended my call with Chris, but I meant every word of what I had said. Barry was a spineless bully, and like all bullies he needed taking down a peg or two. I found Frank's number and pressed dial. It rang and rang, but just as I was mentally composing a message, he picked up.

"Well, well, well. I knew you'd call eventually."

"Hi, Frank," I replied, surprised at the jolt of electricity I got when I heard his voice. "I need a favor."

Frank listened quietly as I told him about what had happened. He didn't really comment much, just made the right noises of agreement or disgust at key points in the story.

"So what do you want me to do about it?" he finally asked.

"I think if you popped round to see Barry and explained that he is not welcome at my flat ever again, he would listen to you. That's all. I mean it's not like I can pop round there, is it?"

"Anthony, please be clear about what you are asking me to do. Do you want me to scare him off or just have a nice cozy chat?"

I thought carefully about what he was saying before I answered.

"I think he will respond best to the former," I said.

"Text me his address and leave it to me. Do you want me to go and check that Chris is okay too?"

I felt a sudden and overwhelming wave of gratitude.

"Would you? Really? That's so kind of you; you don't have to, but I think Chris would appreciate it. I'll let him know you are on your way, as he probably isn't going to open the door to you otherwise." I hesitated before continuing. "How will I ever repay you?"

"Don't you worry about that, mate. I'll think of something," he said with a laugh.

I called Chris and began by filling him in on my late-night encounter with our sexy taxi driver. Sensing he would welcome the opportunity to discuss something other than his own problems, I regaled him with every sordid detail. Eventually I made up some cock-and-bull story about Frank having left something at the flat that he needed to pick up and Chris agreed that he would wait in for him. I chose not to tell him about Barry's impending visit from Frank for fear Chris would do something stupid like warn Barry. People do stupid things when they are frightened. Chris acted so irrationally around Barry that I decided it was best to keep quiet. Barry was going to get what was coming to him, and I trusted Frank not to take things too far. Just warn Barry off, that's all.

Glancing at my watch I suddenly remembered I hadn't yet called to smooth things over with Bill from the lettings agency. Thankfully, when I called it went straight to voice mail, so I left a groveling apology and left it at that. Realizing I'd been on the phone for nearly an hour, I headed back to work before I was missed.

No sooner had I stepped foot into the castle than Gloria ambushed me with a list of jobs that needed doing. There was the silver pantry to tidy and selected items to polish. The glass lanterns in the marble hallway needed to be cleaned, and the brass finials on the main staircase needed to be buffed. There were shoes to be polished and suits to be steamed. It wasn't hard to see why the last butler had thrown in the towel. It was good to be busy, but even the intermittent phone reception couldn't stop me from repeatedly checking my phone for messages from Frank.

When four o'clock came around I swapped my rubber gloves for white cotton ones to serve afternoon tea to Lord Shanderson in the Long Library. By the time it came to pouring the Earl Grey, I could barely keep my eyes open.

"Anthony, you look a little tired, if I may say so," His Lordship said as I offered him a plate of cucumber sandwiches.

"Forgive me, m'lord, I thought I was doing a good job of disguising it," I said, stifling a yawn.

" 'Fraid not, Gowers; it's as plain as the nose on your face. Now, listen to me. It isn't my intention to wear you out before your first week is even up, so why don't you take tomorrow off. I won't be around, as I have to go up to London. You relax, explore the estate. Do what you like, and come back refreshed the following day."

"Sir, it really isn't necessary," I protested, fearful he would think me not up to the job.

"I insist. Anyway, you might want to pack your things, as I understand Rose View will be ready for you to move into in the next couple of days."

I was feeling rather overwhelmed by the volume of work and a bit of free time would be great, but now I had to tell Gloria that His Lordship had given me the day off for seemingly no reason. I needn't have worried about how best to break it to her, as by the time I got from the Long Library to the kitchen the castle jungle drums had already been beating loud and clear.

"Well, if His Lordship sees fit to give you a day off, it's not really my place to argue, now is it?" she said as I entered the room.

"Honestly, Gloria, I'd be happy to help you around the house if there is work to be done."

"You will do nothing of the sort!" she snapped. "And what would Lord Shanderson have to say about that, I wonder? He would tell me I was going against his wishes. Which, I hasten to add, is something I would never do. No, you will do as you're told and have a nice, relaxing day." She drew out the word "relaxing" in a way that suggested she wanted my day off to be anything but.

CHAPTER 8

The thought of having a whole day off had quite an energizing effect on me, so when the alarm went off the next morning, rather than roll over and go straight back to sleep I practically sprang out of bed.

It struck me that I might be able to manage a trip to Brighton to grab a spot of lunch somewhere on the seafront and maybe have a wander around the Royal Pavilion. I'd also heard there was a great men-only sauna underneath one of the hotels, catering to the gay crowd. But then again there are only so many hours in a day, so when it came down to a choice between an afternoon spent working up a sweat in a dark and steamy sauna or one spent in a dusty old museum, I knew which one would win.

But before any of that I needed to track down George and speak to him about the cottage, so I pulled on some jeans and trainers and set off for Rose View.

It was bitterly cold, and a frost lay on the ground, causing the grass to crunch pleasingly beneath my feet as I walked. When I arrived at the cottage I stopped at the gate, hoping to catch a glimpse of George through the window, but there was no sign of life. Just when I was about to turn around, the front door slowly swung open. I moved up the gravel path expecting to see George emerge, but instead someone I had never seen before came backward through the door carrying a dilapidated old chair.

"Hello," I said, causing him to stop half in and half out of the cottage, trapped in the doorway beneath the weight of the chair. "Here, let me help," I said, rushing to free him.

"Cheers, mate," he said when I took some of the weight off him. With a bit of maneuvering, together we managed to get the chair through the door and dumped it on the small patch of lawn in front of the cottage.

"Thanks for that," he said.

"No worries. I'm actually looking for George," I replied.

"Too late, I'm afraid."

"Gone to work, has he?"

"Not quite. Lord Shanderson has given him his marching orders. Not so much as a by-your-leave. Happened a couple of days ago, apparently. Told him he had to be out by the end of that day."

"That can't be right—are you sure?"

"Positive. I was told to come and give the place a bit of a cleanup and make it fit for someone to move into straightaway. Some people would jump in your grave whilst it was still warm, I swear. But that's Shanderson for you," he said with a shrug of the shoulders. "You never quite know where you are with him; one minute you are flavor of the month and the next . . . Wouldn't trust him as far as I could throw him personally. But don't go telling him I said that."

"Right, I see. Did George leave an address or anything?"

"You could try asking Barbara in the estate office; she might have something as she'll no doubt have to forward his final pay to him. What did you say your name was?"

Thankfully, before I was forced to expose myself as the person moving in before the fire in the grate was even dead, I felt my phone vibrating in my pocket.

"Thanks, er, I gotta take this," I said, pulling the phone out of my inside pocket and hurrying up the garden path out of earshot.

"Looks like Barry got a visit from your friend," Chris said, launching straight in.

"Hmm, yes," I replied, preparing myself for an ear bashing. "About that."

"Anthony Gowers. You are the best friend anyone could hope for."

"I am?"

"Yes, and you can tell Frank when you see him that he isn't too shabby either. And I can definitely understand what you see in him. He's awfully butch, isn't he?"

He was starting to sound more like the Chris I knew and loved. Whatever Frank had done or said to Barry, it clearly met with Chris's approval.

"So what exactly happened?" I asked. "I haven't managed to speak to Frank yet."

"I have absolutely no idea, babe, but whatever it was, it convinced Barry to get straight on the phone to me and offer to buy out my half of the flat. Just like that. Offered me fifty percent of the full market price—I had to have a good old sniff of the smelling salts, I can tell you!"

"What are you talking about? I thought that useless lump had no money."

"Turns out that was never the case, and all this time he's been sitting on a small fortune. Goes without saying that I never saw a penny of it, but for all the years we were together he's had a couple of hundred grand stashed away somewhere; he thought I would never find it."

"How?" I asked, utterly dumbfounded.

"Left to him by his grandma by all accounts. I thought he

hated her guts, but seems like the feeling wasn't mutual. All it took was one little word from your Frank, and Barry's spilling the beans and handing out Granny's money left, right, and center—unbelievable!"

I savored the words "your Frank" for a moment whilst Chris carried on excitedly.

"So, thanks to you my future is looking a great deal rosier than it was this time yesterday."

"That's great news, Chris; it really is. Frank's quite the man of the moment, isn't he?" I said, wondering what the hell he must have done to Barry to make him change his mind like that. "He didn't er . . . How shall I put this? Give him a taste of his own medicine?"

"Do you mean did Frank knock ten bells of shit out of him? No, sadly not. He relied purely on his powers of persuasion. Which, I might add, must be considerable as Barry is well known to be a stubborn pig."

I thought for a second about exactly how strong Frank's powers of persuasion were and felt a flurry of butterflies in my stomach.

"So when are you seeing him again?" Chris asked.

Now that was a good question. The truth was, I thought I'd never be seeing Frank again. I'd convinced myself that he and I were just a casual fling, and apart from anything else all the evidence pointed to his having a wife or girlfriend. I don't mind married guys if it's just for sex, but as an only child, sharing my toys doesn't come naturally.

That was the theory, but the reality was that I just couldn't stop thinking about Frank. It was starting to feel like he had some sort of gravitational pull on me, and I was finding it very hard to resist.

"I don't know yet. I'm still thinking about it. He has a few questions to answer before I decide if I want to see him again," I said, the image of the note I had found flashing across my mind.

"Well, don't let the grass grow under your feet with that one—he's quite a catch."

"Really? " I said, keen to change the subject. "A taxi driver? I don't think so."

"Oh, purleeeese!" Chris squealed. "Just admit it."

"Admit what?" I asked testily.

"You are a snob, Anthony. Pure and simple—you are looking for a prince on a white horse to come and make everything better. Open your mind. You never know, maybe perfectly good princes arrive in black taxis, not on horseback. That's all I'm saying."

"You done?" I asked.

"For now."

CHAPTER 9

⟫━◆━⟪

I walked slowly back to the castle, trying to make sense of George's swift departure. I couldn't believe Lord Shanderson would have kicked him out of his job and his home for no good reason, but what could that reason be?

The truth was that I knew nothing about George or what kind of arrangement he had with Lord Shanderson. Perhaps it was only ever a temporary setup. Vera had said he was only just out of the army, so maybe Castle Beadale had been just a stopgap, somewhere to help him adjust to Civy Street. Everyone knows how difficult it is for soldiers to settle back into civilian life.

When I got to the kitchen the only person there was Gloria. I would have made my excuses and left her to it, but she was in an unusually chatty mood.

"Heard about George then, I suppose," she said, pouring two cups of tea and handing one of them to me.

"Yes, that was all very sudden, wasn't it?" I said.

"Oh! You think so, do you? I thought young George had it coming to him." She sipped her tea and peered at me over the top of her glasses.

Gloria obviously knew something I didn't, but as much as I was dying to know, I was damned if I was going to beg her to tell me what it was.

"Lovely cuppa," I said, sniffing tentatively at the steaming brew. Less than a week ago I'd been an avowed caffeine addict, and all I'd been offered in the way of coffee since I had arrived was ghastly instant granules. The very thought of it brought me out in hives. Back in London the day was sure to go downhill if it didn't start with at least three double espressos courtesy of my beloved Gaggenau.

A flicker of irritation flashed across Gloria's face as she realized I wasn't going to press her for what she knew. I cradled the teacup, and when I eventually took a sip I was taken aback to find it actually was quite delicious. It was different than the tea Vera brewed; this was delicate and light, and Gloria had not laced it with milk. The perfume rising from it was floral and smoky and not like anything I'd ever tried before.

"This really is amazing tea, Gloria. What is it?"

"I'll tell you what it isn't," she said smugly. "It's not that muck Vera brews up! It's half Lady Grey and half Lapsang souchong—it's what Her Majesty the Queen Mother used to drink."

It was obvious that in her own ham-fisted way she was trying to let me know that she had, at some point, served royalty. I immediately saw an opportunity to get Gloria to open up.

"Were you at Clarence House?" I asked.

"Good God, no!" she said, looking horrified at the suggestion. "I was the head housekeeper at The Castle of Mey." Gloria looked most pleased with herself at having imparted this information. What she no doubt hoped to convey was that she was cut from slightly superior cloth (probably tartan cloth at that) to the rest of us and this, more than anything else, explained why she looked down her nose at everyone.

But I knew all about The Castle of Mey. It was the low point in the Queen Mother's calendar for all her staff. It was in the farthest reaches of the Scottish Highlands and was renowned for being bleak, cold, and inhospitable. It was so remote that it carried the dubious honor of being the most northerly inhabited castle on the British mainland, and never was that more apparent than in those few weeks every summer when the Clarence House staff made the long journey north. It's a truism that no one ever went to Scotland for the weather, and that's particularly true of the Highlands. Even in the height of summer it could be bitterly cold, but should the weather ever warm up enough to merit removing one's tweeds, one could be sure to be eaten half to death by midges.

Clarence House staff was expected to drive from London to the Highlands in a convoy of old Land Rovers packed to the rafters with Fortnum and Mason food hampers and cases upon cases of fine claret. Even with a tailwind the nonstop drive took the best part of a whole day in vehicles whose broken suspensions left passengers barely able to walk by the time they arrived. On more than one occasion I remember Chris's having suspiciously fallen ill just days before he was due to leave for the Castle of Mey. I was now beginning to understand Gloria a little better.

"I'm ex-Palace," I said.

"Really?" Her harsh angular features visibly softened at the mention of Buckingham Palace.

"Yes. I loved working for the Queen and the Duke. It was a real privilege, and I learned so much." Now it was my turn to lay it on with a trowel, and she was falling for it hook, line, and sinker.

"I could tell you were ex-Royal Household," she said, positively beaming now. "You know what they say, don't you? It takes one to know one!" She let out a reedy little laugh.

Gloria and I sat in the kitchen for a good half an hour, exchanging old war stories about working for the Windsors, before I steered the conversation back round to George.

"So, Gloria, why do you think George had it coming to him?" I asked.

"Well, of course it's not really my place to say, but so long as this stays just between you and me I will tell you exactly why George was asked to leave."

Obviously I was all ears.

"George came to us after he was discharged from the army on medical grounds. He was in the same regiment as Lord Shanderson. Household Cavalry, no less."

"Evil be to him who evil thinks," I said under my breath, remembering Lord Shanderson's tattoo.

"Sorry, dear, what was that?" Gloria asked.

"Oh, nothing. So Lord Shanderson took him in then, did he?"

"Well, yes. George had nowhere to go, and I suppose His Lordship felt sorry for him. I can only assume that Lord Shanderson didn't know the real reason George was discharged though," she said, folding her arms and waiting for me to take the bait. This time I was powerless to resist.

"Go on then—what was the real reason?"

"Officially he was turfed out due to ill health, some rubbish about a bad back, but I happen to know from a very reliable source that young George was caught with his pants down."

"Really?"

"Oh, that's not the best bit," she said, warming to her theme. "It was with another man!" She delivered this last line with absolute triumph, no doubt assuming I would find it as shocking as she did.

"Never!" I said, trying to look and sound suitably appalled. "I would never have guessed he was . . . like that."

"Nor me, but my nephew assures me that is exactly what happened. Of course these days the army likes to keep these things quiet, so they sent him packing without a stain on his name, which I find rather lenient if I'm honest. In my day it would have been on the front page of the *Evening Standard*.

It's a dark world we live in when there are sodomites guarding Her Majesty the Queen."

I didn't know whether to laugh or cry at the drivel pouring out of Gloria's mouth. If she only knew what I had been up to with George less than forty-eight hours earlier.

"It was good of Lord Shanderson to take him in, but why would he get rid of him out of the blue like that?" I asked.

"Well, it's obvious, isn't it?"

"Is it?"

"He must have found out what George was really like. Perhaps someone told him. A gentleman like Lord Shanderson has a reputation to protect. I mean he can't have people like that living under his roof."

I wondered if Gloria had been the one to tell Lord Shanderson George's secret. She was certainly mean-spirited enough, but I couldn't help but think that His Lordship wouldn't act so irrationally on the say-so of his housekeeper. And somehow, I couldn't imagine him being as mortally offended by what George got up to in private as Gloria was. There was definitely more to it than she knew.

After our cozy little chat I made my excuses and left Gloria thumbing through the newspaper at the table.

It was still early and, keen not to waste my day off, I grabbed my coat and wallet and set off for Brighton.

With no car at my disposal I figured if I could get a lift to the local village I could jump on a train and be by the sea by lunchtime. As luck would have it, Tom was in the yard washing the Bentley.

"Morning, Tom," I said as I approached. "What are the chances of a lift to the train station?"

"Oh, I'm not sure His Lordship would approve of my taking you in the Bentley," he said apologetically.

"That's not what I had in mind," I said, pointing to the mud-splattered Land Rover on the other side of the yard.

"In that case jump in!"

After a short drive Tom dropped me at the small station in Westcourt Village.

"Here's my mobile number; if you give me a call when you are leaving Brighton, I'll come and pick you up."

"Tom, that's really kind of you. I will. Bye now."

"Don't do anything I wouldn't do," he said through the open car window. "I hear it gets quite wild in Brighton!"

CHAPTER 10

When I arrived on the platform I was annoyed to see the next train to Brighton wasn't due was for another forty minutes. I bought a cup of watery coffee and a newspaper from the small kiosk and huddled in the waiting room. There wasn't anyone else on the platform, but when the train arrived it was packed with mainly young, good-looking Europeans chatting loudly in French, German, and Italian. I glanced up at the map of the train's route and noticed that two stops before Westcourt was Gatwick Airport, where most of the passengers had probably boarded. The aisles were piled high with bulging rucksacks covered in embroidered badges. Edinburgh, Amsterdam, and Barcelona would soon be joined by Brighton on the fabric trophies of a modern-day grand tour. Many of the passengers were clutching guidebooks that I imagined would extol the virtues of the ultimate English seaside town of Brighton. There would be pictures of the Royal Pavilion's eccentric interior and moody shots of the skeletal West Pier blanketed with a flock of starlings. The atmosphere in the carriage was an excited one, and it was even starting to rub off onto me.

The journey to the coast was due to be less than twenty-five minutes, so with no seat available I perched on a pile of bags in the space between the train doors. I didn't really have enough elbowroom to read the paper, so I contented myself with the view of the South Downs flying past the window at high speed. At one point the train crossed a high viaduct where the landscape opened out as far as the eye could see in every direction. Everybody on the train glanced in unison at the spectacle of the frosty rolling fields way below. I'd never realized how stunningly beautiful Sussex was until that train journey.

The train slowed to a stop at a small provincial station where none of the passengers in my carriage disembarked, but where an elderly couple squeezed on just in time before the automatic doors slid closed behind them. They looked most alarmed when they realized there was nowhere for them to sit, but then a couple jumped to their feet and waved the old man and his wife over. And then another two passengers rose, and then another two jumped to their feet as well. In a matter of seconds most of the carriage was offering to give up their seats.

"Please, señor, señora." A young guy was waving frantically at the couple to come and take his and his companion's seats just behind where I stood.

The old man looked relieved and guided his wife by the hand through the crowd as it parted to allow them the vacated seats.

The young Spanish guy appeared at my side, but his female friend stayed in the aisle chatting to her friends.

"That was a very kind thing you and your girlfriend just did," I said to him as he perched on the bag next to me.

"In my country, old people command a great deal of respect," he said in a heavy, Spanish accent. "And she is not my girlfriend."

"Oh! Sorry, I just assumed . . ."

"She is my sister, Inez, and I am Juan Carlos," he said, shaking my hand firmly and locking his dark eyes onto mine.

"I see, and are you and your sister planning a holiday in Brighton?" I asked, suddenly a little more interested in my new Spanish friend.

"Maybe a holiday, maybe we find work—I don't know yet. I hear Brighton is very friendly place." He winked, and I felt a shiver run down my spine.

Moments later the train began to slow down as it pulled into the huge sweeping Victorian arches of Brighton Station. Having no luggage I was able to position myself nearest the door for a quick getaway and to avoid the inevitable crush at the ticket barriers. As I prepared to say good-bye to Juan Carlos I felt his hand slide over mine and press a small scrap of paper into my palm.

"Maybe we meet later when I have dropped my bags at the hostel? No?" he said as he hoisted a huge rucksack onto his back.

Inez appeared at his side with a similarly sized bag and smiled broadly at me as she grabbed his arm and pulled him into the crowd and out of sight.

It wasn't until I was out of the station and halfway down Queens Road heading toward the sea that I unclasped my hand to see what was on the scrap of paper.

It was Juan Carlos's phone number scribbled on a page ripped out of *Gay Times,* and whether by design or default he had scrawled it across an advert for a men-only sauna called Champions in Brighton.

"Subtle!" I thought, as I folded the paper carefully and placed it in my wallet.

It was lunchtime, and maybe it was the sudden rush of sea air but I found myself in the mood for something I hadn't eaten in years: fish and chips.

There was cold wind blowing in from the sea, but I didn't mind it. In fact the salty air on my face felt good, and I decided that the best place to eat fish and chips would be at the end of the pier. I headed toward the gaudy flashing lights marking the entrance and ordered cod and chips from the first stall I could find.

They were searing hot, and even with a chill wind blowing around me I had to blow on each chip to cool it enough to eat. The chips were greasy and salty with just the right amount of vinegar on them. They were crisp on the outside and fluffy within, but the batter surrounding the fish was the best I had ever eaten. It crunched noisily when I broke into it with one of those ridiculous tiny wooden forks, and plumes of sweet-smelling steam spiraled into the air.

By the time I had made my way along the wooden board-walk, past the Donkey Derby, the old Victorian Helter Skelter, and the noisy Haunted House, I was at the very end of the pier looking back at the seafront with nothing left in the poly-styrene tray bar a single chip. A large, fat seagull was perched on the railings eyeing up the remains of my lunch, so before I tossed the tray into the waste bin I threw the chip high into the air and over the side of the pier. The bird swooped down and caught it midair, gulping it down in one bite before flying off in search of more of the same.

I realized I was still holding the fork so I placed it in my in-side pocket as a souvenir of a perfect lunch.

I then took out Juan Carlos's number and texted him a brief but to the point message:

MEET ME @ CHAMPIONS SAUNA 2PM —ANTHONY

If he showed up I'd consider it a bonus, but as a rule gay saunas are full of men like me who just want some uncompli-cated fun, so even if he didn't I felt sure somebody else would be able to give me what I was looking for. My instructions from Lord Shanderson were to take the day off and relax a little, so who was I to disobey my master? After a little light relief in the darkness of an all-male sauna I was guaranteed to return to work feeling a hell of lot more relaxed.

My phone signaled the arrival of a text message.

Meet U there.

Well, if you insist, I thought as I headed in the direction of Champions.

Following a tiny map on the cutting Juan Carlos had given me, I found the sauna tucked discreetly down a side street and just a short walk from the pier. Even though it was the middle of the afternoon, there was a queue of guys waiting to get in. Most of them seemed to know each other and were chatting like they were waiting in line at the post office. Behind a glass screen there was a good-looking older guy with closely cropped salt and pepper hair. He was dressed younger than his years in a tight fitting vest and gym shorts, but his impressive physique just about allowed him to get away with it.

"Fifteen pounds please, mate," he said when it was my turn to pay. "There's condoms in the lockers, and there's a free buffet on at 7 p.m. if you are still here."

This was starting to feel like some kind of social club rather than like the seedy saunas I'd visited in London. The ones I was used to were the last resort on a drunken night out and not the kind of places where I'd ever want to bump into friends. This guy seemed to know most of his customers by name and greeted them warmly as he handed out towels and locker keys attached to rubber wristbands.

Forget the aquarium and the Royal Pavilion, I thought as I handed over my cash. *It looks like Champions Men-Only Sauna is the hottest ticket in town today.*

As I waited for my change I glanced around the reception area and noticed that all the guys in the queue filed through a swing door marked CHANGING ROOMS. All, that is, except one.

I watched as a short, smartly dressed guy strode purposefully across the reception area to another door. He looked like
some kind of businessman, with his formal suit and leather
briefcase, so compared to the other guys I'd seen entering he
looked rather out of place. He stood in front of the door and
removed a card from his wallet, pausing only long enough to
swipe it in an electronic reader on the wall. He quickly entered,
allowing the door to slam shut behind him, but before he did I
caught a glimpse of the card in his hand. It was black and shiny
and had the words BLACK ORCHID CLUB printed on it in gold.

A voice behind me broke my train of thought.

"Lockers are through the door on the left, mate," the guy behind the desk shouted over.

"What's through there?" I asked, pointing to the door on the
right.

"Strictly members only," he said simply, before turning his
attention to a new customer.

I must be seeing things, I thought as I followed a couple of
the regulars in the direction of the changing rooms. *There's no
way Lord Shanderson would ever come to a place like this,
surely.*

The changing room was buzzing with the sound of guys in
various states of undress gossiping like a bunch of old women.
As I walked through in search of my locker I inhaled the heady
mix of chlorine and male sweat and in a matter of seconds was
transported back to the school changing rooms. Even now that
particular smell is guaranteed to arouse me like no other, and as
I began to undress I felt a shiver run down my spine. I quickly
stuffed my clothes into the locker, but when I wrapped the
threadbare towel around my waist I found it was too small to
cover what little modesty I possess. Having never really suf-
fered from any form of body consciousness, and there being
only one reason for being in an all-male sauna in the middle of
the afternoon, I decided there was no reason to be coy. So,

completely naked but for the towel casually draped around my neck like an Italian playboy's sweater, I headed for the door. On the way I passed a cute blond guy self-consciously attempting to remove his underwear from beneath his own small towel. He glanced up as I passed, but quickly looked away when I winked at him. He was about my age, maybe a bit younger, and despite his chiseled features he managed to look like an embarrassed schoolboy. Maybe it was the flush of pink in his cheeks that did it, but whatever it was, I found him very attractive. It was clear he was not a regular here, and if I had to guess I'd have said it was his first time. His girlfriend probably thought he was at the gym working on his glutes, for all I knew, but I really hoped he would stick around for me to introduce myself properly.

Behind the Scandinavian pine door marked SAUNA, the idle chitchat I'd heard so much of in the locker room was gone. It was eerily quiet and almost completely dark, but as soon as I entered I could feel the sexual tension in the room crackling like static electricity. I felt my way along the wall until I came to a wooden bench and laid the towel down to insulate my bare cheeks from the hot wooden slats. My eyes began to adjust, and as they did I became aware of someone inching toward me along the bench. Moments later I felt a hand brush my thigh before moving away again. Seconds later it tentatively returned, but as the hand began to explore, somebody else entered the sauna, and for a few brief seconds when the door was open the steam cleared enough for me to see who was sitting next to me.

"How did you know it was me?" I whispered.

"I've been waiting for you," Juan Carlos answered. Leaning forward he stroked my cheek tenderly, but before I could say anything he clamped his mouth onto mine and began to kiss me passionately. Our tongues fought feverishly before he pulled away and worked his mouth down my torso, lingering on my stomach, kissing and licking before continuing to head south. I could barely see a few inches in front of my face, but I felt his hands caress my chest and a finger circle a nipple before pinching it tightly. I gasped, and his hand sprang away.

"Don't stop," I said quietly.

Juan Carlos's hands and lips explored every inch of me, but eventually the hot, damp atmosphere became stifling, and I was gripped by a sudden need for some air.

"I need to get out of here," I said, pulling my lips away from his.

He said nothing, but I felt his strong hands grab mine, and he heaved me to my feet.

"You want to hang out?" Juan Carlos said as we toweled ourselves off.

I retrieved my watch from the locker and checked the time before answering.

"It's been nice meeting you, but I really have to go," I replied, genuinely surprised at how late it was.

"No problem. Maybe we meet again, yes?"

"Sure, that would be great. Enjoy Brighton."

"I already have." He grinned.

I finished dressing and headed out, back through the reception area, but before I left I knocked on the glass partition where the receptionist was.

"Hi there."

"Well, hi yourself," he said, looking up from his magazine.

"I was just wondering, what kind of club is 'The Black Orchid'?"

The smile immediately left his face and was replaced by a look of mild suspicion. "Why do you want to know?"

"Well, maybe I want to apply for membership. I mean, how would I know if I want to join if nobody will tell me what kind of club it is?" I said, giving him a cheeky little wink.

"I'll be honest with you, mate—you don't look the type. But saying that, one thing you learn in this job is that you never can tell."

I looked at him and nodded my agreement even though I was none the wiser.

"BDSM," he said finally. "Get all sorts up there. Literally queuing up to pay top whack, if you'll forgive the pun, to have ten bells knocked out of them. Like I say, all sorts—bankers, lawyers, doctors. We even have one regular who they reckon is a lord of the manor. Proper titled gentleman, he is. Imagine that. Still interested in membership?"

"I'll think about it."

"Sure you will," he replied without looking up.

I stood for a moment, rooted to the spot, trying to process the information I'd just been given.

If what this guy was saying was true, my new boss, the terribly upright Lord Shanderson, Third Earl of Beadale, had a hobby other than country pursuits. If, and it was a really big *if,* he was a member of The Black Orchid Club, he clearly enjoyed a bit more than a little slap and tickle. Bondage, domination, and sadomasochism—he just didn't look the type. I'd met plenty of people who like it rough in my time; hell knows I'm not averse to a bit of domination in the sack myself, but Lord Shanderson, really?

My head was swimming as I pulled my jacket tightly around me and hurriedly made my way back up the hill to the train station.

"Well, well, well. Lord Shanderson, you're a dark horse, aren't you?" I said to myself.

When I arrived back at the station, crowds of people were milling around on the concourse, all staring up at the departures board. My heart sank when I saw that all trains out of Brighton were canceled.

"We regret to announce that all trains leaving Brighton are canceled due to a power failure in the Gatwick area. We will make further announcements when more information becomes available. Thank you for your patience and understanding," said a disembodied voice from the PA system somewhere above my head.

"How the hell am I going to get back to Castle Beadale now?" I muttered, feeling neither patient nor particularly understanding. "It'll be a miracle if I'm back in time to serve his breakfast at this rate."

I remembered earlier walking past a long line of vacant taxis at the front of the station, so I headed back out to see how much it would be to take me all the way back to the castle.

The first driver in the queue wound his window down as I approached.

"How much to Castle Beadale?" I asked.

"Where?" he asked, clearly having never heard of it.

"Just near Westcourt Village—about twenty-five miles north of here."

He looked me up and down with an air of grave suspicion before answering.

"Don't normally do out-of-towners, but for you . . . sixty pounds."

"Sixty pounds?" I yelled. "I want to go to Westcourt not Edinburgh."

I stormed away from the taxi rank, and once out of sight I looked inside my wallet. A quick count up showed that I had just twenty pounds to my name plus a handful of coins. I don't know what I expected to find as I was still waiting for my final pay from the hotel, so as usual at this time of the month funds were perilously low. When I was still at the Landseer I never really noticed when my bank account was running on empty as I was making so much cash on the side. But without that cash to fall back on I was well and truly broke. Not to mention stranded in Brighton.

Twenty quid might not have been enough to get me a taxi, but was sure as hell enough to get me drunk, so I headed to the pub opposite the station.

It was comforting to find that the pub was full of stranded people just like me, sheltering from the cold, killing time, and getting slowly pissed. At first I considered ordering just a large glass of New Zealand Sauvignon, but a quick calculation proved that it would be much more economical to order a whole bottle. At least that's what I told myself.

"How many glasses, mate?" asked the barman as he stuck the bottle in an ice bucket.

"Just the one, thanks," I said, handing over my money.

I found a table by the fire and made myself comfortable. Above the bar was a TV monitor that had a live feed to the departures board so I would be able to see when the trains began running again without the bother of leaving my seat.

Soon the combination of the wine and the heat from the fire had me feeling much more sanguine about my disrupted travel plans.

It was past ten o'clock by the time I stumbled off the train at Westcourt Station. I'd managed to text Tom to ask for a pickup, but God only knows how.

When I staggered across the car park he was sitting in the Land Rover with the engine running, grinning at me.

"You look like you've had a good time," he said as I climbed in the passenger side.

"Sure have," I slurred. "Sorry it's late. The trains were all messed up, and I had to shelter from the cold."

"In the pub?" he asked, laughing.

"How did you know that?"

"Call it a hunch," Tom said as he pulled out of the car park and pointed us back toward Castle Beadale.

CHAPTER 11

"Bloody hell! You're cutting it a bit fine, aren't you?" Vera said, looking up from a pan of sizzling sausages when I entered the kitchen the following morning. "You'll be pleased to know that I've set the table for you."

"Thanks, Vera, I owe you one."

"Bit of a heavy night, was it?" she asked, looking me up and down.

"Oh my God! Is it that obvious?" I said, cupping my hand over my mouth to check my breath for alcohol fumes.

"Don't be daft!" she snorted. "You look fine. Tom told me he picked you up from the station last night. You young 'uns deserve to let your hair down now and again—Lord knows I did when I was your age! Now get cracking and take these through; he'll be down any minute," she said, handing me a silver dish containing heavenly smelling crispy bacon.

I was arranging the dishes on the sideboard when Lord Shanderson came in.

"Good morning, Gowers," he said, taking his seat and unfolding his newspaper. "By God! That bacon smells divine."

"Good morning, Lord Shanderson," I said, pouring him a cup of tea. "Would you like me to serve you, sir?"

"No, thank you, Gowers, I'll help myself in a moment or two."

I was just about to leave him to enjoy his breakfast when he placed his paper down on the table and began to speak.

"Did you enjoy your day off, Anthony?"

"Indeed I did, sir, thank you."

"Did you do anything interesting?" he asked, holding my gaze for a split second longer than was comfortable.

It seemed a strangely personal question, but I was touched that he appeared interested. For a split second I considered telling him I'd been to The Black Orchid to see what his reaction would be, but thought better of it and searched my brain for something more fitting.

"I had the most wonderful fish and chips at the end of the pier," I said, relishing the memory.

"How splendid," he said, beaming. "I haven't had fish and chips for years."

I couldn't really picture Lord Shanderson eating fish and chips with a wooden fork at the end of the pier, but then I couldn't imagine him paying to have his arse spanked either.

"I understand your return journey was not ideal," he continued, suddenly looking more serious.

I felt a little bit nauseous. Had he seen me rolling in drunk last night? I'd be mortified if he'd seen me staggering around like an idiot. I swallowed hard before I answered.

"Yes, trains can be tricky, sir, but I got home safely in the end. That's the main thing," I said with a nervous smile.

"Yes, well, I think we had better make sure that doesn't happen again, don't you, Anthony?" he said, before returning to his newspaper. "That will be all."

I left the dining room as quickly as I could without breaking into a run and stood in the tiny butler's pantry trying to make sense of what he had just said to me. I couldn't work out if he had seen me coming in drunk or if Tom had told him.

"Jesus, Anthony, you've only been here five minutes and already the boss has seen you falling down drunk," I said to myself with a slap to the forehead. "Pull yourself together, man. You really need this job!"

I went through to the kitchen where Tom was sitting at the table devouring one of his mother's doorstop bacon sandwiches.

"Morning, Anthony," he said cheerfully.

"Can I have a word?" I said, hoisting him to his feet by his elbow.

I marched him through into the butler's pantry where I was sure we wouldn't be overheard.

"Did you tell His Lordship about my being drunk last night?" I asked.

"Certainly not! Why would I do that?" Tom said through a mouthful of half-finished sandwich. "He's not mad at me for borrowing the Land Rover, is he?"

Tom looked as worried as I felt, and it seemed pretty unlikely that he'd go round telling tales for no reason.

"He just seemed to know all about the difficulties with the trains, that's all. How would he know about that if you hadn't told him?" I asked.

Tom seemed to think about it for a moment before he just shrugged his shoulders.

"Anyway, I don't make a habit of getting myself into that state, so don't go telling anyone else," I said.

"Relax, Anthony—it's not me you need to worry about around here. I'm one of the good guys."

"And exactly who should I be worried about?"

"I'm just saying, not everybody round here will have your best interests at heart. I'm not naming no names."

And with that he returned to the kitchen to finish his breakfast.

* * *

Later that day I bumped into Gloria in the laundry as I was attempting to remove an ominous-looking stain from one of the fine linen dinner napkins.

"If that's red wine you're trying to get out, then I suggest you soak it in some white wine first," she said, regarding my efforts with a certain amount of suspicion.

"Thanks, I'll try that."

"I hear you are moving into Rose View this week."

"Am I, Gloria? You seem to know more than I do." I laughed.

"Given it quite the makeover, apparently," she said, remaining stony faced.

Something about Gloria made me think that her default setting was that of mild irritation. I watched as she folded a pile of towels as though she had a personal grudge against each and every one.

"So who should I talk to about getting a set of keys and moving in?"

"I suppose you should talk to Barbara, the estate manager. She's in charge of all the cottages on the estate. You'll find her in the office above the stables."

Gloria picked up a basket of clean laundry and left the room without another word. After serving tea I headed out to find Barbara and the estate office. All big country houses rely on their estate managers for the smooth running of the organization. There are tenant farmers to manage, rented cottages to oversee, and a whole host of bureaucratic nightmares to shield the landowner from. But in my experience they were also invariably a bottomless well of insider gossip, so in order to cement our relationship I made sure to take a huge slab of Vera's fruitcake with me.

The offices were formed of three, maybe four old haylofts knocked into one to create a big open-plan room. The walls were covered in year planners and ordinance survey maps of the estate. At the far end I spotted Barbara, but only just, as she was partially obscured by huge towers of paper on the desk at which she was sitting, barking down the telephone.

"Jim, listen to me. The fence bordering your farm is damaged and needs repairing today. If any of your sheep get out, you can't come to us for compensation. The fence is your responsibility—check your contract. It's all there. Today, Jim. Got it?" She banged down the phone and stood up from the desk. "Bloody farmers! They'll be the death of me, I swear! You must be Anthony." She extended her hand between piles of documents and shook mine with a surprisingly firm grip.

"Sit," she said, gesturing to a chair that was also covered in papers. "Just push that lot on the floor."

As I made room to sit I spotted an ancient Jack Russell sleeping in a basket under the desk. It let out a low and menacing growl as I placed the papers on the floor.

"Enough, Agamemnon!" Barbara shouted down at it. "Don't mind him; he's just old and grumpy. Bit like me!" She let out a booming laugh that practically shook the windows.

"Coffee?" she asked, walking over to a small kitchenette. She was one of those country types whose age it was impossible to guess. She could have been anywhere between forty and sixty, but her hair was cut into a short, graying bob, and her ample frame was encased in a thick tweed suit, the skirt of which ended unflatteringly halfway down her enormous calves. Around her neck she wore a double string of pearls that she fiddled with as she waited for the kettle to boil.

"I've brought you some of Vera's homemade cake," I said, passing her the Tupperware box.

"How bloody marvelous!" she said.

I was glad I had brought the cake, as it did a good job of masking Barbara's disgusting excuse for coffee. It tasted like a supermarket's own brand with UHT milk and was served in a dirty, chipped mug that looked like it would benefit from a good scrub with a wire brush. Barb, as she insisted I call her, might not have been much of a housekeeper or tea lady but she was, just as I expected, full of useful information.

"So, Anthony. You must have made quite an impression on Lord Shanderson."

"Really? Why do you say that?"

"You obviously haven't seen Rose View yet, have you?"

"As a matter of fact I visited it last week when George was living there, so I know what it's like—it could be very nice with a bit of TLC."

"Oh! It's had that all right." She laughed, tossing me a set of keys across the desk. "There's no need for you to sign a separate contract, as it will be part of your employment contract, which should be ready to sign in the next couple of days. It's quite straightforward—a month's notice for both parties, that kind of thing."

"Barb, I hope you don't mind my asking, but what happened to George?"

"Ah, him," she said, chewing the end of her pencil. "He broke the terms of his contract with Lord Shanderson and was asked to leave with immediate effect."

"Do you have any contact details for him? I'd like to stay in touch with him—we got on really well."

" 'Fraid not. Transient type, that one."

I sensed I wasn't going to get anything else out of Barb on the subject of George's departure, so I changed tack.

"Have you worked here long, Barb?" I asked, choking down the last of my coffee.

"Years and years—bloody well lost count. My father was the estate manager for the late Lord Shanderson. Lived on the estate all my life."

"Good, then if I need to know anything about the lay of the land, I know who to speak to," I said, getting to my feet.

"Anytime, young man. My door is always open."

I couldn't wait to go and check out my new cottage, but there wasn't time if I was to change for dinner and set the table. It would just have to wait until the morning. I would go down to the cottage first thing after breakfast and see it in the daylight.

Only one more night in that cold, drafty room, and then I'll have my own place! I thought as I excitedly headed back to work.

The following morning, as soon as His Lordship was out of the dining room, I cleared the breakfast things with lightning speed and set off for Rose View.

The cottage was set back from the main road down a short gravel path. A tall line of trees would completely obscure it from view in the summer, but now, in the middle of winter, the bright white-painted façade was clearly visible through the skeletal branches as I approached.

The first thing I noticed was that the picket fence that had been broken and dilapidated the last time I was here had been replaced and painted a beautiful sage green to match the front door. The lawn had been re-turfed, and new flower beds dug on either side. As I slipped the key into the lock I noticed that a smart new sign had replaced the tatty old one bearing the name of the cottage.

"Rose View Cottage. Hello, I live at Rose View Cottage. Yes, that's right, Rose View Cottage," I said to no one except myself.

The interior smelled strongly of fresh paint, and for a second when I stepped into the living room I thought I was in the wrong cottage. Looking around I recognized absolutely nothing about it. I had expected it to have had a bit of a spruce-up, a lick of paint here and there and maybe some basic furniture to replace the beaten-up old stuff that had been in here the last time I visited. These "grace and favor" cottages are usually basic at best, with the landowner providing only the bare minimum of home comforts. But this one looked like it had just undergone the mother of all TV makeovers. A makeover, that is, carried out by someone with exquisite taste.

It had been completely redecorated, and where the battered old Chesterfield used to be sat a big, plump overstuffed sofa scattered with cushions. On the floor were old Persian rugs, and an ornate, Georgian gilt mirror was hanging over the fireplace. The last time I had visited the windows had been partially covered by old sheets held in place by drawing pins, but now they were hung with lovely vintage curtains. Nothing matched, but everything in the room looked like it belonged together.

I stood, just trying to take it all in, when I spotted a small box and an envelope with my name on it sitting on the mantelpiece. I turned the thick vellum envelope over and on the back was Lord Shanderson's crest embossed in gold. I tore it open, and on a slip of Castle Beadale–headed notepaper it simply said:

> *Welcome to your new home. —Drummond*
> *Shanderson.*
> *PS—I see no reason why you can't enjoy your*
> *fish and chips in style next time.*

I picked up the small blue box and noticed the familiar logo for Asprey's of London on the lid. Inside, beneath a layer of tissue paper, was a perfect replica of a wooden chip fork cast in solid silver.

I turned it over and over in my hand, trying to fathom why Lord Shanderson would have given me such a beautiful gift. Maybe Barb was right; perhaps in my short time at Castle Beadale I had made a particularly good impression on His Lordship. But somehow it didn't seem right. This was all a bit much for a staff cottage, not to mention for someone who had worked here for all of five minutes.

My train of thought was broken when I heard a car pull up outside, followed by a knock on the door.

When I opened it, a guy was standing on the porch, writing information onto a form attached to a clipboard.

"Anthony Gowers?" he asked.

"Yes, that's me," I said, admiring the glossy black Mini Cooper he'd just climbed out of. "Nice car," I said.

"Yeh, lucky you. Sign here please." He held out the clipboard and a pen.

"Sorry, I don't understand. What exactly am I signing for?"

"That," he said, pointing to the car with his thumb.

"Sorry, mate, I think you have got the wrong address." I laughed. "I think I'd remember if I'd bought myself a brand-new car."

He rolled his eyes and snatched the clipboard out of my hand.

"Mr. Anthony Gowers. Rose View Cottage, Beadale Estate, West Sussex. Is that or is that not you?"

"Well, yes. It is."

"Good, sign on page one and page three, the top copy is yours," he said, handing me a set of keys.

As I attempted to sign my name with a shaking hand a white van pulled up behind the Mini and sounded its horn. The delivery guy forced a smile before taking the clipboard from me.

"Enjoy your new car," he said, before joining his colleague in the van and quickly driving away.

So, Lord Shanderson, what have I done to deserve all this? I thought as I jumped into the driver's seat and ran my hands over the silky smooth leather interior. *And more to the point, what am I going to have to do to earn it?*

I turned the key in the ignition and felt a thrill run through me when the powerful engine roared to life. With only two bags of clothes and an old espresso cup to move into my new home, if I got a move on I would be fully ensconced by teatime. I drove much faster than was strictly permitted within the walls of the estate and sent herds of deer scattering in every direction as the fat wheels rattled noisily over the cattle grids. I arrived at the castle in a matter of minutes, almost running over Tom when I entered the stable yard.

"Bloody hell, you could have killed me!" he said as I pulled up alongside him and wound down the electric window. "Where did you get this from?"

"It's my new company car," I said, trying not to allow a note of smugness to creep into my voice. "Fancy a ride?"

"Are you kidding? Of course I do; it's beautiful," he said, running his hand over the bonnet.

"Give me a chance to grab my stuff, and then we'll go. I'll give you a guided tour of my new cottage too if you like."

With my bags safely stashed in the tiny boot of the Mini I decided that rather than head directly to Rose View I would take us off the main road and follow the farm track that ran around the perimeter of the estate. I glanced over at Tom as we dipped and bumped our way along the rough, unsealed road and he, just like me, was grinning like an idiot. I was enjoying driving the Mini so much that I considered going off the estate entirely and really opening it up on the country lanes, but it occurred to me that racing around the country lanes of West Sussex in my brand-new car would be the perfect way to spend my next day off.

When we arrived at the cottage, Tom was out of the car and halfway up the path before I'd had a chance to kill the engine.

"Blimey! I heard they'd done the place up, but this is like a palace!" he said, admiring the outside of the property.

"Wait till you see inside. Come and have a look," I said, leading the way.

Once inside, I dumped my bags down and began to show Tom around.

"They've certainly not spared any money on this old place," he said, checking out the living room. "It used to be a right old dump."

"I know, I was here only last week, and you're right, it was in a bit of a state." As soon as the words left my lips I regretted mentioning my previous visit.

"I'd offer you a cup of tea, Tom, but I haven't had a chance to stock up yet," I said as we entered the kitchen. "As you can see the cupboards are bare." I flung open the doors of the large pine dresser to make my point, but far from being empty the cupboards were packed fit to bursting with tea, assorted biscuits, jars of jams and marmalade, sugar, in fact just about everything one could need. I moved over to the fridge, and that was fully stocked too. There were milk, eggs, butter, bacon, and bread—everything had been thought of and placed there in time for my arrival and all bearing the distinctive green and gold labeling of Harrods Food Hall.

"Wow!" I said, staring into the fully loaded fridge. "That's a lot of food."

"You're not kidding. Certainly looks like His Lordship is trying to make a good impression on you," Tom said. "Never quite known him to go this far before."

"Oh, don't you worry, I'm sure I'm going to have to work very hard to justify all of this," I said.

As I cast an admiring eye around the kitchen a shard of sunlight bounced off something sleek and shiny on the countertop. Its modernist stainless steel case made it stand out against all the traditional kitchen paraphernalia, and my heart skipped a beat when I saw what it was. It was a brand new Gaggenau espresso machine. Even better, it was a more up-to-date version of the one I had back in London. At that exact moment in time I thought my heart would burst with happiness.

"ESPRESSO!" I squealed, clapping my hands like an excited schoolgirl. "Coffee, proper Italian coffee—want one?" I asked, flicking the switch to fire up the machine. Tom just laughed and shook his head.

"No, ta, I've got to go and run some errands for my mum.

You enjoy your coffee though, won't you," he said, heading for the door. "And welcome to your new home, Anthony."

As soon as Tom was out of the door I unzipped one of my bags and took out the tiny package containing my favorite cup. I made a double espresso and took it through to the sitting room to savor whilst I tried to get my head around Lord Shanderson's overwhelming display of generosity. It was not particularly cold in the cottage, but I couldn't resist lighting a fire. Moments later with the fire crackling loudly in the grate I lay back on the sofa and drifted off into a light sleep.

I couldn't have been asleep for long, but I was so relaxed and contented I knew that if I didn't get up now, I never would, and it was time to change and head back to the castle to serve Lord Shanderson his dinner.

On my way out of the door I remembered that I hadn't yet written a thank-you note. I also realized I didn't actually have anything to write one on, so in desperation I pulled open the drawer of the writing desk in the living room, and sure enough there was a pile of Castle Beadale notepaper, matching envelopes, and a silver pen.

Sending silent words of thanks to whomever had thought of such details, I quickly wrote a few words. I tried not to gush, but it was a struggle. I managed to keep it simple but sincere. I hoped so, anyway.

I folded the paper and placed it in an envelope before tucking it into the pocket of my tails and jumping in the car.

When I passed through the kitchen on my way to set the table, Vera looked like she wanted to stop and chat.

"Settled in, dear?" she asked, wiping her floury hands on the front of her apron.

"I certainly have—I couldn't be happier," I said, beaming.

"I'm so glad, Anthony; I really am. And I'm happy you are getting on so well with His Lordship. He can be a tricky old sod sometimes, we all know that, but he seems to like you. A lot. It's all about chemistry, the relationship between master and servant you know. If you get it right, everyone benefits."

"And if you get it wrong?" I asked.

"Well, let's just say that plenty before you have got it very wrong indeed, and where are they now, eh?"

I laid the table, taking extra care with each tiny detail. I folded His Lordship's napkin into an extravagant bishop's hat and double-checked that all the silver was perfectly aligned. Finally I propped my thank-you letter against his wineglass. I then retreated to the butler's pantry until I heard Lord Shanderson come into the dining room.

When he took his seat I waited for a few moments before I went through with a decanter of 1999 Chateau Margaux in hand.

"Good evening, Your Lordship," I said, filling his glass. My thank-you letter had been opened and was carefully folded by his butter knife.

"Do you play billiards, Anthony?" he asked, quite out of the blue.

"I'm not sure I do, Your Lordship. I played pool and snooker in my youth, but not billiards."

"Would you like to learn?" he said, a faint smile hovering around the corners of his mouth.

It struck me as less of a question and more a statement of what was about to happen.

"Of course if you have plans after work I would fully understand. It's just that I do like a game of billiards, and I've yet to convince Vera to take up my offer of lessons."

"I have no plans, sir, and learning a new game would be fun, I'm sure. Are the rules complicated?"

"My rules are very simple, Anthony, so I have no doubt you will pick them up in no time. Why don't you meet me in the games room after dinner?"

Lord Shanderson ate more quickly than usual, and all three

courses were done and dusted in less than half an hour. When I returned the empty dessert plate to the kitchen, Vera stood by the Aga with her hands on her hips.

"What is wrong with that man tonight?" she said, shaking her head. "He'll do himself a mischief bolting his food like that. I spend all day cooking, and the whole lot is gone like that." She snapped her fingers above her head.

I just nodded my agreement and went back through to offer him a Cognac. But when I got to the table he was gone. I finished clearing the dinner things away and blew out the candles before heading to the games room for my very first billiards lesson.

CHAPTER 12

The games room was at the far end of the house, but as I walked through the Marble Hall I detected a faint trace of His Lordship's distinctive cigar smoke in the air. The sweet scent grew stronger as I approached the door. I knocked once before entering. The wall lights were turned down so low that only the barest glow emitted from them, and the only other light came from a large brass lamp over the enormous billiards table. I squinted until my eyes adjusted to the gloom. Lord Shanderson was nowhere to be seen. The cigar smoke was strong enough for me to think that he wasn't far away, so I decided to explore the games room while I waited for him to return.

Not only did the room have a distinctly male feel, with its rows of stuffed animal heads and assorted hunting paraphernalia hanging from the blood-red walls, it smelled masculine too. At the far end there were banks of floor-to-ceiling bookshelves tightly packed with ancient leather-bound books. It was probably the antique leather of the bindings mixed with the sweet scent of fine Cuban cigars that contributed to the masculine aroma permeating every corner. It was an unusual smell, and one I found strangely arousing.

As my eyes wandered over all the nooks and crannies of the room, I realized I could hear the sound of classical music coming from somewhere. I moved toward the bookshelves and noticed that between two of them was a chink of flickering light. Up close I realized that the central bookshelf was in fact a false door behind which was another room entirely.

One book had been partially pulled out to form a door handle, so I gently pulled the heavy door toward me to reveal a small study. Mozart's *Requiem* played softly from speakers concealed behind the walls.

"Lord Shanderson?" I said in a quiet voice.

I got no reply, but something pulled me in regardless.

The room was small and windowless, furnished with just a desk, an old leather sofa, and a low coffee table piled high with yet more books. The walls were covered in a mixture of antique copper engravings and quite arty black-and-white photographs. There was barely an inch of wall space between them. It was hard to make out much detail in the half-light, but when I did study one of them up close I was quite taken aback by the subject matter. My eyes darted from one to another until I was satisfied there was a distinct theme running through all the pictures. Each and every one of them depicted scenes, to a greater or lesser degree of severity, of bondage, domination, and sadomasochism.

I went back to the door and fumbled around on the wall until I found the light switch. Once the room was flooded with light I studied the pictures in more detail.

There were lots of grainy early Victorian photographs of women being flogged over the knees of gentlemen with extravagant mustaches, and even more involving riding crops and whips. Sandwiched between a copper print engraving of two Georgian men in powdered wigs spanking a street urchin and a Victorian photograph of a corseted lady pleasuring herself with an enormous ivory dildo, there was a very modern and very famous Robert Mapplethorpe photograph. It depicted Mapplethorpe himself wearing black leather chaps and positioned with his back to the camera. In it he's bent at the waist and has the thick woven handle of a bullwhip inserted deep into his arse, his face turned defiantly toward the camera.

Say what you want about Lord Shanderson's taste in art, it's nothing if not diverse, I thought as I continued to check out his extraordinary collection.

Eventually my eyes rested on some modern-day photographs. They were of much poorer quality than the rest, not much more than snapshots really. There must have been a dozen or so featuring the same guy in the center of the frame. In each photograph he was either hooded or wearing a leather mask so his face was not visible in any of them, but I could tell it was the same guy by his toned physique. In one of them his wrists were intricately bound with rope and hoisted high above his head. His chest bore the red marks of having been recently flogged. In another, he was kneeling naked with his hands tied tightly in front of him, palms pressed together like he was praying. In the next one he was lying facedown over an old-fashioned leather vaulting horse. At first my eye was drawn to the actual horse itself as I was reminded of all those hideous gym lessons I had tried to wriggle out of at school. And then, I noticed the tiniest detail in the photograph; in the center of the photograph, high up on the guy's backside, probably barely noticeable to anyone but me was a small tattoo. It was not legible from the photograph, but I knew instantly what it was. It was the words "Honi soit qui mal y pense"—evil be to him who evil thinks. It was Lord Shanderson's tattoo, and it was Lord Shanderson beneath the mask. And then I heard a voice from behind me.

"Ready for your lesson?" His Lordship said from the doorway, causing me to gasp sharply.

He was holding two billiards cues. "I see you have found my

closet then. Not many people know it exists. I like to hide from people in here. It's where I like to do all my thinking, amongst other things."

"It's hardly what I would call a closet, sir," I said, confused by his choice of words. "More of a study surely?"

" 'But thou, when thou prayest, enter into thy closet, and when thou hast shut thy door, pray to thy Father which is in secret; and thy Father which seeth in secret shall reward thee openly.' King James Bible, Mathew 6:6," he said with a teasing smile on his lips. "I think you'll find that's the correct name for small rooms such as this in houses built around the same time as Beadale. They were built during the Reformation for people to hide away and worship away from prying eyes."

"Well, then I've learnt something new today," I said.

"It's also where the phrase 'to be in the closet' comes from. So, may I offer you a drink?"

"I don't really think I should, sir," I stammered. "I am still on duty, after all."

"Nonsense. Consider yourself stood down for the evening," he said. "And anyway, the first rule of billiards is that you need a very stiff drink to be able to play properly."

I followed him over to the billiards table. He took a bottle of amber liquor from the drinks tray and half filled two crystal glasses.

"Do you like a good single malt?" he asked, passing one to me.

"I do when it's this good," I said, breathing in the peaty fumes before taking a tentative sip.

"Cheers, then," he replied, chinking his glass against mine. Lord Shanderson held my gaze as he sipped at his drink. I didn't feel uncomfortable exactly, but the atmosphere between us was somehow different since he had found me in his study. The subtle nuances of the master and servant relationship were rapidly becoming blurred. So blurred, in fact, that I was standing having a drink with my employer and about to get a lesson in billiards.

As Lord Shanderson rattled off the rules of the game my attention turned to the actual billiards table itself. I stared at it for ages, not really being able to figure out what was so different about it. It was an imposing piece of furniture that dominated the center of the room, and, whilst it was certainly bigger than the pool tables of my youth, there was something else very different about it. For a start it wasn't covered with the familiar dark-green baize but with a midnight blue—but even that wasn't what set it apart.

"Hang on a minute," I said, as it finally clicked what was missing. "This table has no pockets! How is that possible?" I laughed.

"Anthony, this is carom billiards," Lord Shanderson said, laughing. "The original form of the game. In fact this table dates back to the seventeenth century." He ran his hand over the polished mahogany rail before adding, "Let it alone. Let's to billiards. Come!"

I might not have known the rules of carom billiards, but I did, against all the odds, get an *A* in English literature at school.

"*Antony and Cleopatra,* if I'm not mistaken," I said, feeling a little smug.

"Well, young man, let's see if your grasp of the game is as firm as your grasp of The Bard."

The game was fast and furious, and even though I somehow managed to hit a couple of decent shots, it was obvious I had no idea what I was doing.

"This is nothing like pool," I said, pausing between shots. "I think you had better explain the rules before we carry on."

"Never mind the rules," he said, topping up my drink. "Your posture is no good."

"In what way?"

"You need to keep your legs straight and bend from the

waist so that you can look straight down the cue like the barrel of a gun. You would improve no end."

He was leaning on his cue, puffing smoke rings into the air from his Cuban cigar, his fine chiseled features illuminated from above.

The drink must have been working its magic, because although I didn't feel in any way drunk, I couldn't help but say what was on my mind. "Why don't you show me what you mean, sir," I said, looking him straight in the eye.

He took another couple of puffs before he placed his cigar in the ashtray and walked slowly around the table to where I was standing. He silently moved behind me and took me firmly by the shoulders, instantly forcing me to stand ramrod straight.

"Take hold of your cue, Anthony." He said it in a low voice with his mouth surprisingly close to my ear.

I did as he asked and felt him inch nearer to me, so near I felt the warmth of his body against mine. Then he placed one hand on the small of my back and another at the nape of my neck and bent me sharply at the waist until my chest was almost touching the table.

"Do you see how much better that position is?"

"Much better, sir," I replied, though in truth I could see nothing as my eyes were tightly shut. I stayed like that for what felt like ages, but was probably only a few seconds, concentrating hard on regulating my breathing. The last thing I wanted was to give any hint of the fireworks that were exploding in every nerve ending in my body. Even though the effects of the alcohol were amplifying every sensation running through my brain, I wasn't so drunk that I didn't know this was a very dangerous game to be playing with one's employer. And I wasn't thinking about the billiards.

"You take instructions very well, Anthony," he said eventually. "I think you will see immediate results when you listen carefully to my directions."

I felt a rush of blood flood my cheeks as his eyes followed my hand when I attempted to hide the bulge in the front of my trousers.

"Lord Shanderson, it's getting late and I—"

"Nonsense, Anthony. I feel like we have only just started to get to know one another. And why don't you call me Drum?" Something about the way he spoke suggested that, whatever I said, he had made his mind up that we'd be here for a while yet. I took a slug of my drink, and as soon as I did so he topped it up.

"I think that would be, um, most irregular?" I said.

"You will find many things about me irregular, Anthony," he said, taking a step closer. "But I think that you and I could learn to understand one another perfectly. I have been paying a great deal of attention to you, and I like what I see. You have huge potential."

As he spoke I inhaled deeply, and my nostrils filled with the spicy smell of his cologne. It instantly reminded me of when I had smelled it in Rose View Cottage when I was with George. I was desperate to ask Lord Shanderson if he had been there that day.

"Let's get right to the point here," he said, placing his drink down and stubbing out his cigar. "I am looking for the perfect manservant, someone who can take care of all my needs. Is this something you are up to?" His words were as clear as a bell, but their exact meaning was far from obvious.

"Am I not already doing so, sir?" I asked.

"Hmm, there's the million-pound question." He smiled. "You are an excellent butler, but I have very specific needs that have not been fully met for many years, and I won't pretend to you that they are not complicated."

"Go on," I said, wondering what on earth was coming next.

"I make no bones about the fact that I am a complex man, Anthony, but what you probably don't know is that I also have certain proclivities that are more than a little—what's the word, niche?" He lowered himself into a large leather club chair and gestured for me to do the same opposite him. "It has always been my dream to keep the realization of these desires strictly 'in house.' And should ever my dream of finding the perfect servant become a reality, that person would want for nothing. I would make sure of it. That person would be looked after for the rest of his life—just like dear Mr. Johnson was."

I studied his body language and realized he was doing just about anything he could to avoid meeting my gaze.

"As is so often the case in these matters it stretches back to my childhood," he continued.

He spoke at a rapid-fire rate, as if he were afraid that if he inserted any pauses or gaps in his rhetoric I would run for the hills. But nothing could have been further from the truth. I was riveted.

"My father was a distant man, and my mother was simply far too busy being lady of the manor to pay me much attention. I acted up whenever I saw an opportunity in the vain hope it would provoke some kind of reaction from them. I wanted them to get angry with me or shout and scream, but all they did was ignore me and delegate all responsibility for my care to one of the servants."

He gave a gentle shake of the head, which made me wonder if that were the end of the story, but after a few seconds he carried on.

"At first, it fell to my nanny to dole out punishments, but as a teenager I was a keen rugby player, quite a strapping lad in fact, and it wasn't long before I towered over her. It wasn't so surprising that her threats of teaching me a good lesson fell on deaf ears. As I grew taller and stronger her ability to control me withered and died. Of course she complained bitterly to my parents, but they accused her of not doing her job properly." He relit his cigar and poured us both more whiskey.

"The poor woman was distraught at the suggestion of being incompetent, so she confided in Mr. Johnson, our butler. It was then that he decided that young Master Shanderson needed to be disciplined by a man. I was fourteen years old."

"And then what happened?" I asked breathlessly, hanging on his every word.

"He marched me up to the top floor and took me to his room. There he stripped me from the waist down and put me over his knee for the beating to end all beatings."

I shuddered as I conjured up a mental picture of the young Drummond Shanderson having his hide tanned by the older man in the very room I had been sleeping in until a couple of days ago.

"And did that work?" I asked, my hand trembling slightly as I lifted the glass to my lips.

"At first it had the desired effect, yes. I immediately went downstairs and apologized to Nanny, swearing to her through tears of humiliation that I would mend my ways. I regretted my behavior, and I genuinely had no desire to upset her again. But what happened that day wasn't about Nanny and me. It was about the problem brewing in my sex-addled teenage mind." He blew a smoke ring into the air and paused as if reliving the moment.

"And if you don't mind my asking, sir, what exactly was the problem?"

I was desperate for him to come to the point of the story to see where, if anywhere, I fit into it.

"The problem, Anthony, was that for weeks I could think of nothing else other than the burning sensation of Mr. Johnson's hand crashing down onto my bare arse. The problem was that I was aroused by it. Very aroused indeed."

Things were slowly starting to fall into place. Lord Shanderson's membership in the Black Orchid was certainly beginning to make a whole lot more sense now.

"I began to misbehave in front of Mr. Johnson with the sole intention of incurring his wrath. I would wait until we were alone and be purposely rude to him, goading him into action and praying he would take me upstairs and put me over his knee."

"And did he?" I asked.

"Yes, with rather alarming regularity. And it went on for years. In fact it went on until just before he died when I was nineteen years old. I was devastated by his death, as were my parents. Though it's fair to say for very different reasons."

I was now feeling quite drunk, but I couldn't work out whether it was the booze that was making my head spin or everything Lord Shanderson had just told me.

"Drum," I said, finding the sensation of using his Christian name a bit strange, "why have you chosen to tell me, of all people, this?"

He waited before answering, running a hand nervously through his thick, graying hair and pinching the bridge of his nose.

"I am very attracted to you, Anthony. You do realize that, don't you?" he said, making proper eye contact for the first time since this outpouring began. "I also saw you with George that day at Rose View."

A lump formed in my throat as the image of George's beautiful, bare backside bearing the brunt of the riding crop replayed through my mind like the highlights of a well-loved porno movie. "Yes, I had a feeling you might have. And?"

"And my mind has been on little else ever since. It is the reason I have gone out of my way to make your stay here a comfortable one. After seeing the way you dealt with George, I had to make sure you would stay. I had to make sure I got the chance for us to have this chat."

He leaned forward in his chair and slid his hand slowly up my leg. He stopped just short of my aching, swollen crotch and firmly squeezed my thigh, before letting go and sinking back down in his chair. The sensation of being touched by him was like being struck by a bolt of lightning and he knew it, if the small smile that flickered across his face was anything to go by. But then, as quickly as it arrived, the smile disappeared, and he became serious again.

"But seeing you with him was just an unexpected bonus. I had actually gone there that day to pay him off and tell him to leave. He had been the object of my affections for a while, but he was not like you. He did not understand my needs, and when I lost interest in him he turned nasty and threatened to tell the papers what I had gotten up to."

"So he was blackmailing you?"

"Yes, I'm afraid so. Pathetic, isn't it?" he said, looking rather sad. "He didn't particularly share my interests, so it was never going to develop into anything meaningful, but when I saw the way you dealt with him and how you used that riding crop on his blackmailing little arse, I couldn't stop thinking about how we could harness all that sexual energy to our mutual satisfaction."

For a fleeting moment it felt like all the air had been sucked out of the room. Lord Shanderson's lips were moving, but the only sound I could hear was my own shallow breathing. He placed his hand on mine and tilted his head, waiting for the answer to a question I hadn't heard.

"Anthony?" he said, looking nervously up at me. "Have I offended you?"

I looked down at his hand clasping mine, and before I knew it, I was out of my chair and standing over him. I placed a hand on each of his shoulders and pinned him firmly into his seat. His pale blue eyes widened as I towered over him, saying nothing.

"One thing you will discover about me," I said, lowering my face close to his, "is that I am very hard to offend."

I fell onto him and kissed him deeply. I could feel the relief radiating from every pore of his body as I kissed him more deeply and passionately than I had ever kissed anyone before.

His breath was hot and sweet with just a slight taste of cigar, and I couldn't get enough of it.

Despite the vise-like grip I had on him, he struggled and bucked beneath me, so I removed my hands from his shoulders and grabbed each of his wrists quickly, hoisting his arms high above his head and holding them there tightly. His broad chest began to rise and fall dramatically, keeping time with his rapid breathing. At that moment I was sure I'd never seen a man as consumed with lust and desire as he was.

"Drum," I said with my mouth close to his ear, "if this is going to work for both of us, I think we need to set some ground rules. Don't you?"

He nodded vigorously, but seemed unable to form any actual words. I released his hands, causing his arms to fall like dead weights into his lap. I was straddling him in the chair now and was able to slip my hand between his legs. Just as I had predicted, the fabric of his tweed trousers was straining against his swollen mound, and I allowed my hand to explore the contours of it. I had of course caught a glimpse of his manhood that day when I saw him naked on the bed, but on that occasion he'd been less than fully aroused. Now, though, was quite a different story.

As my palm brushed his balls he let out a low moan, raising his hips to increase the pressure between his crotch and my hand. I watched as his handsome, chiseled face contorted into a mask of sheer ecstasy. His eyes were tightly closed and his lips slightly parted as my hand explored him through the thick, course fabric. It would have been so very easy for me to unzip him right then, but I knew instinctively that I'd be wise to play the long game with Drummond Shanderson. I planted one final kiss on his lips before climbing off his lap and dusting myself down. His eyes flew open, and he sat bolt upright in his chair.

"I'll think about it," I said, flicking an imaginary speck of dust off my lapel.

"Think about what?" he said, with a look of abject horror.

"I'll give some thought to exactly what our ground rules will be. And when I have come to a conclusion, I will inform you, but until then we must maintain our employer-employee relationship at all times."

He stared at me in utter disbelief, and it took him a few moments to compose himself before he could speak.

"But, Anthony, I have just bared my soul to you. What do you mean you will think about it—what on earth have you got to think about exactly?" He had a note of irritation in his voice that I couldn't honestly blame him for. But that was all part of my plan.

"Will there be anything else tonight, m'lord?" I asked impassively.

"No, that will be all, thank you, Gowers," he replied, turning his head away as I left the room.

That night I lay awake until the small hours of the morning, trying desperately to make sense of what had just happened. Lord Shanderson had just taken the biggest gamble of his life, inviting me to be not only his manservant but his master too. It was a dizzying thought, but one that also fascinated me. He had hinted that I would want for nothing so long as I fulfilled my role. If I was honest with myself what I really wanted more than anything in the world was the kind of security I hadn't had growing up. If I stayed at Castle Beadale and met all Lord Shanderson's "needs," then I could live out my days in the manner to which I was rapidly becoming accustomed. I'd never have to worry about anything as dull as paying a utility bill or handing over rent to a faceless landlord ever again, and by the looks of it I wouldn't even have to worry about buying my own food!

What's more, it wasn't as if he were asking me to do anything

I didn't want to do. It would be a different story if he was some crusty old wreck of a man, but he was far from that. He was deeply, deeply sexy, and the truth of the matter was that I couldn't wait to get my hands on him. But if this plan was going to work for both of us, he would have to sweat a bit before I gave him my answer.

CHAPTER 13

I managed only three, maybe four hours sleep, and the bags under my eyes were there to prove it.

I wanted to face Lord Shanderson looking as though I had slept like a baby, as though the events of the previous night had not troubled me in the slightest. I poked and prodded my face in the mirror, wondering what I was going to do to remove all traces of fatigue and worry. And then, I remembered a tube of very expensive and very potent moisturizer hidden somewhere in the depths of my wash bag.

I emptied the entire contents of the bag onto the bed and marveled at how much money I must have spent on lotions and potions over the years. In London, buying expensive face creams had been my favorite pastime, second only to buying over-priced cashmere sweaters.

Eventually I found a tube of Beauty Flash Balm—every party boy's secret weapon. I can't remember the number of times I'd turned up for work at the hotel on no sleep, looking like I'd been at a health farm for a week. In fact, looking back I really should have offered to promote the balm for the manufacturer.

I slathered on the thick lotion, made myself a double espresso, and waited for both to work their magic. By the time I'd drunk the coffee I could feel the skin around my eyes tightening.

"Well, don't you look fresh as a daisy this morning," Vera said cheerfully when I walked into the kitchen.

"Well, thank you, Vera. I must say I am in a rather buoyant mood today."

I picked up a piece of buttered toast from a pile in the middle of the table and gobbled it down in seconds.

"Well, I'm glad someone is," Vera said, shaking her head in dismay.

"Why? Who's in a grumpy mood then?" I asked, reaching for more toast. "Not you, is it, Tom?"

"I'm never in a bad mood, me," he said, looking up from his bowl of cereal.

"His Lordship is in the darkest mood I've seen him in for many a long month. The last time he was this foul tempered was when *she* was here," Vera huffed.

I didn't need to press Vera for any more details, as it was pretty obvious I was the problem. The thought of it instantly killed my appetite, so I placed the slice of toast I was holding back onto the plate and headed for the dining room to face the music.

"Where you off to?" Vera asked as I was halfway out of the door.

"To serve him his breakfast," I said.

"Don't bother. His Lordship called me an hour ago saying he didn't want anything. Not even a cup of tea—most unlike him." She scraped a pile of sausages from a silver dish onto a plate and banged it down on the table.

"Waste not, want not," said Tom, spearing two of them with his fork.

I made my excuses and headed up to Lord Shanderson's room to see how he was. He might have been in a foul mood, but it was going to be impossible to avoid each other, so it would be better to have our chat about my future role at Castle Beadale sooner rather than later.

I knocked sharply on the door before entering. Inside the room was, as usual, in complete darkness, so I moved toward the window to open the curtains.

"Good morning, Lord Shanderson," I said as the room flooded with bright morning sunlight. But when I turned to greet him I could see that the bed had not been slept in. The cover was still folded neatly back the way I had left it last night when I had come in to do his turndown.

I walked into the bathroom, and that hadn't been touched either: towels still folded neatly on the washstand and the toiletries by the sink all perfectly aligned.

"Where on earth are you, Drummond?" I said to myself, looking around the room.

With none of the usual mess to clear up I decided to have a quick tidy-up of his dressing room. The small cedar-paneled room where Lord Shanderson's clothes were stored was truly a thing of beauty. Just off the main bedroom, it was fitted with exquisitely built-in rails for his suits and sports jackets, brass-handled drawers for shirts, and custom-built racks for his multitude of handmade shoes. It even had a glass-topped display case just for his collection of cufflinks, lending the room an air of the old-fashioned gentleman's outfitters. I stood looking at my reflection in the floor-to-ceiling mirror, imagining what it would be like to have a room like this of my own one day.

I began to flick through the suits, checking for any that could do with a press or needed sending away to be cleaned, when I heard someone cough. It definitely hadn't come from inside the room, as it was barely audible. I checked the bedroom just in case, but as I suspected, I was alone. I returned to the wardrobe and carried on, but seconds later I heard it again. This time the cough was louder and slightly more prolonged. It seemed to be coming from behind the suits. I parted the garment bags sharply, feeling slightly foolish when all that was revealed was the wooden paneling behind them.

Jesus, Anthony, what did you expect to find? I thought as I slid the suits back into place.

But as I was carefully arranging them, one of the jackets caught on something and wouldn't budge. I tugged at it, but was afraid it would rip, so I took down all the suits on either side of it to see what it had snagged on.

The cuff of the jacket had been caught between a join in two halves of the wooden paneling, but, when I pushed on the part where the fabric was trapped, something clicked loudly, and the paneling creaked open to reveal a very narrow spiral staircase. It was thickly carpeted, and tiny stained-glass windows in the curved walls flooded the stairwell with jewel-colored light. I stood at the bottom of the stairs and listened for signs of life above me.

I heard nothing at first but then, louder than before, I heard someone clear his throat. I squeezed into the narrow space, and before I could stop myself I was climbing the stairs two at a time. When I reached the top I gently pushed open a wooden panel just like the one at the foot of the stairs and peered nervously around the edge of it to see where the stairs had brought me out.

To my amazement, I was in my old room in the turret, and there, lying in bed cocooned in a mountain of blankets, was Lord Shanderson.

"So, this is where you are hiding, is it?" I said, closing the wardrobe door behind me. He emerged from beneath the mound of bedclothes and rubbed his eyes as if to check that what he was seeing was real.

"What on earth are you doing here?" he asked, sitting up. "I thought I had locked the door."

"Maybe you did, but I found another much more interesting way in," I said, pointing to the wardrobe.

"Ah, yes. The back stairs. Always came in so handy when Mr. Johnson was alive." He smiled weakly and shrugged his shoulders. "They haven't been used for years."

He was wearing a pair of fine white cotton pajamas with his initials embroidered on the pocket. The jacket was unbuttoned slightly, exposing a glimpse of his well-defined chest and its light dusting of salt-and-pepper hair. Never in a million years had I ever thought I would be aroused by anyone in pajamas, but something about them on him was incredibly sexy.

"Get out of bed!" I snapped suddenly, taking us both rather by surprise.

At first he looked slightly taken aback by my tone, but a flicker of understanding crossed his face before he did as I asked. I walked over to a thickly upholstered chair positioned in the bay window and sat down. He stood rooted to the spot as I got comfortable.

"I think it's time you were taught a lesson for disappearing like that," I said, patting my knee. "Get over here."

He obeyed immediately and positioned himself slightly to my right.

"I think you know what you need to do, Drum," I said, looking him straight in the eye. He started to loosen the cord on his pajama pants, but I raised my hand to stop him.

"Leave them on," I said.

He lowered himself over my knee and placed his palms on the floor, saying nothing. I let my hand explore the contours of his cheeks and marveled at how firm and round they were. I suppose a lifetime of horse riding would give anyone a bubble butt, but it was still impressive in someone old enough to be my father.

I circled a couple of times before I administered a sharp slap to each cheek, one right after the other. He said nothing, but I could feel his entire body tense and then relax with each blow. I waited a few seconds before I slapped him again, harder and sharper this time. As my hand rained down on his buttocks, I felt something hard stir and press into my thigh. I also felt a slight dampness soak into the fabric of my trousers.

I slipped my hand under the waistband of his pajama pants and pulled them down a few inches to reveal *that* tattoo. I ran a finger over it as I read out the words aloud.

"Honi soit qui mal y pense," I said quietly as I pulled the pants down farther to reveal his entire backside.

When I tugged at the waistband, he raised his hips to allow the pants to fall down to his knees. I left him there for a few minutes, just circling his cheeks with the palm of my hand and allowing a finger to momentarily disappear into the darkness at the base of his spine. When he raised his hips I saw a glimpse of his balls and reached down to feel them. They were hot and felt incredibly heavy.

"Don't stop," he muttered.

"Who asked you to speak?" I barked at him, bringing my hand down as hard as I could onto his bare flesh.

He moaned deeply, but didn't utter another word. I felt him pulse uncontrollably when my hand made contact. Then, just at eye level on the tall chest of drawers to my side I spotted a large silver-backed clothes brush. So with Drummond still positioned over my knee I quickly reached over and grabbed it. It was the perfect shape and size for my purposes, making me wonder if it might have been used to teach Drummond a lesson in the past.

I administered a couple more blows with the palm of my hand before, without warning, changing to the brush and bringing it crashing down onto his bare skin with a loud and satisfying "thwack." It instantly sent the blood rushing to the surface of his pale skin and left a distinct, angry, hand-shaped mark that would last a couple of days at least.

"So, is this the kind of arrangement you had in mind?" I asked.

He nodded his head, but stayed silent.

"Speak up, Drummond!" I barked.

"This is precisely what I had in mind," he said quietly.

"You can get up now; your punishment is complete for today," I said, pushing him off my knee.

He stood before me with his pajamas still around his knees, making no attempt to cover himself up; he looked almost mesmerized. I reached out and gently stroked him, making him gasp sharply. It was obvious he wanted me to carry on by the way he moved his hips toward me. But I knew instantly that giving him what he wanted would serve neither of us well in the long run. I looked into his eyes and saw a look of absolute surrender and contentment. It was then that I realized I had the power to give him the very thing he desired most in the world. But today was about laying down some ground rules and showing him who was in charge. From now on I would be the one to decide when he got what he wanted.

"Pull up your pants," I ordered.

There was a look of disappointment in his eyes, yet he seemed completely at peace. From the expression on his face it was obvious he had just experienced the most elusive kind of release, the kind he had been searching for all these years: the release of power.

I left the room without another word, leaving him to gather himself and reflect on the seismic shift in the nature of our relationship.

For the rest of the morning I kept busy polishing silver and organizing the butler's pantry. By the time I'd finished cleaning every candlestick, table centerpiece, and entrée dish in the silver vault, my stomach loudly reminded me that it was time for lunch, so I locked up and wandered through to the kitchen.

"You staying for a bite to eat, dear?" Vera asked from over the top of a wooden trug filled to the brim with salad from the garden.

"No, thanks, Vera. I think I'll nip back to the cottage and try and get the smell of silver polish from under my nails. I'll grab something to eat there," I said, slipping on my jacket.

"Well, whatever was bothering him earlier," Vera said, breaking apart the lettuce and dropping the leaves into a sink of icy water, "it's not bothering him now. His Lordship just about skipped through here earlier, he did. Even got a kiss on the cheek!" She laughed, shaking her head. "I don't know what gets into that man sometimes; I really don't."

"Any idea where he's gone?" I asked, trying to sound professional rather than plain nosey.

"Out for the day, he said. Not the faintest idea where, and he's driven himself, so I can't even ask Tom where he is."

Back at Rose View I set about making myself a sandwich, but the second I sat down to eat it there was a knock at the door. When I opened it the rear end of a van was just disappearing up the drive, but on the doorstep there was an enormous bouquet of long-stemmed white roses. There must have been at least ten dozen of them, and they were taking up most of the doorway. I struggled into the kitchen and stuck them in the sink until I could figure out what to do with them. As I was removing the cellophane wrapping I saw there was a small card taped to it. I opened it and read the message out loud to myself:

Thank you for making my dream a reality. —DS

"Drummond Shanderson, well, well, well, you old romantic," I said to myself as I placed the card on the mantelpiece.

Just as I was about to go back to my lunch there was another knock at the door. *Jesus, what now, a box of fluffy kittens?* I thought as I went to answer it.

When I opened the door I screwed my eyes closed for a second, but sure enough when I opened them again there she was, large as life and as bold as brass: my mother.

"Hello, Tony. You going to invite me in then?"

CHAPTER 14

One of my earliest memories of Mommy Dearest is of being on the sleeper train from Cornwall to Scotland with her. The train was the old-fashioned type with compartments that ran off a connecting corridor. You could still smoke on trains back then, and my mother took full advantage of that fact from the minute we boarded. The journey's starting and finishing points are so far apart that they effectively bookend the whole of the United Kingdom, and back then it took an entire day and a night to complete the trip. It sounds romantic, and under very different circumstances I suppose it could have been, but as with most of my mother's grand plans it turned out to be anything but.

I was five years old, and it was February 1988. Of this I am 100 percent sure. Why so sure? Because that was the month that Kylie Minogue scored her first number-one hit with "I Should Be So Lucky," and for some little boys that's the kind of fact that leaves a life-long impression. (I still know all the words by heart.) Another thing I am sure of is that it felt like the longest journey in the world and my mother spent most of it trying to drill the intricate details of her plan into me. We were traveling with my mother's new boyfriend whom I didn't particularly like. I had developed a way of ignoring most of her men friends and skillfully deflecting their feeble attempts to befriend me. They usually stopped buying me sweets and toys as soon as they realized my mother couldn't care less whether I liked them or not. Alan was a nice enough guy from what I can remember of him, but I had a built-in disdain for anyone who was stupid enough to fall for my mother. As the train snaked its way the entire length of the country I would have been perfectly content to watch the scenery and count telegraph poles, but my mother had other ideas.

"Now, remember, Tony, this is your Uncle Alan and, if any grown-ups ask you any questions about him, you tell them that—Mummy's brother, got it?"

"He's not my uncle," I said, turning my attention back to the window. "He's your boyfriend."

Even at that age I knew exactly how to get to her. Usually, if I was being difficult or misbehaving, she would have just hit me round the head and sent me to my room, but I can remember thinking that whatever the reason it meant an awful lot to her that I went along with her plan.

"If you don't call him Uncle Alan this won't work, and then we will all be in a lot of trouble, and you wouldn't want that, would you, Tony?" she said, breathing a heady mix of cigarette and booze fumes into my small face.

I have no recollection of arriving in Scotland, but I do remember waking up in my granny's house. I didn't know at the time that it was my granny's house; in fact before that train journey I hadn't even been aware I had a granny. For some reason, not only had my mother omitted to tell me I had a grandmother, she had also conveniently forgotten to tell my granny she had a grandchild.

Her house was a tiny railway cottage on the outskirts of

Glasgow. Not much more than a two-up two-down with an outside loo, so when we turned up it was quite a squeeze. I must have been carried upstairs the minute we arrived, because when I woke up I was alone in a huge brass bed in a room I didn't recognize. The room was as neat as a new pin and smelled sweet like freshly cut flowers. I later learned that the smell that followed my granny wherever she went was Lily of the Valley, and even now I can't smell that perfume without thinking of her. Even though I was alone in a strange house, I must have felt safe, as I made no attempt to go and look for my mother. The room was in darkness, but somebody had conveniently left the door ajar so I could hear voices in the room below.

"How do I know you are telling the truth?"

"Here, this is his birth certificate. That should be all the proof you need. Your son's name is right there under *Father*. See? That's your grandson up there."

"Why have you never contacted me until now? Why wait until my son is dead?"

"Too busy bringing up his kid, that's why. And you aren't exactly local, are you?"

The voices trailed off, and a few moments later the woman I came to know as Granny entered the room and flung her fleshy arms around me and sobbed herself to sleep right next to me.

The next day I was woken by the smell of a huge breakfast being prepared. When I wandered down the stairs, Granny was dishing up bacon and eggs whilst my mother and "Uncle Alan" chain-smoked by the back door. Granny seemed to be more or less ignoring them, but when I walked into the kitchen her face lit up. What struck me even at that tender age was how very different she was from my mother. I loved her straightaway, and it certainly felt like the feeling was mutual.

"Come on, my boy—get some breakfast down you. You don't look like you've had a decent meal in days. I've seen more meat on the butcher's dog," she said, shooting my mother a look that could turn the milk sour. She fussed over me endlessly, which delighted me and infuriated my mother.

"Valerie, leave the boy alone—he'll be unbearable when we get home if you carry on like this," my mother said, snatching a couple of rashers of bacon off my plate.

"You can't blame me for wanting to make up for lost time, can you, Carole?"

The two women were now staring at each other over the kitchen table, and it was clear that they were both biting their tongues.

"Tony, you can stay here with your granny whilst me and Uncle Alan pop into Glasgow to run a few errands—you'll be okay, won't you love?"

"He'll be fine," Granny said before I had a chance to speak. "We'll have a nice time getting to know each other, won't we, love?" She slipped an arm around my shoulders and pulled me close.

"Yeah, do whatever you like—we won't be long."

Grown-ups have a habit of thinking that they are being discreet around children when most of the time they are being anything but. It was just such an attempt at discretion that morning that made certain I sat up and took notice of what was going on.

Granny retrieved a large brown envelope from the dresser drawer and removed some official-looking documents from it. She signed the last page in a slow and unsteady hand that made me think she either didn't want to or that she wasn't used to signing things. My mother stood over her whilst she did it, and no sooner had Granny lifted the pen from the page, my mother snatched it up and stuffed it back into the envelope.

"It's for the best," she said, quickly shoving the envelope into her handbag. "He'd have wanted it to go to his only kid. Come on, Alan; we need to get going."

That afternoon Granny did everything in her power to keep

me entertained. She taught me how to play gin rummy and pontoon, but as lovely as it was to spend time with her, I kept one eye on the hands of the kitchen clock, marking the hours my mother was away.

Eventually they rolled in after Granny had put me to bed. Even at that age I knew when my mother was drunk, so it came as no surprise to hear them arguing. I heard Granny raising her voice, and at one point I even heard the usually quiet Alan chip in, but I couldn't make out any details so I must have drifted off to sleep.

My memories of leaving Scotland are hazy, but I do remember my granny begging my mother to stay longer. I can only assume it was so that Granny could spend time with me, as there was definitely no love lost between the two women.

We boarded the sleeper train late the following night, and I clearly remember waving to my granny as she stood sobbing on the train platform and my mother's pulling me back into the carriage by the seat of my pants. I couldn't quite work out why Granny was so upset, but looking back I think she probably knew it would be the last time we'd ever see each other.

My mother never spoke about that trip again. Growing up it never struck me as at all strange. Many stranger things happened in my childhood to relegate meeting my granny to a dim and distant memory, but as I got older I started to pick over the details and wonder why on earth my mother would have bothered to go all that way for the briefest family reunion on record.

She had hinted all my life that she had never really known who my real father was, but long after I had left home and was preparing for my first foreign holiday, I was forced to contact her to see if she had my birth certificate so that I could apply for a passport.

To my utter amazement it turned out she had kept my birth certificate safe all those years, but refused point-blank to post it to me so that I'd have no choice but to pay her a visit. I half expected her to have lost it by the time I got there or for it to be buried forever beneath one of the huge piles of discarded magazines in her squalid little flat.

Even then our relationship had broken down sufficiently to make a visit to see her something I approached with absolute dread. So when I saw an old battered shoe box on the coffee table with *Anthony's Stuff* written on it in my mother's distinctive scrawl, I felt a huge surge of relief that I wouldn't have to spend hours in her company whilst she searched for the birth certificate.

"It's all in there," she said, jabbing a nicotine-stained finger at the box. "Birth certificate, your first tooth, a couple of old photos of you as a baby. I don't know why I kept all that crap for so long, but anyway, there it is. So, why do you need your birth certificate?"

"I'm going to Greece on holiday," I said, instantly regretting it.

"Ooh! Greece, is it?" she said in a ridiculously posh voice. "All right for some, I suppose. Don't forget to bring me a present back, will you?"

"I'll be off then," I said, ignoring her amateur dramatics and heading for the door.

"Thanks for popping in, love," she called as I closed the door behind me and tried not to break into a run.

It wasn't until I sat down and began to actually fill in the passport application that I studied my birth certificate in any detail. I'd never actually seen it before, so when I saw my father's name for the very first time in black and white, I felt a lump form in my throat.

John McCrae, Profession—Merchant Sailor

As I stared at the yellowing document all the memories of that strange little trip to Scotland came flooding back, but before I went to place the certificate back into the box, I decided to take a look at all the other bits and pieces in there. I rummaged through the contents and amongst the faded photographs, a tiny lock of hair tied with a ribbon, and a single baby's shoe there was a small letter addressed to me. It had been opened at some point, but certainly not, to the best of my knowledge, by me.

As soon as I began to read, I realized it was from my granny, and was dated August 1988, just over six months after our visit. The address on the envelope was that of our old house in Cornwall, the one we were evicted from later that year. I immediately wondered how many more letters she might have written to me that I would never get to see.

It took quite a bit of concentration to read, as the writing was tiny and old-fashioned, but in it she explained that after my father had died in a car crash she had thought she had nothing left of him. That is, until she met me. She went on to say that when we showed up, she had been shocked at first, but, once my mother had told her how broke we were, she saw a chance to provide for me just like my father would have wanted her to. She hoped that signing over my father's death in service benefit would allow my mother to give me a better life. She inquired how I was getting on at school and asked if I might like to go and stay with her in the holidays one year.

I must have read and reread that letter twenty times. I felt sick at the thought that my mother dragged a small child the entire length of the country to use as leverage to fleece an old woman of a small fortune left to her by her only son. But worse still, I felt like she'd robbed me of the chance to have a loving relationship with my granny forever. It was beyond cruel; it filled me with a sense of shame so deep that of all the things I'd forgiven her for over the years, that was never going to be one of them.

I think it was around that time that I began to describe myself as a happily orphaned only child, and who could blame me?

CHAPTER 15

"**W**hat the fuck are *you* doing here?" I said, grabbing her by the arm and pulling her inside before she was spotted. "How did you find me here?" She staggered over the threshold, and as soon as I let go of her, she was on the far side of the living room.

"Wow!" she said, letting out a whistle. "My boy done good for himself."

"Oh, no you don't, Carole," I said, turning her round and pointing her back toward the door. "You are not welcome here. You have to go. Now!"

"Calm down, Tony," she said. "I've just come to say a wee hello to my only child—what's wrong with that?"

"I'll tell you what's wrong with that," I spat. "The last time I saw you, you told me you were dying of cancer—remember that?"

"It was a false alarm."

"Yeah? It must have been because that was three years ago. And what happened to the five grand I gave you to see you through your final days? I'll tell you what happened to it—you spent it on fucking sangria on the Costa del Sol with someone half your age called José."

"You seem to know an awful lot."

"Aunty Jean had the decency to tell me what you were up to. And, just so you know, she was as appalled at what you did as I am, so well done. Your only two living relatives hate you."

"Bit harsh," she mumbled, pushing past me and sinking into a chair.

"Don't get comfortable," I said, yanking her back onto her feet by her scrawny arm.

"Ouch! Take it easy, Tony," she squealed, slipping out of my grip and staggering into the bookcase, sending a silver-framed photograph of Chris and me crashing to the floor.

"Awe, sorry love," she said, stooping to pick up the pieces. "Is that your boyfriend?"

"None of your fucking business," I said, snatching the picture frame out of her hands. "Carole, you and I are done. I no longer have a mother. She died three years ago around the same time as you told me you had weeks to live and fleeced me of a small fortune." Her rheumy eyes began to fill with tears, and I could see exactly where we were heading.

"Does family mean nothing to you?" she said, beginning to cry.

"As a matter of fact it means everything to me, so you'll be pleased to know I have found myself a new one. A family I'm not actually ashamed of. A family who actually cares about me." I placed my hands over my face, willing her to disappear or even better to have never been there in the first place. "Tell me how you found me here; I need to know."

"I paid your friends at the Landseer a little visit. They couldn't wait to tell me that you had run away to the country." She let out a laugh, and I felt my palms instantly ball into fists. "That nice Mr. Henderson told me exactly where to find you."

"Get out of my house before I do something we both regret."

"You should watch that temper of yours," she said. "You get that from your father, you know."

"Don't drag my father into this," I said, the hairs on the back of my neck suddenly standing on end. "He must have had a screw loose to get involved with you; no wonder he ran off the minute you got pregnant."

I hated that she made me speak to her like this, but my mother and I in the same room is like pouring petrol on a roaring fire.

"When I saw you in the paper," she said, tears gone just as suddenly as they had appeared, "I was so proud to see you'd been promoted to hotel manager. I mean, you must be earning a small fortune." She was sounding almost sober now.

"Oh! I get it," I said, everything suddenly falling into place. "Old habits die hard, don't they, Mother? Let me guess; you've run out of money again."

Her face was close to mine now as she unsteadily shrugged her shoulders. "Come on, if a mother can't come to her only son for help, then what kind of world do we live in? I know you've got plenty," she said, jabbing a nicotine-stained finger at my Cartier watch.

"You really are a piece of work, aren't you?" I replied, slipping the watch off my wrist. "If that's all you care about, just take it. Go on, take it!" I threw the watch at her, and it landed with a dense thud on the rug by her feet. Without a moment's hesitation and with surprising agility she bent down to scoop it up.

"You see," she hissed, "it wasn't that hard to do the right thing by your mother, was it?"

"You disgust me," I said, exhausted by the sudden intrusion of the past into the present. "You really do, so just take the watch and leave. You should get more than enough money to drink yourself into oblivion—so be my guest."

"You are a good boy, Anthony."

"Just go."

Just then a car sounded its horn outside, and she immediately headed for the door.

"Keep in touch, Tony," she said as she left.

"Don't. Call. Me. Tony," I hissed as the door slammed shut.

A few seconds later I tentatively peered out of the living room window just in time to see her climbing into a waiting car. If I hadn't known better, I could have sworn there was a spring in her step. I watched as she leaned over and kissed the driver passionately on the mouth before holding up the watch for him to see the fruits of her labor. Even from where I was I could see how smug they both looked.

As the car finally disappeared from view I began to laugh. Just a chuckle at first, but in a matter of seconds I was almost hysterical, clutching my sides and tears rolling down my cheeks.

"Oh! Carole, you are going to have the shock of your life when you try to sell that watch," I said, looking at my bare wrist.

I fell back onto the sofa, trying to catch my breath. The Cartier watch she had walked away with was about as genuine as her motherly concern for me. A total fake bought for twenty pounds from Chinese Bob in the Landseer staff canteen. The irony of it all would have been poetic had it not been just so damned tragic.

I returned to the castle after lunch and got stuck with yet more polishing. I've always found the repetitive nature of cleaning highly therapeutic, and after my mother's visit I was certainly in need of a bit of therapy. In fact I became so engrossed in buffing the brass banisters in the Marble Hall that I didn't hear Lord Shanderson enter the room.

"Jolly good work, Gowers," he said, making me jump. "You have a lovely shine on that."

"Thank you, sir," I replied, turning to face him.

He was dressed more casually than usual in jeans and a Barbour jacket. His hair was messed up slightly from wearing a cap, and his cheeks were flushed. He also had a distinctly mischievous glint in his eye.

"Been anywhere nice today, m'lord?" I asked.

"Indeed I have, Gowers. I decided I needed some sea air so I drove down to Brighton and did a spot of shopping," he said, his face breaking into a broad smile.

He was holding a plain, black plastic bag that he began to swing by his side, drawing my attention to it.

"In fact, if I can tempt you to a game of billiards after dinner, I will show you my purchases."

"Very well, sir," I said, returning the smile. "As you wish."

When I served dinner later that evening I was relieved that the atmosphere between Lord Shanderson and me felt perfectly normal.

Neither of us said much over and above that which was strictly necessary during service. I asked if he would like more wine. He answered no. I inquired if he would like second helpings of Vera's steak and kidney pudding, and he responded with a resounding yes. Lord Shanderson and I were clearly in agreement that there was a time and a place for everything, so the absence of any discussion about what had occurred in the last thirty-six hours seemed to suit us both.

"We can have a drink together over billiards," he said, refusing his customary Cognac at the end of dinner.

"I hope you are not planning on getting me drunk again," I said as I cleared his plate.

"Knowing what you know now, I don't think that will be necessary. Do you?" He winked and placed his hand fleetingly on top on mine.

I felt a familiar charge of electricity crackle between us.

"I'll get cleared up and meet you in the games room," I said, slowly removing my hand from beneath his.

I cleared the dining room and washed the plates with lightning speed, suddenly desperate to be alone with him again. This time, when I got to the games room, I didn't bother to knock.

"That was quick," he said, looking up when I walked in.

He was leaning on the billiards table, drink in hand and another one poured for me at his side. Just as before the room was sparsely lit, but he was standing in a pool of light coming from above. He had loosened his tie and unbuttoned his shirt slightly, revealing a tantalizing glimpse of his chest. He looked so handsome I had to restrain myself from launching myself at him right there and then.

"Thanks," I said, taking the glass from his outstretched hand.

I inhaled the rich aroma rising from the glass before taking a sip.

"This is different than before," I said.

"Well spotted, Anthony. You have an excellent palate. I thought you deserved only the finest, so I dug out one of my father's best from the cellar." He held up an ancient-looking bottle covered in dust.

I took it from him and carefully wiped some of the dirt from the label so I could see what I was drinking.

"Bloody hell, Drum, this must be worth a fortune!" I said as I saw the year and make. "This is a 1957 Bowmore Islay—we had two of these in the cellar at the hotel, but I don't recall anyone's ever shelling out to buy one!"

"Yes, the year I was born," he said nonchalantly. "My father bought cases and cases of wine and whisky that year. It was a good vintage apparently."

"I'm honored."

I took another sip of the heady liquor before placing it carefully down on the side of the table and moving closer to him. I took the glass from his hand and placed it next to mine before pushing him back against the table.

"First roses and then this," I said, leaning in to kiss him. "I can see I'm going to have to work hard for my keep."

I pressed my body against his and held his head in my hands as I kissed him passionately. After a while I tore my mouth away from his and worked down to the crook of his neck. As I nibbled and sucked his whole body tensed, his back arched, and he moaned softly into my ear.

Usually, when I'm with a man for the first time, the sexual dynamics take time to assess. There are fundamental questions that need to be answered before any satisfaction can be guaranteed or, for that matter, expected. Is he top or bottom? What sexual proclivities does he have? Are his taboos the same as mine? Is he here to pleasure or be pleasured? The whole thing can take hours to figure out and quite often with disappointing consequences. I've lost count of the number of guys I've dragged home only to discover that we have so little in common sexually that they might as well be from a different planet.

But with Drummond things felt different. Everything with him seemed so natural and somehow just right. I knew exactly what he wanted, and so did he. And I had a strong feeling I was going to enjoy giving it to him.

I tugged at the collar of his shirt until a couple more buttons popped open to reveal a broad expanse of chest. I ran my fingers over every inch of it, lingering only fleetingly on his rock-hard nipples. When I did though, he gasped loudly.

"Oh! You like that, do you?" I said, pinching one firmly and twisting it.

"God, yes," he moaned. "For Christ's sake, don't stop."

I reached behind his back and slid my hands down onto his arse and began to roughly knead his cheeks. I felt the muscles tense sharply and then relax as he took a deep breath before whispering into my ear.

"Look in the bag on the table."

I removed my face from the crook of his neck and glanced over his shoulder. And there, carefully placed in the center of the billiards table, was the black plastic bag he had been carrying earlier.

"So, what have we here?" I said, reaching over and grabbing it.

As he looked on with barely concealed glee, I emptied the contents onto the table piece by piece.

First out of the bag was a length of thick silk rope, the purpose of which was fairly obvious.

"Hmmm, I can see that you are going to need restraining at some point," I said.

The next item was a small, beautifully carved wooden paddle with a short, leather-clad handle. I turned it over in my hands, and on the reverse side carved into the surface were the initials *DS*.

"It's a spanking paddle," he said proudly.

"Yes, I can see that. And how clever of you to have your initials put on it. That way if you leave it in a hotel room somewhere it's more likely to be returned to you."

He laughed and took the paddle from me before slapping it loudly against the palm of his hand.

"I do not intend to leave it lying around." He smiled.

Next was another paddle, but this one was larger and made from black leather. It was smooth and cool to the touch and obviously had more give than its wooden counterpart. I felt a thrill at the thought of the different effects the two paddles would have on Drummond's backside.

"We'll definitely have some fun with these," I said.

I leaned in and kissed him hard on the lips before taking him firmly by the shoulders and spinning him round to face the table.

I pushed the toys aside as he fumbled with the buckle of his trousers. Seconds later his tweeds were round his ankles, and in the flash of an eye he was bent over the table with his palms spread wide and his face pressed into the baize.

"So, Drummond. Shall we see if these toys of yours were worth the money you paid?" I asked, picking up the wooden paddle and performing a few practice swings in the air as if I were about to play a round of golf.

"Yes, please," he panted.

"In that case I want you to count the strokes. Can you do that for me?"

"Yes."

"Yes, WHAT?" I said with my mouth close to his ear.

"Yes, sir."

"And just so we are clear, if you miss any or purposely miscount, I will start all over again. Am I making myself clear?"

"Crystal," he said breathlessly.

I set to work and used the paddle on one cheek after the other as he kept count. I began with a moderate amount of force, but everything about Drummond's body language told me not to hold back for long. As I increased the pressure his back arched, and he pushed up his hips to anticipate the blows. With every strike his moans became lower and more animalistic. In fact, the harder I brought the paddle down on his bare skin, the more ecstatic he became, and by the time we arrived at the twentieth stroke his cheeks were glowing.

"Let's see if this one is any better," I said, teasing him gently with the tip of the leather paddle.

On the first actual stroke he gasped sharply, and his whole body spasmed. For a second I thought it might be too much for him and paused to take stock of his reactions.

"Twenty-two," he said through gritted teeth.

I was just about to carry on when I realized he had miscounted.

"Well, well, well—turns out you can't count after all," I barked, seeing a shudder of excitement run through his body as I began the count all over again.

By the time I reached twenty-five strokes I had to stop. My whole upper body was aching, and the biceps in my right arm were beginning to throb and burn as if I had just done a workout. He showed no signs of wanting me to stop, but something told me that if I didn't we'd be here for hours.

"I think that's enough for today," I said, dropping the paddle onto the table.

He straightened up carefully before turning to face me. His eyes were half closed, and a thin smile played on his lips. He slowly pulled up his trousers and winced as the rough cloth grazed his angry red cheeks. But as he tucked in his shirt and smoothed down his hair, he said nothing to give away how he was feeling.

"Are you okay?" I asked, placing a hand on his shoulder.

"Okay?" He laughed. "You have no idea how very okay I am—you are quite an expert spanker, young man." He leaned over and kissed me lightly on the lips before reaching for a cigar from the ashtray. He lit it and puffed two large smoke rings into the air. "You can leave now," he said.

I wasn't sure what the protocol was for being dismissed after having spanked one's employer, but I certainly didn't expect to be stood down quite so quickly afterward.

"As you wish," I said, before leaving him to his thoughts.

CHAPTER 16

A few days later I was sitting at the kitchen table reading the newspaper whilst Vera opened the post.

"Christ on a bike!" she shrieked.

"What's wrong?" I said, quickly getting up from the table and rushing to her side. "Has somebody died?"

"No, it's worse than that," she said, sounding as if she were about to burst into tears. "Lady Shanderson is coming to stay."

The letter was from Lady Shanderson's personal secretary, explaining that Lady Shanderson would be arriving the following weekend, and included a list running to two pages of what special arrangements were required for her stay.

As Vera began to read the letter she shook her head and snorted indignantly at the list of special requests.

"Well, that's a new one on me—*Lady Shanderson requires only pasteurized caviar from Harrods*—bloody Harrods! When am I going to find time to go to Harrods? She's obviously on one of her weird diets," Vera huffed, sliding the letter across the table for me to read. "Last time she was here I was up half the night shucking oysters, and she brought a cheese that smelled so bad I thought something had crawled into the pantry and died. At least we don't have to deal with that this time."

The list was mind-boggling. There were requests for organic spelt flour, bottles of rare glacial mineral water, fat-free goat's milk yogurt, unsweetened soy milk, and yeast and wheat-free bagels. And then, as if that weren't enough, on the second page there was a list of special toiletries to be ordered and placed in her bathroom prior to her arrival.

"Anyone would think we didn't have soap in West Sussex," Vera said with a shake of her head. "Why can't they ever give us more notice? This is a nightmare—and now I'm going to have to break the news to Gloria."

"What news is that?" said Gloria, entering the kitchen.

The news of Lady Shanderson's impending visit was broken to Gloria in the way in which one might explain to a particularly sensitive child that his or her puppy had just died. Hot sweet tea was made (good for shock, according to Vera), and I wouldn't swear to it but I'm pretty sure Vera slipped a tot of brandy in it for good measure.

"Well, that's just great, isn't it?" Gloria said as Vera rubbed her back soothingly. "I'll never get the house ready for her in less than a week. I mean, where am I supposed to find white phalaenopsis orchids, whatever they are, around here?"

Gloria and Vera were sent into a tailspin that threatened to last most of the day, so I made myself scarce and left them to it.

I mean, how bad can she be? I thought as I headed for the library to tidy the newspapers and empty the wastepaper basket. *She's probably a pussycat compared to what I had to put up with at the Landseer.*

The library was in its usual state of disarray, and as I began to reassemble the *Financial Times, Telegraph,* and *Daily Mail,* I made a mental note to give Lord Shanderson a few extra strokes later that night as a reminder to tidy up after himself.

The desk looked like it had been ransacked, as usual. There

were messy piles of papers and documents all over the place, but there was one letter in full view that I couldn't help but notice. After checking to see if anyone was hovering around in the hall, I smoothed out the thick cream vellum and began to read.

It was handwritten, and embossed at the top was the address of the Shandersons' London residence, Dugdale House, and it was signed, *Lovingly yours, Elizabeth x.*

In it, Lady Shanderson wrote about how much she was looking forward to coming back to Castle Beadale, and although I didn't have time to read the whole thing it did strike me as quite chatty. In fact, the whole tone of the letter struck me as most odd and not what I would have expected from someone who was widely acknowledged to be a prize bitch.

But it was the last line that jumped out at me as being the most interesting:

I'm so glad we have finally done what we set out to achieve.

As I pondered the meaning of the letter I heard someone coming down the corridor and quickly put it back in where I found it.

It had just gone 11 a.m., so the kitchen was buzzing with people congregating for their morning tea break when I got there. I was dying for a decent cup of coffee, but rather than head back to the cottage to fire up the Gaggenau I decided to stick around and see what I could find out about Lady Shanderson.

Thankfully, things had calmed down a bit, and Vera even managed to stop fretting long enough to cut up one of her fruitcakes for elevenses.

"So, the lady of the manor is coming for a visit, is she?" I said to no one in particular.

"Indeed she is, so we'd all better batten down the hatches," Vera said, pouring tea for everyone.

"No tea for me, thanks," I said, holding my hand up as Vera lunged toward me with the teapot.

"I've got two words for you," Vera said, banging the huge fruitcake down in the center of the table. "New. Money. It's just not the same. They want everything yesterday, no understanding of how things are really done."

I began to regret asking the question, but the genie was out of the bottle now, so I pressed on.

"Come on, Vera, she can't be all that bad, can she?"

"I'm not saying she is a bad person; of course I'm not. I'm just saying that she is a very demanding woman. That's all. I'm not showing her no disrespect. Just pointing out that she's different from us. Just a bit, you know . . . foreign in the way she goes about things."

"Like what?" I asked, stifling a laugh.

"She drinks vodka at dinner. And it doesn't get more strange than that. Even you, with your fancy London ways, have to admit that," Kylie chipped in, causing everybody to stop and look up.

"Is that right? Do tell me more," I said with a smirk that instantly sent Vera's eyes skyward.

"You need to learn your place, young lady," Vera barked, snatching back the slice of fruitcake she'd just put in front of Kylie. "I don't recall anyone's asking your opinion."

"Just because I don't share them at the drop of a hat doesn't mean I don't have opinions," Kylie shot back defiantly, before winking at me.

"Do you know what, Vera, I might have a cuppa after all," I said, inching my chair nearer to Kylie.

After that Vera managed to skillfully steer the conversation away from Lady Shanderson, but as people began to finish their tea and get ready to go back to work I saw my opportunity to find out more.

"Leave those," I said to Gloria, Tom, and Vera, pointing to

the dirty teacups and cake plates. "You lot look busy; Kylie and I will wash them up."

"That's sweet of you, dear," Vera said as she hurried out of the kitchen after Gloria. "Orchids! I need to talk to you about orchids."

"So, tell me what you know about Elizabeth Shanderson," I said to Kylie as soon as we were alone.

"You wash, and I'll dry," she said. "Then I'll tell you what I think."

At first, the pair of us just stood washing the dishes, staring out across the fields in front of the kitchen window.

"Beautiful here, isn't it?" I said, breaking the silence.

"Sometimes," Kylie replied.

"Sometimes? What's that supposed to mean?" I said, draping the tea towel over the lid of the Aga to dry.

I looked at Kylie now, and it was clear she was choosing her words carefully. She suddenly didn't look like a little girl anymore. She looked more serious than before, and I felt a sudden pang of guilt for never really having taken notice of her until now.

"What I mean is that sometimes things can get ugly around here. It might look all lovely to you, but I've heard them say things no husband and wife should ever say to each other," she said.

"Do you mean Lord and Lady Shanderson?"

"'Course I mean them—she's up to something I can tell." Kylie was standing with her hands on her hips now, clearly relishing the fact that she had my full attention. "I mean, why does she never spend time with her husband? It's not normal. It's like they don't even like each other. I think she's leading a double life. And I'm not the only one who thinks that. I've heard Gloria and Vera talking. I swear they think I'm deaf sometimes. Or stupid."

"No one thinks you are stupid, Kylie," I said. "Far from it."

"Anyway," she continued, "I think she's got someone else."

Poor Kylie had got it so very wrong that part of me wanted to tell her how wrong. To tell her that it was Lord Shanderson who had someone else and that that person was standing right in front of her. On the other hand, it suited me very well indeed that, so long as all suspicion lay at the feet of Lady Shanderson, her husband and I would be able to carry on with our agreement undetected.

"And I'll tell you what else I think. I think she's one of those lesbians."

Kylie's words took me so by surprise that I couldn't help but let out a tiny, high-pitched laugh before clamping a hand over my mouth.

"What on earth would make you think that?"

She looked me slowly up and down before shaking her head. "Isn't it obvious? If she's not a lesbian why wouldn't she want to be with him, like, *all* the time? I mean you must be able to see how handsome he is."

"Jesus! Would you look at the time?—I've got to get back to work," I said as I pulled my jacket on and headed for the dining room to polish some silver.

By late afternoon the fumes from the silver polish had given me a raging headache, so I decided to try and clear it with a good dose of fresh air. I headed out of the back door and kept walking until I was at the edge of the lake where I perched on a tree stump to admire the view. It really was stunning, and it felt good to be alone for a while to admire it. The air was crisp and cold, and I could feel my head clear almost immediately.

I was just about to head back to the house when my phone began to vibrate. It was a message from Maria:

> **Ciao, bello! How is country living? Have you swapped your Gucci loafers for Wellington boots yet? Call me xx**

I immediately punched in her number and waited for her to pick up. Until I saw that brief message I hadn't realized how much I was missing her.

"Anthony, *mia caro!*" she said when she eventually answered. "I have missed you."

"Oh, God, Maria, me too," I said, meaning every word.

"So, tell me. Are you enjoying the work? How is Lord Shanderson treating you? Is he a slave driver?"

Given what was going on between Lord Shanderson and me, that simple question felt incredibly loaded, and for a second I contemplated telling her everything. I was unaccustomed to keeping secrets from Maria, and in all the years I'd known her I had never lied to her, so it didn't feel right to start now. But I instinctively knew it wasn't the right time to drop such a bombshell. I made a snap decision to keep the facts of exactly how well my employer was treating me to myself for the time being and quickly changed the subject.

"Maria, can ask you something?"

"Anything, my darling, you know that."

"What's the deal with Lord and Lady Shanderson? I mean, do they get on or not? I just can't work it out."

The line went quiet, and for a second I thought I'd been cut off, but then I heard Maria slowly exhale, which usually meant she had sparked up a Marlboro Red and was choosing her words carefully.

"Why would you ask such a question?" she said eventually.

"Oh, you know, just being nosy I suppose."

"I'm not going to lie to you, Anthony; she can be tricky. She gets that from her mother. She's moody too. I hear her staff have to tread on eggshells most of the time. Does she get on with her husband? Depends on how you define 'get on,' I suppose. Whatever their arrangement is, it seems to be working."

There were so many direct questions I wanted to ask, but

unless I wanted to answer some pretty probing questions myself, I would be forced to keep it vague.

"She's coming to stay next week—I just wanted to make sure I knew what I was in for."

"I have heard whispers that she's not been herself lately. She's hardly left the apartment in New York for weeks. Not even to go shopping, which is totally unlike her."

"Any idea what's up with her?"

"Anthony, of course I know what's wrong with her, but you know I hate to gossip, don't you?"

"Of course I do, Maria—we all know wild horses couldn't drag a secret from between those luscious red lips of yours." I laughed. I knew perfectly well that she'd spill the beans eventually, but not before she made me work for it.

"I mean if anyone were to find out that I was being indiscreet, well, I shudder to think what would happen."

"Come on, Maria, just tell me what you know."

"Have you ever heard of Lloyd Maxwell?"

"The artist?"

"The very same. Well, let's just say that Lady Elizabeth Shanderson has been a most generous patron of the arts where young Lloyd is concerned."

"Are you saying she's having an affair with him?" I said, trying to keep the note of delight out of my voice.

"Past tense, darling. She dropped him like a hot brick last month—the poor lamb is devastated. He's canceled a huge show at the Gagosian Gallery in LA. He says he might never be able to paint again."

I knew exactly who Lloyd Maxwell was. He was the sexiest thing to come out of the art world for years, and he knew it. He'd even modeled for *GQ* magazine a few months earlier, smoldering in front of some of the huge abstract canvases that made him famous, wearing nothing but his designer underpants.

"Well, say what you want about Lady Shanderson, she's got excellent taste in men," I said with a genuine note of admiration.

"Are you talking about her ex-lover or her husband?" Maria asked.

"Maria!" I protested. "Her toyboy lover, obviously."

"Oh, I don't know, Lord Shanderson is quite handsome if you like that kind of thing. You can't seriously expect me to believe that you haven't noticed."

"Oh, Maria, I've just seen the time—I've got to get back to the cottage to change for dinner, otherwise I'll be late. Love you! Call me next week."

For the rest of the week I managed to not allow myself to be drawn into the mounting hysteria generated by Lady Shanderson's visit. Vera and Gloria whipped themselves up into such a frenzy about every tiny detail that I avoided the kitchen whenever possible, thinking it best to let them argue it out between them as to whether pink roses or white lilies were a more suitable replacement for orchids.

But whilst chaos reigned below stairs, things continued as usual between His Lordship and me. In fact, at no point was the subject of his wife's visit raised by either of us, and that suited me fine. I could understand that she had to show her face from time to time if only to keep up the pretense.

"I'd like you to come to London with me tomorrow," he said to me as I was pouring his wine at dinner.

"I see. And will this be business or pleasure?" I asked.

"Let's agree that it could well turn out to be a bit of both," he said with a smile.

"So what is the occasion?" I asked, feeling a thrill at the thought of being in London and away from Beadale with him.

"Well, I have to see my solicitor, and you have an appointment too."

"Why would I need to see your solicitor?" I asked.

"No, *I'm* seeing the solicitor. You have an appointment to be fitted for a suit at Gieves and Hawkes on Savile Row—it's a little gift in recognition of all your hard work."

I was standing rooted to the spot with the wine bottle hovering in midair when he reached up and hooked his arm around my neck, pulling me in for a deep, lingering kiss.

His breath was hot and tasted of red wine. I could barely bring myself to pull away, but I needed to know more.

"Oh, wow! Thank you," I said. "I've always dreamed about having a bespoke suit."

"I had a feeling you might," he said, draining his claret. "Now, Anthony, we will need to set off quite early tomorrow, so why don't we both have an early night? We can save all the real fun and games for The Dorchester."

"So we're staying the night in London?" I said.

"Yes, just one. I have my usual suite at The Dorchester. One never knows when one might need to get away from all the prying eyes at Dugdale House. The suite has an adjoining room for a manservant, so no eyebrows will be raised. Just make sure you ruffle up the sheets before housekeeping comes in!" He stood up from the table and kissed me again before heading for the door. "Get some rest. I want you in top form tomorrow."

I was so excited about our trip to London that I wasn't the least bit tired when I got back to the cottage. I packed a case, selecting only smart clothes. I would, after all, have to play the part of Lord Shanderson's valet to the full, and although we would be sharing a bed for the first time, I would still have to look like staff to any prying eyes.

I picked up my phone and brought up Chris's number. It was a bit too late to call, so I decided to text him instead.

Batten down the hatches, bitch! I'm coming to London tomorrow—R U in town? I have an

**appointment in the West End. Could meet for
drink in Soho around 5ish? Let me know. —X**

Now I was doubly excited about my trip at the thought of
being able to catch up with Chris—I had so much to tell him
I'd be hard-pressed to fit it all into a quick drink. Then my
phone vibrated.

**Baby Girrrl! You are shit out of luck—I'm in LA
until Friday. When you next in town? Does Frank
know you are coming? —He's been asking about
you. Are you staying at the flat? If so, I have
drunk all your decent wine soz.**

My first thought when I read Chris's text was *Frank's been
asking about me?* I had a split-second flashback and felt a flutter of butterflies at the thought of a naked Frank standing in my
kitchen with his arms around my neck. I had had no idea Chris
and he had kept in touch.

Maybe I would call Frank and see if he wanted to meet me
for a drink instead.

I was up, dressed, and over at the castle by 7 a.m. the following morning.

By the time I was ready to wake His Lordship, I'd steamed
both suits he'd left out, polished the shoes, and had everything
packed and ready to put in the car. I prepared a tea tray and
went up to his room to wake him.

"Good morning!" I said cheerily as I flung open the curtains.

As usual he was lying naked in a tangle of sheets, and I delib-
erately averted my eyes in case I found myself diving on the
bed and ravaging him right there and then. He stretched and
yawned for a few seconds before eventually opening his eyes.

"That's a fine sight to wake up to," he said with a grin.

"I take it you are talking about the tea, Drummond," I
replied, placing the tray over his lap.

"I'm talking about you." He took my hand and pulled me toward him. "And the tea of course. You make a lovely cup of tea." He kissed me briefly before letting me go.

"Tom has the car ready, and I have all your bags packed. Your navy double-breasted suit is hanging in the dressing room, and I've taken out the Dunhill cufflinks and your regimental tie. We are ready to go whenever you are."

I scooped up his discarded trousers from the floor and had begun to fold them neatly over the back of the chair when he began to speak.

"You think of everything, Anthony. Absolutely everything. And that's why I love you."

Thank God I had my back to him, otherwise he might have seen my eyes grow to the size of dinner plates. I was certain he meant it in the very broadest sense, but even so, those last few words hit me like a cricket bat around the head.

"Come on," I said, still not looking at him. "The sooner you are up and dressed, the sooner we can go."

I left him to bathe and dress whilst I took the cases down to the car. I convinced myself that what he had just said was a slip of the tongue or a figure of speech. But whatever it was, it was proving difficult to convince myself he hadn't said it at all.

"That it?" Tom said when I placed His Lordship's bags by the car.

He was suited and booted and looked pleased to have a driving assignment that would require him to drive farther than Westcourt Village.

"No, I have a bag too; I just need to go and grab it."

"Are you going with him?" Tom asked.

"Yes, I have an appointment in London too," I said, before heading off to fetch my bag from the hallway.

If Tom was suspicious of my reasons for accompanying His Lordship, he didn't show it. For all I knew Drummond always took his butler with him when he traveled, but to be honest until now I hadn't really given it any thought. Another thing I hadn't stopped to think about was whether or not I should sit in the front of the car with Tom or in the back with Drummond. There'd be no time to ask him before he came down, so I just hovered around with Tom as we waited.

Ten minutes later Drummond came out of the front door of the castle and crunched his way over the gravel toward the car. Tom immediately stood to attention and held open the rear door whilst I stood by his side.

Before he climbed in Drummond slipped off the thick cashmere overcoat he was wearing and handed it to me.

Once he was in his seat Tom went to close the door, but Drummond held his hand out to stop him.

"What are you waiting for?" he said, looking at me. "Get in; we haven't got all day."

I climbed in beside him and stared out of the window so that he couldn't see the stupid grin creeping across my face. Seconds later I felt his hand slowly move under the overcoat I had placed over my lap and slide up my thigh. He hadn't looked at me since we got in the car and was still looking out of the window as we drove through the estate gates and onto the main road. He tightened his grip on me before he spoke in a voice just low enough that I would be able to hear but not Tom.

"I can't wait to get you all to myself tonight."

The drive to London seemed quicker than usual somehow. Drummond and I barely spoke, but it wasn't uncomfortable, just normal really. I couldn't exactly strike up a conversation with him about where he was going to take me for dinner with Tom in the driver's seat, so as Drummond buried his head in the day's papers I discreetly took out my phone and checked my messages.

The first one was from Maria, and I instantly felt bad for not calling her. She didn't take kindly to being ignored and said as much in her text:

ARE U DEAD OR SOMETHING?

I had so much to tell her that I decided to call her when I got to the hotel rather than text. With any luck she'd be able to swing by for a drink and I'd be able to fill her in on the madness of Castle Beadale. I stifled a laugh when I imagined what her reaction would be when I finally told her what I'd been up to with her boss's son-in-law.

The second message wasn't so easy to deal with.

Where U stayin in London? Can I come and say hello?
I really want to see you. —Frank X

Fuck! Chris must have spoken to him, I thought as I stared at the tiny screen. *I'll kill him when I see him.*

Of course I could have just ignored the text. I could even have told Frank I was busy. I could have lied about where I was staying. But I didn't.

IM staying at the Dorchester, but with boss.
Could meet for coffee at 4?

I pressed Send before I had a chance to change my mind. Anyway, it was only a coffee with a mate. No harm in that.

Tom steered the Bentley off Park Lane and onto the small forecourt of The Dorchester Hotel. The second he killed the engine not one but two uniformed doormen simultaneously opened the rear doors of the car. I instinctively went to the rear of the car to retrieve the bags, but yet another Dorchester employee was already on it.

"Pick us up at 4 p.m. tomorrow," Drummond said to Tom, before marching into the hotel lobby.

I waved and smiled at Tom before following His Lordship inside.

The lobby of The Dorchester is as rich and opulent as its well-heeled clientele. Everything about it screams money, from the oversized chandeliers to the enormous bronze urn in the center of the room overflowing with exotic flowers. It's one of those places where you have to squint to take it all in.

I must have been too busy checking out the room, because when I looked around I couldn't see Drummond anywhere.

I expected to see him at the front desk checking in, but caught a glimpse of the back of him as he marched round the corner toward the lifts. I quickly followed him, managing to jump through the lift doors just as they were sliding shut. Drummond pushed the button for the fifth floor and tapped his fingers impatiently on the wooden paneling as we slowly moved up through the building.

When the doors opened we were greeted by one of the hotel butlers, standing to full attention.

"Good morning, Your Lordship. I trust you had a pleasant journey."

"Yes, fine, thank you, Philip. Not too bad at all."

Realizing Philip knew Lord Shanderson from previous visits, I smiled and nodded at him, but he just blatantly turned his back and marched down the corridor.

When we arrived at suite 501 Philip swiped a card and held open the door for Drummond. But, when I went to follow him, Philip pushed past me and was hot on Drummond's heels, leaving the door to slowly close in my face.

You cheeky bastard! I thought as I pushed my way into the room.

Once inside Drummond slipped his coat off and slung it over the back of a chair before heading through to the adjoining bedroom. Philip quickly moved over to scoop it up, but I positioned myself between him and the coat and looked him straight in the eye.

"Touch that fucking coat and I'll break every one of those scrawny fingers," I said, not blinking.

His face was a picture, and I nearly cracked up when he pursed his lips and his nostrils flared like a racehorse's.

But before he had a chance to think of a bitchy reply, Drummond shouted through from the other room. "That will be all, Philip; we'll call if we need anything."

"Very well, sir," Philip said, looking like someone had just snatched his favorite teddy bear from him.

"And Anthony, if you could sort out Philip and then put the Do Not Disturb sign on the door, I have things I need you to attend to."

I knew exactly what this guy was up to. I hadn't worked all those years at the Landseer without learning how to maximize my earning potential, and this guy was no different. When he had seen Lord Shanderson turn up with his own hired help, he probably knew his chances of making any tips were greatly reduced. I couldn't really blame Philip, but it's not the way *I* would have dealt with it.

"Here, Philip," I said in a voice just loud enough for Drummond to hear. "Let me give you something for all your kind help."

I rummaged around in my pocket, eventually taking out a ten-pence piece and holding it up in front of his face before placing it carefully in his hand, closing his fingers around it, and squeezing tightly.

Philip left the suite as quickly as he had arrived, and I was sure we wouldn't be seeing him again before we left.

When I went through to the bedroom Drummond was lying on the bed. He'd loosened his tie and kicked his shoes off and was grinning like an idiot.

"We have an hour to kill—any ideas?" he said, patting the bed next to him.

But before I could say anything there was a loud knock at the door.

"Deal with that, will you," he said, rolling his eyes.

When I opened the door it was a porter with the luggage.

I ushered him in and pointed to where I wanted the cases.

I opened my wallet and took out a tenner. But then I had a better idea.

"Listen, mate, you know Philip the butler, right?"

"Yes, sir, I know Philip," he said, his lip curling slightly when he said the name.

"Well, in that case I need you to do me a favor," I said, taking out another note, twenty pounds this time. "When you see him, be sure to let slip how generous the guests in 501 were."

"Very kind of you, sir, and I can't think of anything I would enjoy more," he said with a wink.

When I returned to the bedroom Drummond had fallen asleep. I perched on the bed next to him, and when I began to stroke his hair he opened his eyes and smiled up at me.

"I might just have forty winks," he said. "Wake me in an hour so I can get ready for my meeting."

I pulled a blanket over him and went to unpack.

As instructed, around an hour later I gently woke Drummond and ushered him into the shower to get ready for his meeting.

"So what are your plans this afternoon?" I said as I sat on the edge of the bath whilst he showered.

"I'm having lunch at the Wolseley with Nigel, my solicitor. Knowing him it will probably take all afternoon," he said, stepping from the shower.

I grabbed a towel and began to dry him off. I tried not to let my eyes wander over his naked body for too long as neither of us could afford to get waylaid.

"And you?" he said.

"Gieves and Hawkes at 2:30 p.m., and then I might meet a friend for coffee."

He lowered the towel he was using to dry his hair and looked at me.

"Anyone interesting?" he asked.

He was smiling, but something about his tone told me to lie. "Maria," I said.

"How nice." He slipped into a robe. "Do give her my regards."

I followed Drummond down to the lobby and waited with him whilst the doorman hailed him a cab.

"So shall we meet back here at 6 p.m.?" he asked as we waited. "I've booked a table at China Tang for 8 p.m."

"That sounds great—I love Chinese food," I said, opening the door of the cab as it pulled up in front of us. "See you later," I mouthed through the window as it pulled away.

I checked my watch and, realizing I had a fair bit of time to kill, I decided to walk over to Savile Row and stop for a coffee en route. But just as I was about to walk off another cab pulled up directly in front of where I was standing.

"Need a cab, mate?" the driver said through the open window.

"No, thanks . . ." I began to say, but when I looked into the cab I stopped mid sentence. "Frank. What are you doing here?"

"Just get in, will you? I'm holding up traffic."

Not wanting to cause a scene I climbed into the back just as he accelerated, sending me totally off balance and headfirst into the lap of a woman I had never seen before on the backseat.

"Oh! Christ, I'm so sorry," I said as I struggled to right myself.

"You all right there, Anthony?" she said, helping me up by my arm. "I'm Karen," she said, taking my hand and shaking it firmly.

"I'm really sorry, but I don't think we've met," I said, reaching over to flick the switch that would allow me to be heard by the driver.

"Frank, what's going on?" I said, banging on the glass partition.

"Hang on a minute—I'm just going to park up," he said, pulling into an empty parking bay just off Curzon Street.

The woman next to me just sat there and smiled. She looked vaguely familiar, but for the life of me, I couldn't put my finger on how I knew her.

"I see you two have met then," Frank said as he climbed into the back of the cab with us.

"Frank, seriously, what the fuck is going on? Why are you here and who is this?" I said, before adding, "Excuse my language."

"Anthony, this is my sister Karen."

"That's really nice for both of you, but why did you feel it was necessary to kidnap me in order to introduce us?"

Karen began to rummage around in an oversized leopard-print handbag whilst I just stared at Frank, shaking my head.

"Karen's got a bit of explaining to do, haven't you, sis?"

"Yeah, s'pose I have," she said, letting out a throaty laugh.

Then I realized why she looked so familiar. I definitely hadn't met her before, but she had exactly the same eyes as Frank, and when she laughed it was obvious they weren't just brother and sister. They were twins.

"Frank said I'd better explain why you found this in the glove box of my car," she said, holding up the note from the glove box. "I'm surprised you could read my handwriting if I'm honest," she said, letting out a machine-gun laugh.

"What she's trying to say is that I drove you to Sussex in her car that day. She's my twin sister. Not my girlfriend. And she wrote that stupid note!"

"Oi! Watch your mouth, brov," she said, punching his shoulder. "I lent you my car, didn't I?"

Frank was laughing now and playfully ruffling her hair. It was sweet seeing them together, and for a second it even made me wish I had a sister like Karen.

"So," I said to Frank, "turns out you're not a liar after all."

He didn't say anything; he just shrugged his shoulders and smiled.

"Right, I'm off then," Karen said suddenly, climbing out of the cab. "Looks like you two have a bit of making up to do."

Frank followed her and hugged her tightly, but before she walked away she leaned back into the cab and placed her hand on my knee.

"Be nice to him, Anthony. He's a lovely bloke and not as tough as he looks."

She kissed Frank on the cheek and disappeared down the street.

"So, where to, gov?" he asked through the partition after climbing back into the driver's seat.

I felt myself beaming at him, but I honestly couldn't stop myself.

"Number One Savile Row, please, driver," I said. "And if you are not busy maybe we'll have time for that coffee afterward."

CHAPTER 17

———◆———

I had dreamt of being fitted for a bespoke suit for as long as I could remember, so going to Gieves and Hawkes was a bit of a dream come true.

When I arrived I was shown straight through to a private room and told that my tailor would be along shortly.

The room was small and wood-paneled with a curtained-off changing area in the corner. It had a window that looked out over bustling Savile Row and a large oak table piled high with hardbound books containing fabric swatches. As I waited I began to flick through them, wondering what kind of fabric I should choose. Some of the pages contained Harris Tweeds in every possible color combination, but I laughed at the idea of Drummond and me in matching suits.

I was flicking through a book of fine Italian gabardine when the door opened.

"Mr. Gowers? I'm Patrick, Lord Shanderson's tailor," a tall, bearded man said, dropping a heavy bolt of fabric onto the table before offering me his hand.

He was immaculately groomed and was, as you'd expect,

wearing the sharpest suit I'd ever seen, complete with a tape measure round his neck.

"Pleased to meet you, Patrick. I've just been trying to choose a fabric from all of these," I said, waving a hand over all the swatch books. "I might need a bit of help. Although I did see a nice navy blue gabardine that I thought . . ."

"Actually, Mr. Gowers, the fabric for your suit has already been chosen for you by His Lordship." He pointed to the bolt of cloth he had been carrying.

I hadn't taken much notice when he walked in, but I examined it more closely now I knew I was stuck with it.

"Oh, I see. And I take it this is it," I said, running my hand over it.

It was a sort of nondescript mid-gray flannel, and, whilst it was nice enough, it wasn't what I would choose for myself.

"Yes, a very fine cloth this one," he said, slipping off his jacket. "If you could stand completely naturally with your back to me, we can begin."

He took what seemed like a million measurements, jotting each one down into an old leather-bound book.

He bent my arms into various positions and pulled my shoulders back. At one point he announced that I had one arm significantly longer than the other. He seemed very matter-of-fact about it, but I couldn't help wondering how I'd managed to never notice I was so hideously deformed.

"I was thinking maybe a three-button jacket, you know, kind of sixties?" I said as Patrick silently worked away.

"Actually, sir, Lord Shanderson was very clear about what he wanted. He has requested that we measure you up for a double-breasted suit."

"I see. In that case I'll shut up then, shall I?"

Patrick just looked up and smiled weakly before continuing to measure my inside leg. The whole thing took no longer than half an hour, which I was glad about, as not having the chance to choose my own suit had rather taken the gloss off the whole experience.

Patrick said he'd be in touch about a second fitting, but to be honest all I wanted to do was get out of there and see Frank.

I burst out of Gieves and Hawkes's door expecting to see Frank parked right outside, but he wasn't. I scanned the street in both directions, but I couldn't see him anywhere.

When a black cab pulled up alongside me, I excitedly bent down, expecting to see Frank's rugged face staring back at me, but it wasn't him.

I thought maybe he'd got bored of waiting and picked up a fare. Perhaps he'd had a change of heart, and he didn't want to have coffee with me after all. I tried to suppress my disappointment, but in truth I felt like someone had just punched me in the stomach.

After realizing I'd been stood up by one man and deemed incapable of choosing my own clothes by another, I decided there was only one thing for it and that was to spend some money. And what better place to do it than Bond Street?

I headed past Burlington Arcade and was just about to head down Cork Street when I heard footsteps behind me. I spun around just in time to see Frank skid to a halt right in front of me.

"You deaf?" he panted. "I've been shouting after you from right back there."

As he bent over, trying to catch his breath, I felt a huge surge of relief.

"You came," I said to the back of his head.

"'Course I bloody came. Did you think I was going to piss off and leave you? I just went to park the taxi, and when I came back the geezer in the shop said you'd just gone." He straightened up and stared at me like he was waiting for me to speak. "Well?" he asked.

"Well, what?"

"Are we going for this bloody coffee or not?"

We crossed over Bond Street and headed down to Berkeley Square where I knew an ancient coffee shop that did great espresso. As we walked Frank chatted nonstop, telling me about the various characters he'd had in his cab that day and how he'd nearly got a parking ticket. In fact, he talked so much I started to think he was a bit nervous.

"I don't know how you can drink that stuff," he said when the waitress brought over my double espresso.

"Well, that just goes to show you what different people we are, doesn't it?" I laughed. I raised an eyebrow at him as he stirred four sugar cubes in his tea, one after the other.

"You and me aren't all that different, you know," he said.

"Aren't we?"

"No. I think we want the same things."

As he spoke I studied his face. He looked serious, and there was something about the way he was speaking that made me think he'd been rehearsing what to say.

"Listen, Frank. It's been great seeing you, but I think you should know that I've started seeing someone, so you and I should just stay mates."

He looked up from his tea and cocked his head to one side.

"Seeing someone? Like who?"

"Never mind who. That's private, and anyway, he and I have to keep it totally on the quiet," I replied.

He shrugged his shoulders and tried to look nonchalant, but I could tell it wasn't what he wanted to hear.

"Yeh, mates would be good," he said eventually, before reaching across the table and putting one of his huge hands on top of mine. "But why all the secrecy?"

"It's complicated."

"Come on! How complicated can it be? I mean it's not like you are shagging, I dunno, the boss or something, is it?" He laughed.

The air in the café suddenly felt thick and oppressive; I felt my cheeks flush red-hot. I stared at my empty cup, but when I went to speak my tongue felt like sandpaper and refused to work. I needed to get out of there and away from all of Frank's questions.

"Anthony, you're not, are you?"

I looked up and saw he was staring at me and slowly shaking his head; his lovely blue eyes were now full of concern. Concern for me.

I got up from the table and pulled a fiver out of my wallet.

"Gotta go," I mumbled as I pulled on my coat.

Frank suddenly grabbed my elbow and steered me out of the café.

"You are going nowhere until we have had a little chat," he said as he frog-marched me across the road and into Berkeley Square. He found an empty bench and pointed to it.

"Right, sit down and get talking. I've got all afternoon."

I told Frank everything. It was as if he'd pulled a ripcord or something. I just couldn't seem to stop. I told him about all the gifts I'd been given, and I told him exactly what I had to do to Drummond to deserve them. When I finally stopped talking I held my breath, expecting him to be angry with me or even a bit jealous, but he was neither.

"You need to pack in your job," he said matter-of-factly. "In fact go and tell him to shove his job up his arse. Actually, on second thought, maybe that's not such a good choice of words."

I began to laugh, even though the situation I had got myself into suddenly seemed far from funny. Frank put his arm around me and pulled me tightly to him so my head was resting on his chest.

"Frank, what am I going to do? I need this job and . . . I like him. He looks after me."

Frank looked more than a little dubious, but chose his words carefully.

"Anthony," he said, running his fingers through my hair, "all these things he's done for you are not because he has your best interests at heart. The car, the cottage, all that shit is just so he can control you. You must realize that."

I wanted him to shut up. I wanted to get up and walk away and forget this conversation ever happened, but then again sitting on a park bench wrapped tightly in Frank's arms felt pretty damned good too.

"He says he loves me," I said.

Frank took a deep breath before speaking.

"Anthony, if you believe that you are a bigger mug than I thought. There's no easy way to tell you this, but he loves being fucked by the help. Plain and simple."

His words stung like a slap in the face, and I pressed my nose into his sweatshirt so that he couldn't see the tears welling up.

After I'd blinked away any tears that threatened to embarrass me I glanced at my watch and gasped when I saw the time. It was 5:30 p.m., and I'd promised to meet Drummond at six back at the hotel.

"Frank, I *really* have to go. I'm going to be late for him," I said, jumping to my feet.

"Promise me you will think about what I've said," he said, getting to his feet.

We stood for a few seconds just staring at each other, saying nothing, and then he pulled me into a bear hug so tight it squeezed the breath out of me.

I pulled away and, saying nothing, headed in the direction of The Dorchester. When I reached the far side of the square I looked back, but I couldn't see whether or not he was still there as the tears had begun to flow.

Jesus, Frank. What have you done to me? I never cry, I thought as I wiped my eyes and headed off to meet Drummond. He was on the phone when I got to the suite and barely looked up as I walked through, so I headed for the adjoining room, where I'd unpacked my clothes. I quickly stripped off and turned on the shower, sitting on the edge of the bath whilst I waited for the room to fill with steam. It would be the first proper shower I'd had for weeks as Rose View's bathroom offered not much more than a dribble of water compared to this shower. It was a gray marble cubicle as big as the whole bathroom at the cottage with a showerhead the size of a dinner plate fitted into the ceiling. When I stepped under the torrent of hot water, the pressure of it was a shock at first, but I quickly relaxed, and it soon began to feel as if every inch of my body were being massaged. It was deafening too. So much so that I didn't hear Drummond enter the room.

"Need a hand?" he said, pulling open the shower door.

"Jesus, Drum!" I gasped, almost losing my balance. "You scared me."

I quickly turned off the shower and stepped out. Drummond was holding one of the hotel's enormous, white, fluffy towels for me.

"How was Maria?" he asked.

"Fine. She sends her regards," I said from behind the towel.

I slipped on a robe and began to lay out what I was going to wear for dinner. I took out my dark gray Helmut Lang suit and carefully laid it on the bed. It was my absolute favorite thing in my wardrobe and had cost me a small fortune, but the way it made me feel when I wore it made it worth every penny.

"You're not wearing that, are you?" Drummond said from behind me.

"Why not?" I snapped, turning to face him. "Got any better ideas?"

"As a matter of fact I have," he said, holding out a bright yellow Selfridges bag. "Take a look."

I took the bag from him and removed a parcel wrapped in

tissue paper. Inside was a black velvet dinner jacket with satin lapels.

"Put it on; let's see if it fits," he said excitedly.

I slipped out of the robe and pulled on the jacket. The silk lining felt cold and strange against my bare skin.

"That looks very smart," Drummond said, smoothing down the lapels and fastening the buttons. "Do you like it?"

I looked at my reflection in the full-length mirror on the wall opposite and quickly looked away again. It looked hideous on me. The fit was perfect, but the cut was so old-fashioned, I wanted to rip it off immediately. I could tell by the feel of it that it was expensive, but it just wasn't me.

"It's lovely," I said, kissing him on the cheek. "I love it, thank you."

"Come on, hurry up or we'll be late for our booking. That Chinese maître d' is an absolute beast about timekeeping—the last time I was here he gave my table away to some bloody Russians whilst Tom was looking for a parking space." Drummond laughed.

I retired to the adjoining room to finish dressing and when I returned, he looked me up and down with an approving nod.

"You look very handsome," he said, placing a hand on the small of my back and guiding me toward the door.

Stepping into China Tang is like stepping into a 1930s Shanghai opium den crossed with an English gentleman's club. But whilst it has the power to transport its guests to another continent the minute they walk through its doors, the restaurant is actually accessed via a discreet door just off the main reception area of the Dorchester.

Inside the restaurant it's all dark wood paneling and oriental lanterns with a smattering of chintz, so, even though I was uncomfortable in the jacket Drummond had bought me, I had to admit that it suited the surroundings rather more than it suited me.

"Would you like a cocktail or shall we move straight onto wine?" Drummond asked as soon as we sat down at our table.

"Either," I replied.

"We'll have two of your Sandy Slings, please," Drummond said to the waiter. "You seem a little subdued tonight," he said when the waiter left us.

"I don't mean to be," I said, offering him a weak smile. "I'm just a little tired, that's all."

"I see. Well, let's hope you perk up a bit later," he said with a wink.

Annoyingly, Drummond insisted on choosing everything we ate, but I have to admit that he chose exceptionally well. In fact dinner was quite remarkable. It seemed to be a never-ending stream of food, with little dishes of dim sum following hot on the heels of hot and sour soup and crispy Peking duck.

"That was amazing," I said, finally pushing my plate away in defeat.

"Yes, I particularly enjoyed the lobster in black bean sauce. . . ." He let his sentence trail off, and his eyes suddenly focused over my left shoulder.

I turned around in my seat to see what he was looking at, and when I saw who was approaching our table it felt like someone had just punched me in the stomach.

"*Mia caro!*" Maria squealed as she clamped a hand on each of my shoulders and kissed me on both cheeks. "I cannot believe you didn't call me to say you were coming to London."

She obviously clocked the look of horror on my face, because she immediately changed tack and turned to Drummond.

"Lord Shanderson, how are you?" she gushed, extending her hand. "Aren't you the perfect employer bringing young Anthony to such a wonderful restaurant!"

I watched Drummond's face carefully as he took her hand and kissed it.

"He's worked very hard, so I thought he deserved a little

thank-you," he said, before adding, "Won't you join us for a drink?"

Maria glanced at me for a fleeting second, but that was all it took for her to register the look in my eye that pleaded with her to say no.

"Lord Shanderson, you are too, too kind, but I am here with friends. Perhaps another time." She smiled politely and turned to me. "Call me," she said simply before heading to a table on the far side of the room.

Drummond waited until she was fully out of earshot before he spoke.

"I thought you said you spent the afternoon with her," he said in a low, calm voice. "It would appear as if that were not the case."

He waved the waiter over and asked for the bill. He didn't speak to me again until the bill was paid and we were leaving the restaurant.

"I was going to suggest we go for a drink, but I think we had better go upstairs and get to the bottom of where you were all afternoon," he said as we entered the lift.

"Look, Drummond . . ." I began, but he turned on me and pushed me hard against the wall of the lift.

"Maybe I didn't make myself clear," he hissed into my ear, "but I will not be lied to."

"You're hurting me. Let me go!" I said, pushing him away as hard as I could.

Thankfully, just then the lift doors slid open, and an American couple stepped in.

"Good evening," Drummond said to the couple, all smiles. "Lovely evening."

If I was shocked at his outburst in the lift, I was more shocked at how he could switch back to being his charming self so effortlessly. The lift finally arrived at our floor, and we nodded our silent good-byes to the Americans before heading down the corridor to the suite.

As soon as we were inside, Drummond put the DO NOT DISTURB sign on the door and locked it behind him.

"Get undressed," he ordered.

"Drummond, I'm sorry I told you I was with Maria. I don't know why I lied, but it was nothing, honestly." I began to try to explain myself, but he cut me off mid flow.

"Did I or did I not just tell you to get undressed? Trust me, Anthony, you do not want to make me any more angry than I already am."

My first instinct was to stand up to him and tell him to calm down, but something about his tone and a menacing look in his eye had me doing exactly as he asked. I began to take off my clothes.

He said nothing as I slowly removed each item of clothing and waited until I was completely naked before he spoke.

"Get over here, you dirty little liar," he said, moving over to the writing desk where he'd been making phone calls earlier.

And then with one sweep of his arm he sent everything on it crashing onto the floor.

"Jesus, Drum, what the fuck are you doing?"

He didn't bother to answer; he just grabbed me by the scruff of the neck and pulled me over to the desk, forcing me over it and holding me in place with one hand. I could hear him fumbling around for something with his free hand, and seconds later he landed the first agonizing blow to my naked arse.

"Fuck! Drummond, no . . . Please, please stop. You know I'm not into this," I screamed, but he just continued.

Ignoring my pleas he began to rain blows down onto my bare flesh. It felt like he was never going to stop, and, whatever he was using, it sure as hell wasn't his hand.

I struggled at first, but he had such a firm grip it felt like a waste of energy, so I focused instead on breathing through the excruciating pain he was inflicting on me.

Eventually, after what seemed like an age, he stopped and let whatever it was he had been using to beat me fall from his hand and land with a thud on the thick carpet. I opened my eyes and saw the black leather paddle he'd bought in Brighton lying on the floor next to me.

"Get up," he said calmly. "It's time for that chat."

I straightened up and immediately felt the skin on my behind tighten and scream. Not wanting to meet his eye, I walked over to the bedroom and took a robe from behind the door. Whilst I was out of his line of vision, I wiped my face with the sleeve and took a deep breath before going back to face him.

"So who was it?" he asked.

He was sitting on the sofa now, inspecting his nails.

"It was somebody I met just before I came to Castle Beadale. I met up with him to let him know that I didn't want to see him again. Happy now?"

"I wouldn't go that far, Anthony, but I will admit to being a touch *happier*." He let out a little laugh, which made the hairs on the back of my neck bristle. "And I take it you have severed all ties to this person now."

"Yes, I won't be seeing him again. I promise," I said.

"Good. That's what I like to hear. I think you should sleep in the valet's room tonight. I need a good night's sleep."

"If that's what you want," I said, secretly glad I wouldn't have to sleep next to him. "What time would you like me to wake you?"

"Let's have a nice breakfast together around eight thirty?" he said as he headed for the bedroom. "And, Anthony, I'm glad we have sorted things out, aren't you?"

I was stunned at his jovial tone given what had just happened between us, so I found myself just nodding at him.

"Tomorrow's another day, as they say, so we'll soon be back

to our normal routine. Good night." He blew me a kiss and closed the bedroom door behind him.

I stood rooted to the spot, trying to make sense of what had just happened. Did he really think we could get back to normal after *that?* Feeling suddenly exhausted and more than a little confused, I took myself off to bed in the adjoining room, hoping to God that I'd be able to sleep.

CHAPTER 18

The next day we ate breakfast together in the suite as if nothing had happened. He read the papers, commenting on various news stories, whilst I poured his tea and buttered his toast.

"I asked Tom to pick me up at 10 a.m.," he said from over the top of his *Financial Times*.

"I'll make sure we are both packed and ready to go by nine thirty then."

"Actually, I'd like you to return to Beadale by train."

"I see. Any particular reason for that?"

"Yes—I have some errands I need you to run for me in town. Shouldn't take you more than a couple of hours. You'll be back at Beadale in time for tea."

Tom was waiting outside the hotel at 10 a.m. sharp with the engine running and the boot open. Drummond climbed in the back and waited whilst the porters loaded in the bags.

"Thank you, Anthony," he said simply, before the electric window slid shut and the car pulled away.

I returned to the suite to grab my jacket and the list of errands Drummond had left me on the desk. There was a trip to

Penhaligon's to collect some more of his favorite cologne, a pair of handmade shoes to be collected from John Lobb on St. James's, and interestingly a parcel to collect from Rigby and Peller in Knightsbridge.

Now, I'm no expert on women's underwear, but even I know that Rigby and Peller is London's poshest bra shop. So posh in fact, that they even supply Her Majesty the Queen with her undergarments.

Jesus, Drummond, don't tell me you're a cross dresser as well as a sadist, I thought as I walked out of the hotel.

I left Rigby and Peller for last; I figured I could get a bus from right outside to Victoria Station.

Next to the cash desk at Rigby and Peller were piles and piles of dark gray gift boxes tied with silver ribbon. Some were tiny, and some quite large, and they were balanced so precariously on top of one another that it looked as if one false move would bring them all crashing down.

"I'm here to collect a parcel for Lord Shanderson," I said to the middle-aged lady behind the desk.

She peered at me over the top of her half-moon glasses and smiled warmly.

"Ah! Yes, Lord Shanderson. Bit more than one parcel, dear," she said, waving a hand at the leaning tower of lingerie.

"What—*all* these?" I said.

"Yes, lucky girl, isn't she?"

"Sorry? Who exactly is a lucky girl?"

She looked at me like I was a complete idiot and reached over for one of the small boxes on top of the pile. She lifted up a label attached to the ribbon and held it out for me to see. It was printed with the words:

LADY ELIZABETH SHANDERSON

"All of this is for her?"

"Indeed it is, and may I just say how refreshing it is to still have clients who want quality undergarments at a time like this," the saleswoman said, patting her lacquered hair. "Most people are straight down to Marks and Spencer, but not the Shandersons. Of course, she'll have to be measured again in a few months time, but this should see her through."

I didn't have a clue what this woman was going on about, and to be honest I didn't care. But what I did care about was who was going to pay for it all.

"Erm, and the bill?" I asked.

She looked at me as though I had just had an outburst of Tourette's.

"A bill? Good Lord, no. Lord Shanderson always puts his wife's items on account and settles at the end of the month. All you need to do is get it in the car. I take it you are in a car."

"Erm, actually no. I'll need to hail a cab, I think."

She rolled her eyes and waved over a uniformed doorman.

"Norman, be a love and hail a cab for this young man, would you?" she said before silently mouthing the word *Shanderson* like a secret password.

Against the odds I managed to get all the bags and boxes to the train station and onto a train that was leaving almost immediately without losing any of the packages.

Thankfully, the train was not busy, as all the bags and parcels took up a ridiculous amount of room on the luggage rack. I made myself comfy and watched with a tinge of sadness as Battersea Power Station slid slowly past the train window picked out against the dark clouds that were gathering high above the Thames.

I took out my phone and saw two missed calls from Maria and a text from Frank. I couldn't face calling Maria to explain what had happened the previous night, even though I knew she'd be so desperate to know she was probably foaming at the mouth by now. I'd need time to figure it out in my own head before I let her in on it. But Frank was a different story. His text was, as ever, straight to the point:

> **So, U thought about what I said?**
> **U gonna pack it in or what? I can help you.　XX**

What do you mean, "I can help you"? I thought as I read the text over and over again.

I considered calling and telling him what had happened, but quickly thought better of it. God only knows what he'd make of Drummond's little outburst.

I chose my words carefully and began to reply to his text.

> **Hi, Frank—yes, I have thought about what you said, but**
> **I need to stick things out for a bit longer at Beadale.**
> **Everything will be fine. Thanks for being a mate.　X**

I quickly pressed Send and slipped the phone into my pocket before I had a chance to add anything I'd regret later.

It was gone four by the time the train pulled into Westcourt Station. When I struggled onto the platform with all my bags and parcels, I was pleased to see Tom waiting for me.

"Done a bit of shopping, have we?" he said, scooping up an armful of bags and heading out to the waiting Land Rover.

"Yes, I thought I'd treat myself to some new lacy underwear," I replied.

With the car all loaded up Tom put his foot down and had us back at the castle in next to no time.

"Drop me at Rose View, will you? I need to change for dinner," I said.

"Oh! Sorry, Anthony, I forgot. Vera asked me to tell you that His Lordship is out for dinner tonight, so you're not needed."

I felt a huge surge of relief at the thought of not having to serve him whilst I could still feel the heat of his hand on my backside.

"No worries. I guess that means I can have an early night then," I said, staring out of the window so he couldn't see the look on my face.

Tom and I unloaded the car and took all the shopping bags into the kitchen, where Vera and Gloria were sitting drinking tea.

"He's spoiling her this time. I wonder what she's done to deserve all this," Gloria said through gritted teeth as the bags began to pile up in front of her.

"Rigby and Peller, eh? Can't be bad," Vera said, taking a sneaky look inside of one of the boxes.

"Makes Her Majesty the Queen's bras you know," said Gloria.

"Yes, so I'm told. Anyway, I'm going to unpack his bags and then head off for an early night," I said, making for the door.

"Good idea. We should probably all do the same. Tomorrow is going to be a hell of a day what with *her* arriving and everything," replied Vera.

Until then I'd almost forgotten about Lady Shanderson's visit.

"Oh! She's arriving tomorrow, isn't she?"

"Unfortunately, yes," said Gloria with a sniff. "So God only knows what we have in store for us."

The next morning Barb came over from the office to inform us that Lady Shanderson and her butler would be arriving by helicopter later that afternoon. The rest of her staff would need picking up from the local train station a little later.

"Sweet lord!" exclaimed Vera. "How many is she bringing this time?"

"Just four," Barb said, shrugging her shoulders. "Lady's maid, chef, and butler. There's a doctor coming up from Harley Street tomorrow, but he's not staying."

"Is someone ill?" I asked.

"I doubt it; Lady S is a bit of a hypochondriac. She's forever popping pills, that one," Barb said, rolling her eyes. "And don't forget that His Lordship will expect all of us to be lined up to greet her when they land."

"I suppose I should be practicing my bloody curtseying?" Vera grumbled.

At three o'clock precisely, Vera frog-marched all the staff out of the side door and around to the front of the castle, where she organized us schoolma'am-style into a neat line just to one side of the front door.

Gloria stood ramrod straight with eyes fixed on the spot on the lawn where the chopper was due to land, whereas Tom and Kylie could barely conceal their excitement, scanning the empty sky above their heads for signs of its arrival.

"Does she always arrive this way?" I asked Vera as we waited.

"No, this is her new toy. Bit gauche if you ask me."

And then in the distance, I could hear the sound of rotor blades slicing through the air before a red spot became visible in the distance. Everyone stopped chatting and stood to attention as the red dot grew larger and circled a few times before coming in to land in the middle of the lawn. As the helicopter lowered slowly toward the ground, the grass parted and the nearby trees bent under the force of the displaced air before the helicopter came to rest and the blades slowed to a stop.

A uniformed pilot was the first to disembark, jumping down from his seat and quickly opening the rear passenger door. He extended a hand, and moments later Lady Shanderson slowly emerged, looking like a sixties film star sent to the future in a time machine.

Stepping gingerly down onto the lawn, she shook her perfect hair free from a Hermès silk scarf and removed her enormous dark glasses. Her butler quickly appeared by her side, draping a cream trench coat around her shoulders.

Her progress across the lawn was impeded ever so slightly by the sinking of her spike-heeled boots into the lawn, but nevertheless she looked thrilled to be at Castle Beadale.

"Hello, everyone, I'm back!" she shrieked as she approached the welcoming party.

First in the lineup was Vera, who stood impassively as Lady Shanderson placed a hand on each of her shoulders and kissed her on both cheeks. I stifled a laugh when Vera flinched.

"How are you, Vera?" Lady Shanderson asked. "It's been ages; you look well.

"Tom, handsome as ever," she said, moving down the line. "Kylie, still here, I see. Gloria, hello again. And YOU," she said when she got to me, "must be Anthony. Mummy tells me you come highly recommended by the lovely Maria, and what's more, my husband tells me you are most attentive." She fixed me with a smile that sent a shiver down my spine.

"A pleasure to meet you, Lady Shanderson," I said, extending my hand.

But suddenly her attention was drawn away from me by the arrival of Lord Shanderson. He came out of the house and stood by my side for a second before stepping forward to greet his wife.

I expected no more than a polite kiss on each cheek or a brief embrace, but instead he moved straight in and kissed her full on the lips, locking his arms around her like they were love-struck teenagers. And then he placed one hand tenderly on her stomach.

"And how's this little chap doing?" he said.

"So much for keeping it a secret, Drum!" she laughed, playfully slapping his shoulder.

"Forgive me, darling; you know how I am with secrets. I've never been able to keep one for long," he said, looking straight at me as he passed on his way into the house.

I glanced over at Gloria and Vera, whose mouths were literally hanging open.

"Well, I didn't see that coming, did you?" Gloria said to Vera when Lord and Lady Shanderson were out of earshot.

"No, I did not," Vera replied.

Long after the welcome party had dispersed, I was still standing alone by the front door, trying to make sense of what had just happened.

Lady Shanderson, Lord Shanderson's trophy wife with whom he shares a marriage of convenience, is up the duff. What a turn-up for the books, I thought. *All that bullshit about separate rooms and separate lives would appear to have been nothing more than a big fat lie.*

I suddenly felt as if my stomach were about to do a somersault, and every last drop of moisture evaporated from my mouth. And then, quite out of the blue, I was violently sick into the rose bush next to me.

When I finally pulled myself together I heard a small, timid cough from behind me.

"Erm . . . Vera told me to come and look for you. Lord Shanderson is calling for you," Kylie said, looking quite shocked at having seen me barfing up into the bushes.

"I'll be there in a minute," I said, taking out a hankie and wiping my mouth.

"He's not a good man, you know," she said in a tiny voice.

"What did you just say?" I said, clasping my hand over my mouth, worried I might throw up again.

"Oh! Nothing, ignore me. What do I know? Sometimes I just say silly things. Vera's always telling me I have a vivid imagination," she said with a nervous laugh.

"No, seriously, Kylie, what makes you think he's not a good man? What have you heard?"

She looked at me carefully before answering, as if she were undecided about what route to take.

"I used to go out with George, you know," she said.

"I didn't know that," I replied, suddenly very worried about what she was about to say next.

"Lord Shanderson made George's life a misery. One minute he's flavor of the month, and the next he's throwing him out on his ear. George and me, we hit it off just fine until Shanderson took a shine to him, and then I was discarded like yesterday's newspaper. I thought George really liked me, and then he goes and dumps me without an explanation. Next thing you know he's being escorted off the estate. I still haven't got to the bottom of why he was sacked, but I will."

I studied her face as she spoke and felt an overwhelming urge to put my arms around her and tell her a few home truths, but she looked hurt enough without my telling her that her ex-boyfriend was a bisexual blackmailer.

"I'm sorry to hear that," I said, clasping her hand between mine. "Shall I tell you something, Kylie?"

She nodded silently.

"I think you can do a lot better than George; I really do. I think George might have been a bit rough around the edges for a nice girl like you."

"Maybe you're right. But you have to admit he was bloody sexy though, wasn't he?" she said with a little wink.

"He certainly was," I agreed.

When I eventually pulled myself together, I headed back into the house, but as I crossed the Marble Hall on my way to the kitchen, I did a double when I saw Lady Elizabeth's maid and her butler arguing like an old married couple.

"Sharon, how many times do I have to tell you? My doctor says I simply mustn't lift heavy loads. You'd be the first to complain if I was off work altogether with a bad back," the butler said, lifting a tiny vanity case and flouncing up the stairs with it.

"Lazy, fat, old queen," she hissed under her breath, before heaving a huge tote bag over her shoulder and picking up two suitcases.

"Here, let me help," I said, running over and wrestling one of the cases off her.

"Cheers," she said with a toothy grin. "Glad to know there's at least one gentleman in this house."

Lady Shanderson's suite was in the East Wing, directly above the games room, but when I turned left at the top of the stairs, Sharon turned right.

"Erm, excuse me, I think you'll find Lady Shanderson's suite is this way," I shouted down the hallway.

"Don't worry. I know where I'm going," she said over her shoulder, before turning the corner and disappearing out of sight.

When I finally caught up with her, she was just about to march into Lord Shanderson's suite.

"Hey!" I shouted. "You can't go in there." But before she had a chance to answer, the door opened, and Lady Elizabeth appeared with her hands on her hips, looking quite put out.

"You took your time," she said. "Come on, hurry up and get those bags unpacked." She pulled Sharon into the room before spotting me. "Ah! Anthony, how kind of you—would you be a dear and bring that parcel in, please?"

She pointed to a large, flat, brown-paper parcel leaning up against the wall. I placed the suitcases down, but when I went to lift the parcel it was much heavier than it looked.

"Quickly now," Lady Shanderson said as I struggled through the door with it.

I staggered into the room, but I almost dropped the damn thing on my foot when I saw Drummond sprawled out on the bed reading the paper whilst his wife arranged her things on the dresser. I noticed she'd also cleared the top of the nightstand and replaced what was there before with silver-framed photographs of her and Lord Shanderson.

"Where have you been, Anthony?" he said when he saw me. "I've been looking everywhere for you."

"My apologies, sir. I was just helping load the bags in."

He looked over the top of his reading glasses and mumbled

something that I couldn't quite hear, but that made his wife titter like a schoolgirl. The thought of them sharing a joke at my expense made me want to jump on the bed and punch him in the face.

"Anthony, can you call down and tell my chef I want a kale and açai berry smoothy sent up ASAP," she said as she began opening the boxes I had lugged back from London. "Drummond, you naughty boy!" she squealed, holding up a pair of lace trimmed panties. "These are adorable!"

"Only the best for you, my darling," he said, leaning over and planting a kiss on her lips.

"Will there be anything else, Your Lordship?" I asked, trying not to show how uncomfortable I was watching him shower his wife with gifts and affection.

"No," he said without even bothering to look at me.

"Actually," Lady Shanderson interrupted, "there is something you can do, Anthony. You can unwrap the parcel you just brought in for me."

I began to rip open the packaging whilst Lady Shanderson looked on.

"Now it's my turn to give you a gift, darling," she said, clapping her hands and turning to her husband.

"What on earth is it, Elizabeth?" Lord Shanderson asked, looking up from his paper. When I removed the final layer of bubble wrap, I heard him gasp.

"Oh, darling. You didn't. . . . Oh my God! You did. It's stunning, absolutely stunning," he gushed, flinging his arms around his wife and showering her with kisses.

I glanced down and saw that it was a painting. I stared at the thick layers of dark, muted paint caked onto the canvas and felt a little surprised that something so modern and abstract had solicited such rapture from His Lordship. I took a second look to see if I could work out what all the fuss was about and realized

I was holding one of Lloyd Maxwell's most iconic paintings—
Les Éternels Amoureux. The eternal lovers.

Jesus, these two really deserve each other, I thought as I left
the room.

Down in the kitchen Jacques, Lady Elizabeth's chef, was
slowly but surely taking over Vera's kitchen, much to her obvious displeasure.

"Do you have a vegetable juicer?" he asked Vera in his thick
French accent.

"When you say vegetable juicer . . ." she said, looking utterly
bemused.

He rolled his eyes and began laying out a set of expensive-
looking chef's knives like a surgeon preparing for surgery.

"I take it you managed to get all the items on my list," he
said.

Vera shot him a look and simply pointed her thumb in the
direction of the larder. Jacques headed off in search of organic
yak's milk or whatever it was he was looking for, but as soon as
his back was turned Vera stuck two fingers up at him in a gesture so childish and unexpected I burst out laughing.

"It's not funny," she said, pulling a serious face. But in a matter of seconds she was laughing along with me, which seemed
like a blessed relief for both of us.

"Don't worry, Vera," I said, slipping an arm around her
fleshy shoulders. "They aren't staying long."

She pulled away, suddenly looking deadly serious.

"Are you sure about that, dear? Because if I know Lord
Shanderson, he won't let her out of his sight in her condition."
She took my hand and squeezed it firmly.

I thought I must have been imagining it, but something about
her expression made me think she knew something I didn't.

"So have they been planning a baby for long?" I asked.

"It's hot in here, don't you think? Lady Elizabeth always in-
sists on the heating being on full tilt when she's here; drives me

mad, it does. Let's get some fresh air." She let go of my hand and headed out to the garden.

I followed her, feeling nervous about what I was about to hear but at the same time desperate to make sense of what was going on right under my nose. When we got to the far side of the lawn, she led the way through a wooden door in the high, stone wall that ran along its perimeter, closing the door gently behind us. On the other side was Vera's pride and joy: the castle's original Victorian kitchen garden. She guided us past immaculately planted rows of cabbages, leeks, and pumpkins, and other crops I couldn't quite make out as they were hidden beneath ancient glass cloches to protect them from the frost. It was a good choice for a place to have a "little chat" as we were sheltered from not only the biting wind but also from prying eyes. Something I'd realized there was never any shortage of at Castle Beadale.

"Do you know the difference between the French and the English?" she said out of the blue.

"I'm sure you are about to tell me."

"They say the French build castles to keep people out, and the English build them to keep people in." She laughed.

"I can think of worse places to be a prisoner."

"Anthony, do you realize how much this house means to His Lordship?" she asked, turning to face me.

"Yes, of course. It means the world to him."

"If I tell you something in confidence, will you swear to me that you will keep it to yourself?"

"Of course—I promise."

She pointed to a wooden bench, and we sat, turning to face each other.

"The future of all of this," she said with a sweeping wave of her arm, "depends on one thing and one thing only, and that is a male heir to succeed Lord Shanderson."

"I see. I'm guessing that's exactly what he's about to get."

"Yes, God willing, it looks like it is. This baby has been a long time coming, believe you me. And it's something we *all* want because without it a lot of people around here will be out of a job and out on the streets—me included."

"Oh, come on, Vera. Lord Shanderson would never turf you out."

"No, you're right; *he* wouldn't, but Old Ma Szabo wouldn't think twice about it. If her daughter doesn't produce an heir and a spare before her eggs are fried, this house will be up for sale quicker than you can say Jack Flash. Madame Szabo made it perfectly clear that she won't fund Castle Beadale if there's no one to carry on the Shanderson name. Those Szabos are nothing more than a bunch of Hungarian peasants without a title, and without an heir there is no title. It's as simple as that." Vera was wearing a look of such maternal concern that I suddenly wanted to bury my head in her ample bosom and suck my thumb until everything seemed better. But thankfully I didn't.

It was sort of making sense, but what I really wanted to ask Vera and obviously couldn't was "And where does this leave him and me?"

"So, dear, this baby represents a future for all of us at Castle Beadale—you included."

I felt myself beginning to well up, but the last thing I wanted was to treat Vera to a display of waterworks, so I jumped up and pretended to look at my watch.

"Jesus, would you look at the time; we'd better get back."

Vera stayed put and simply smiled up at me.

"If you want to stay around and be part our big Castle Beadale family, then I think you should put your head down and get on with it. I know His Lordship values your services very highly." She took hold of my hand again before adding, "But if it's anything else you are looking for, perhaps Beadale is no longer the place to look for it."

She eased herself up off the bench using my hand as leverage, and as she did I noticed a small, weathered plaque on the back of the bench, right where I'd been sitting.

ALBERT JOHNSON 1908–1977
PERFECT SERVANT, PERFECT FRIEND

Dinner that night had the distinct air of a French farce about it. Malcolm, Lady Elizabeth's butler, hovered over his mistress like a serpent guarding its nest, so much so that at one point when I attempted to fill her glass with sparkling water, he just about barged me out of the way.

"Only still water for Her Ladyship," he mouthed at me as he filled her glass. "Gassy water is bad for baby."

Lord and Lady Shanderson remained locked in conversation throughout the meal, so I doubt they were aware of the simmering tensions between their respective manservants.

I went to place a dessert fork in front of Lady Elizabeth, but before it had even made contact with the tablecloth Malcolm snatched it up as if I had just placed a freshly laid turd in front of her.

"Are you fucking mad?" he hissed under his breath later as we stood side by side in the butler's pantry. "It's a crème brûlée, for God's sake. What use would she have for a fork?" He shook his head and rolled his eyes like a pantomime dame.

"Whatever you say, Malcolm. Though it's not how it's done at the Palace," I added, knowing those particular words would wound him like a dagger through the heart.

"I like to be addressed as Mr. Chisholm, *actually*," he said, placing an emphasis on the last word for added effect.

"I bet you do, Malcolm. I bet you do."

Before the situation between us really started to escalate, the bell from the dining room sounded. Malcolm quickly smoothed down his thinning hair and pushed past me. Smiling to myself, I followed him through to the dining room.

"Anthony," Lord Shanderson said, looking straight through Malcolm, "there don't appear to be any fruit forks here."

"My apologies, sir. Malcolm will see to it right away."

I shot Malcolm a look that said, "Jump to it, bitch!" and he quickly replaced the missing cutlery with a flourish. I was happy that the natural pecking order had finally been established and that dinner was a lot less painful than it could have been.

In the end I actually found myself being grateful to have Malcolm around. For, during all the time I spent trying to get one over on him, I wasn't fretting about how on earth I was going to extricate myself from my car crash of a relationship with Drummond.

When it came to clearing dinner, Malcolm's back suddenly became so painful that he wasn't even able to lift a plate, so he took himself off to bed and left me to it. After everything was washed and put away, I thought I'd stop by the kitchen before I turned in for the night to see how Vera was.

"Ah! Anthony, dear," she said when I popped my head around the door. "I'm glad I've seen you. His Lordship has invited people over for a pheasant shoot tomorrow, so it's all hands to the pump. There will be a shoot in the morning, and then he's asked for lunch in the bothy on the edge of the woods. Nothing fancy, just a beef stew and dumplings and a nice, warming steamed pudding for afters."

"Stew!" Jacques said. "A stew? My God, it's more primitive down here than I thought."

"I'll have you know that my beef stew and dumplings is Lord Shanderson's favorite meal," she barked at him, before continuing in a softer voice. "They'll probably go out for another couple of drives in the afternoon if the weather holds up."

"Don't you mean if they are not too pissed to shoot straight," Jacques said over the top of a tumbler of what looked like His Lordship's fine single malt. "I'll make something more suitable for Lady Elizabeth. I'm sure I read somewhere that beef stew and dumplings can harm the baby."

By the time I got to Rose View I was gasping for a stiff drink. I was all out of vodka, so I cracked open a bottle of white wine from the fridge and poured myself a huge glass of it. In fact I filled it so enthusiastically I had to sip at it whilst it remained on the table until it was safe to pick up the glass. It was cold and crisp and as welcome as a mother's milk.

I sprawled out on the sofa and turned on the TV, mindlessly flicking through the channels whilst I sipped at the wine. Eventually, when I went to top up my glass, I realized that I'd finished off the bottle. Images of Drummond as the proud husband and father were still playing on an endless loop in my head, so in an attempt to roll the final credits on that saga I cracked open another bottle.

And then, halfway through the second bottle, I decided it would be a really good idea to text Frank.

The next thing I remember was waking up about 4 a.m. still fully clothed and clutching my iPhone as if my life depended on it. I didn't bother to check what I had written to Frank, knowing I'd need to grab some sleep if I were to be fit for work in less than three hours, so I left my phone on the hall table and collapsed into bed.

CHAPTER 19

━━━➤◦◄━━━

I'm sure the popularity of shooting game birds for sport would come as quite a surprise to most city folk, but in the countryside it has never lost its appeal. Under any other circumstances I'd have been thrilled at the idea of a shooting party. The combination of blasting small animals out of the sky and drinking hard liquor before lunch is guaranteed to get people in a jolly mood, and if it's a good shoot there's always the chance the guests will tip generously at the end of it.

The royal family's shoots at Sandringham were an absolute hoot, and more often than not the staff wound up as drunk as the guests. Nobody ever seemed to question whether or not it was a good idea to drink four martinis in a row whilst carrying around a loaded 12 bore, but that's the royals for you: good drinking legs, the lot of them.

But my first shoot at Castle Beadale threatened to be a whole different story and not nearly as much fun.

I arrived at the castle early, hoping to be able to get His Lordship's gear ready before he was up, but when I got to the kitchen it was already buzzing with people.

"Morning all," I said.

Jacques looked up from a huge pile of fruit he was chopping and just nodded in that way the French do when they really can't be bothered to speak.

"Oh, Anthony, dear, thank goodness you are here. He's up and about already, barking orders left, right, and center," Vera said with a shake of her head.

"Bloody hell, he must have wet the bed to be up this early." I laughed.

Vera shot me a look that said "Enough of your cheek!" before thrusting a silver dish piled high with sausages and bacon at me.

"Here, take this through to the dining room, would you? He's waiting for it."

I took the dish through and placed it on the hotplate. Lord Shanderson was fully dressed and sitting in his usual seat, but there was no sign of Lady Elizabeth.

"Good morning, sir," I said, pouring his tea. "Will you be having breakfast alone today?"

He lowered the paper before he spoke.

"All alone, Anthony," he said with a tiny smile. "My wife will take breakfast in bed, but no doubt Malcolm will see to that."

It pained me to admit it, but he looked particularly handsome in his shooting gear, and even tweed plus fours looked strangely sexy on him. I tore myself away and began to tidy the breakfast buffet.

"I've been meaning to ask—is everything all right between us, Anthony?"

I took a deep breath before turning around to face him.

"Yes, sir, everything is absolutely fine," I said calmly.

"Jolly good, because I wouldn't want any tension between us. That would be a total bore, don't you think?"

I had a million questions I wanted to ask him, starting off

with "When were you going to tell me you were trying for a baby with your not so estranged wife?" Quickly followed by "Does she know you like it up the arse?" But it was clear he was in no mood to answer those kinds of questions.

"A total bore," I echoed, before leaving him to enjoy his breakfast in peace.

Back in the kitchen Vera was packing a huge picnic basket with bottles of her homemade sloe gin, slabs of fruitcake, and Thermos flasks filled with beef consommé laced with vodka.

"Are there any sausages left from breakfast?" she asked when I entered the room.

"Yes. I was going to make myself a sandwich with them."

"Oh, no you don't, young man. His Lordship likes to keep them for the gun dogs as a treat. Can't you have some toast or something?"

"Sure, toast it is then," I said, taking a seat at the table next to Tom. "You got a day off?" I asked, noticing that he wasn't wearing his usual chauffeur uniform.

"Not likely! His Lordship has asked me to be one of the beaters."

I looked over at Vera, who said nothing, but was beaming with maternal pride. It was as if her only son had been asked to carry the Olympic torch or something.

"Well done, Tom," I said, genuinely pleased for him. "Does that mean you'll be having lunch with the guns?"

" 'Fraid not," he said. "Perhaps next year. I wouldn't mind, but Mum's made one of her famous beef stews for it."

"I guess I'll see you after lunch, then," I said, "but don't worry, Tom. I'll save you some beef stew."

"Don't forget to save him a bit of apple and blackberry crumble as well, then," Vera chipped in.

Later I gave Tom a hand in packing all the shooting paraphernalia into the back of the Land Rover whilst Lord Shanderson went to freshen up after breakfast. There was a mountain of food and drink, the guns, extra boxes of cartridges, and extra coats and blankets. To be honest it looked more like a nineteenth-century polar exploration than a shoot, but I kept my mouth shut.

Tom and I jumped in and drove the car around to the front of the castle. We waited with the engine running until His Lordship came out.

"You should ask His Lordship if you can be one of the beaters next time," Tom said, hopping from foot to foot and rubbing his gloved hands together.

"Not really my scene, to be honest. I'll stick to what I know and serve lunch."

The truth is, I couldn't actually think of anything worse than traipsing through the undergrowth with a big stick, trying to lure pheasants to their certain death, but Tom seemed so thrilled at the prospect I couldn't bring myself to tell him that. I'd be much happier helping Vera sort lunch out at the bothy.

Usually, a bothy is no more than a basic stone hut built on large estates to temporarily house gardeners or migrant estate workers. They are common in the Scottish Highlands, where they are left permanently unlocked so that walkers can shelter for the night.

But the Beadale bothy was something quite different. It was situated on the edge of the forest, near where the shoot was taking place. It was a long, single-story stone building hidden completely from view until you were practically on top of it. There was a patch of land in front big enough to park a dozen cars, and unlike a typical bothy it had a kitchen, a huge fireplace, and, most atypically of all, electricity. It was basic compared to the castle, but as far as bothies go it was the Palace of Versailles.

I'd have never known the bothy was there had I not stumbled over it when I was out running one day. At first I had thought it must be someone's house, but when I looked through the window I knew instantly what it was. It had long wooden refectory tables surrounded by old chapel chairs and a bare flagstone floor. On the walls were yellowing framed photographs of shooting parties of old: proud, if somewhat pissed-looking men in tweeds holding up braces of pheasants for the camera.

"Anthony, give me a hand getting all this down to the bothy, would you, dear?" asked Vera, after I got back from waving Tom and Lord Shanderson off.

"No probs. What car are we taking?" I said as she began to load me up with pots and pans.

"I'm afraid we'll have to make do with my old banger. The Bentley is low on fuel."

Out in the stable yard, Vera's clapped-out old pickup was parked right by the back door with the boot open. It was already packed to the gunwales with food and booze, so it was a struggle to squeeze the pots and pans in.

"Plenty of room in there still," she said, forcefully shoving in a crate of wine and slamming shut the boot before anything had a chance to escape. "Right, jump in; I'm driving."

I had never been a passenger when Vera was driving before, and it was something of an experience to say the least. She steered her old car carefully at first out of the yard, and then rather than follow the unsealed road in the direction we needed to go, she headed straight over the fields in a dead straight line with her foot to the floor.

"Jesus, Vera, we're not on the Paris to Dakar rally, you know," I said, holding onto my seat as pots and pans began to break loose in the back.

"Don't worry, dear; I'll get us there in one piece—I have done this before, you know," she replied, swerving to avoid a tree stump.

At one point the branches of a tree whipped the windscreen so violently it made me gasp, but Vera plowed on obliviously until we arrived at the clearing in the woods.

The first time I'd seen the bothy, it had looked as if it hadn't been used for months. I'd even go so far as to say it had looked a bit creepy. But today it looked anything but. Somebody had been in ahead of us and had lit the fire that was crackling furiously when we entered. The bare wooden tables had been laid with white linen cloths, and the chairs had cushions on them. The table was laid with old, mismatching china, and cheap wine glasses were set in place of His Lordship's usual fine crystal.

The final flourish was a row of old jam jars, tightly packed with wild foliage, placed carefully down the center of the table.

"This looks lovely," I said, taking the whole room in. "Who did all this?"

"Tom, Kylie, and I came down here last night and gave the place a clean and laid the table, and one of the farm workers came in and laid the fire this morning," Vera said with a note of pride in her voice. "It's nothing fancy, but it's homely." Vera and I set to work adding the final touches to the table, and then she put her stew on to warm and her pudding to steam. As I began to open the claret to breathe, the whole room began to fill with the smells of her cooking, and for the first time since Lady Elizabeth had showed up with her little surprise I began to relax.

Maybe today won't be such torture after all, I thought to myself as I headed into the tiny kitchen to see if I could be of any help to Vera.

The shooting party was due to break for refreshments at 11 a.m., so there seemed no point in my going back up to the castle. Instead I hung around chatting to Vera about nothing in particular until we both heard the sound of cars pulling up outside.

"That'll be them," she said, smoothing down her apron. "Crack open that Thermos and start pouring the bullshot, would you, dear?"

Every shoot I've ever worked on has involved the tradition

of drinking the world's weirdest cocktail. It's basically beef consommé laced with vodka and lemon juice and served hot. I wasn't at all convinced when I first encountered it, but after just one sip I could totally see what all the fuss was about. I nicked a good shot of it when Vera's back was turned, and by the time the bothy was filled with people and wet dogs, I was waiting by the door with a tray of pre-poured shots.

"Jolly good," one old guy said as he downed his in one before taking another from the tray. "Always hits the spot."

Vera emerged from the kitchen with a plate piled high with slices of fruitcake that were demolished even before she'd had a chance to set it down. The party consisted of about twenty-five men, ranging in age from around my age right up to one man old enough to be my grandfather. The atmosphere was lively and loud with everybody talking excitedly about how many birds they had bagged.

"I say, Vera, what's for lunch?" the oldest member of the group shouted over.

"Beef stew and dumplings, Lord McCallum—your favorite!" Vera replied with a wink.

"Loves my beef stew, does Lord McCallum," Vera said to me in a low voice as she passed. I watched as she worked the room, topping up drinks whether they needed to be topped up or not. It was clear she was totally in her element. There was a flirtatious spring in her step that I'd never seen before, and it was a wonderful sight to see.

One gentleman attempted to discreetly refuse a top up when Vera lunged toward him with the jug of bullshot, prompting another to shout "There's no use putting your hand over the glass, Charles; she'll pour it through your bloody fingers!" and sending the whole crowd into fits of raucous laughter.

When a few of the guests left the bothy to have a cigarette, I noticed Lord Shanderson on the far side of the room, leaning on the fireplace. A younger man was talking to him, but it was clear His Lordship wasn't listening. Instead his eyes were firmly fixed on me. At first I thought I was imagining it, but sure enough, as I moved around the room clearing away glasses and sweeping cake crumbs from the table, his eyes stayed locked onto my every move.

"Anthony, be a sweetheart and fetch some more of this from the kitchen. We're running low already," Vera said, holding up the empty jug.

"No problem," I said before heading into the tiny kitchen. As I ladled the steaming liquor into a jug, I heard the door close behind me. I turned around expecting to see Vera and gasped when I saw Lord Shanderson.

"Can I get you anything else, sir?" I asked.

"You know we could just carry on where we left off once the baby is born," he said in a low voice.

"I don't think that would be a good idea if I'm honest."

"Well, I'm telling you it is a very good idea," he said, sharply moving toward me so that his face was just a few inches away from mine and grabbing my wrist. As he spoke I got a whiff of whiskey fumes on his breath, and I noticed that in his other hand was a silver hip flask.

"Drummond, let go of me and go back to your friends."

He lunged forward and tried to kiss me, but I jerked my head away and pulled my wrist free from his grip.

"You're drunk, Drum, so let's pretend this never happened, shall we?"

He was swaying slightly, but then he seemed to pull himself together before he spoke. "Anthony, I am unaccustomed to not getting what I want, so please think very carefully before denying me," he said, before taking another swig from the hip flask. "I mean, what would you do without this job, eh? Not to mention Rose View. Be a shame to throw it all away just because you don't know your place," he said, before leaving without another word.

"Fucking arsehole!" I muttered as I grabbed the jug and stomped out of the kitchen.

The party only stayed for as long as it took them to knock back a few more drinks before heading off to shoot more birds, and as soon as the last Land Rover disappeared I felt like a huge weight had been lifted. For the time being anyway.

There was plenty to do before they returned for lunch, but it was hard for me not to dwell on Drummond's threats. He was basically telling me that if I didn't do what he wanted, he'd turf me out of a job and out of a home. And I had absolutely no doubt in my mind that he meant every word of it.

"Right, young man, I think we are ready to receive the hunter-gatherers for their feast," Vera said, emerging from the kitchen with a huge, steaming pot of stew.

No sooner had she placed the pot in the middle of the table than the noise of approaching cars signaled the guests' arrival. They began to file in to take their seats. It was as if they had been lured by the smell of Vera's cooking, and there were lots of loud and appreciative cries of "Yummy!" and "Top scoff, Vera!" as the men began to tuck in.

I worked my way around the table with the red wine, quickly followed by dishes of mashed potatoes and carrots.

But when I got to the head of the table, Lord Shanderson had hardly touched his food.

"Get me a whiskey," he barked when I held out the wine to fill his glass.

"I'm afraid we only have the claret with lunch, sir," I replied.

"Well, I don't want wine. I *said* I want a fucking whiskey."

A couple of the guests on either side of him fell silent and turned to see my reaction.

"And I said, we haven't *fucking* got any." This time I made sure I spoke loud enough for everybody to hear.

Every single one of the guests had stopped chatting now and was staring at Lord Shanderson and me.

At first it was just his cheeks that were flushed with color, but in a matter of seconds his whole face began to turn a sort of purple, and he sprang from his chair, sending it crashing to the floor. He came at me with such force I didn't have time to swerve around him before he pushed me hard in the chest, sending me flying backward, narrowly avoiding the open fire. When I hit the deck the impact completely winded me and the wine bottle I was holding shattered on the flagstone floor.

Vera came running from the kitchen to see what all the noise was and promptly dropped a dish of mashed potatoes onto the stone floor when she saw Lord Shanderson launch himself at me.

"Lord Shanderson, what on earth are you doing?" she shrieked, moving in to pull him off me.

There was a lot of noise and confusion as people moved in to break up the fracas, so I didn't hear the sound of another vehicle pulling up outside. I was flat on my arse on the cold stone floor, backed into a corner, with Lord Shanderson trying desperately to take a swing at me.

"You little fuck! How dare you speak to me like that!" he spat.

But then the crowd seemed to suddenly part, and an unseen force literally lifted Lord Shanderson clean off his feet before hurling him into the table.

"Taxi for Mr. Gowers?" Frank said, reaching down and hoisting me onto my feet.

"Frank! What are you doing here? I don't understand. . . ."

"I say, who the hell are you?" Lord Shanderson yelled as two of his friends pulled him out of the wreckage of the lunch table and onto his feet. "You are trespassing on private property I'll have you know!"

Frank turned around to face His Lordship and took a deep breath before looking back at me.

"Hang on a minute," he said.

He turned around again to face Lord Shanderson, and Frank

pulled himself up to his full height so that he towered above him. Lord Shanderson began to protest again, but before any words came out of his mouth, Frank drew back his arm and punched Lord Shanderson hard in the face, knocking him clean off his feet.

The crowd gasped loudly, and one of the younger guys even stepped forward to square up to Frank. But then the younger guy took a second look at his opponent and quickly thought better of it. Some of the guests were now hovering over Lord Shanderson as he muttered incoherently, but when Frank stepped over they sprang out of the way.

"What's wrong, posh boy? I thought you liked it rough," Frank said, standing over him.

"Somebody call the police!" Lord Shanderson started to scream. "This is common assault!"

Frank started laughing.

"Really? Are you absolutely sure you want to get the police involved? Because my problem is, once I start talking, I never know when to stop."

Lord Shanderson instantly fell silent, and noticing one of the guests fumbling with his mobile phone, started to panic.

"Erm, no need for that," he spluttered. "Just go."

Frank slipped his arm around me and began to steer me toward to the door.

"Erm, Gowers, where do you think *you* are going?" Lord Shanderson shouted.

"I'm going home, Drummond. Good-bye."

Outside the bothy Frank's London taxi was waiting with the engine running.

"You getting in or what?" Frank said.

"What made you come for me?"

"Bloody hell you were drunk!" Frank laughed. "This was your idea. You texted me last night, remember?"

I thought about it for a second, and tiny fragments of what I'd written started coming back to me.

"Well, I'm glad you did," I said, kissing him on the lips. "But we'll need to stop off and get my stuff from Rose View."

"All sorted, mate," Frank said, pointing to two large bags in the back of the cab. "A nice kid called Kylie answered the door when I turned up at the castle. She told me where to find you. She even came with me to Rose View and helped me pack up your gear."

I couldn't believe it: Of all people to come to my rescue, it was Kylie! Who'd have thought?

"So?" Frank said, holding the passenger door open as if I were a paying customer. "What's the hold up?"

"I think it's about time I got to sit in the front, don't you?"

"You've obviously never noticed before, Anthony." He laughed. "But London taxis don't have a passenger seat in the front. Just jump in the back and be quick about it. We've got quite an audience."

I looked over his shoulder and saw practically all of the guests staring open-mouthed from the windows of the bothy. And then in one final act of defiance I flung my arms around Frank's neck and kissed him hard on the mouth before breaking away and sticking two fingers up at the lot of them.

As Frank slowly drove away, I chanced one last look back. I'm not sure what or whom I wanted to see, but what I wasn't expecting was to catch a glimpse of Vera, standing just out of sight of the guests, clutching her sides and laughing uncontrollably.

As the tall iron gates to the estate came into view, I suddenly thought of something I knew Frank would never have known to collect from the cottage.

"We have to turn around, Frank," I said.

"Don't worry. Everything you need is in those two bags; let's just get out of here."

"No, you don't understand—just take me back to Rose View. I have to get something really important."

Frank didn't look convinced, but he turned the taxi around anyway and drove the short distance to Rose View.

"You wait here; I'll be really quick," I said, before dashing into the cottage.

A few minutes later I was back in the cab and passing through the gates of Castle Beadale for the very last time.

"Where are we going by the way?" I asked, sticking my head through the sliding glass panel.

"You are coming home with me," Frank said, keeping his eyes on the road, but reaching over to stroke my face. "So what's so important you had to go back to the cottage?" he asked.

I stuck my hand in my pocket and stroked the cool, smooth surface of my Bar Italia espresso cup like a talisman.

"Oh, it's nothing really. Just something I like to keep with me for luck."